KILLER INSTINCTS

JACK BADELAIRE

WOLFPACK
PUBLISHING
— EST 2013 —

WOLFPACK PUBLISHING
— EST 2013 —

Copyright © 2019 (As Revised) Jack Badelaire

Paperback Edition

Published in the United States by Wolfpack Publishing, Las Vegas

Wolfpack Publishing
6032 Wheat Penny Avenue
Las Vegas, NV 89122

wolfpackpublishing.com

Paperback ISBN: 978-1-64119-681-9
eBook ISBN: 978-1-64119-891-2

Library of Congress Control Number: 2019953855

KILLER INSTINCTS

Chapter 1

I'm standing on the bow of a 160-foot Benetti luxury yacht, sipping a cup of velvety black coffee from a robin's-egg blue china cup. It's two o'clock in the morning, and I'm forty miles off the coast of Senegal, well into international waters. From the top of my head to the soles of my feet, I'm wearing black: knit watch cap, a long-sleeved wool pullover on top of a polypropylene undershirt, tough black Cordura nylon cargo pants and high-top black cross-trainers. It's all very ninja.

Over all that, I've got a Kevlar-lined tactical vest with six magazines of nine-millimeter frangible ammunition. The magazines are for the suppressed Uzi submachine gun slung over my back. I've also got a black tactical belt rig around my waist, suppressed Ruger .22 automatic riding low on one hip, with two spare mags and a combat knife balancing the load on the other side. I've got a short-range secure radio set clipped to my back, the wire running up to a headset tucked around my ear, throat mic hanging loose at the moment. One frag grenade and two flash-bangs round out my arsenal. I've got a small LED flashlight, a multi-tool, a couple of plastic zip-tie restraints, and that's it. I like to keep my loadout light so I'm quick on my feet; I've seen too many guys bite it because they were turtled by their combat gear.

I feel like a G.I. Joe commando. Hell, all I need is a code-name.

The yacht isn't mine, of course. It belongs to a seventy-something year old millionaire expatriate by the name of Steiger. He made it big at the start of the Silicon Valley craze, earning mega-bucks locking in government and military contracts all through the 70's and 80's as war went from high-tech to micro-tech. He's spent the last twenty years sailing around the Med on this floating mansion, living out his sunset years in style.

I hopped onto the yacht thirty hours ago, jumping aboard from the side of a Portuguese fishing vessel. Steiger was on the deck wearing a bullet-proof vest, a .45 caliber Glock in one hand and a life preserver in the other, just in case. I immediately found I liked the guy in spite of myself. Steiger was rich as fuck, fit with a full head of hair, tanned and toned. He might have been in his seventies, but they were California seventies, south of France seventies, not living in Philly eating grinders and drinking rye whiskey seventies. While giving me the tour, Steiger showed me his gun locker, just off of the main hatchway. A scoped Heckler & Koch 91 and a bandolier of mags keep company with a stainless steel Mossberg pump shotgun. Along with the guns, Steiger has a pair of flare pistols, an air horn, a couple of smoke and tear gas grenades, even a can of mace. Steiger had opened the locker and stood there like a proud parent showing off his kid's first-place science project.

"You have fine taste in hardware, Mister Steiger," I had said.

Steiger winked at me then. "I learned a lot from our mutual friend."

He was referring to my contract-broker, Richard. Apparently the two had some history back in the seventies. That's how Richard got the call when Steiger's granddaughter Maryanne was snatched four days ago, while visiting Steiger during summer vacation. The downside of having a super-rich grandparent is that you look great to professional kidnappers, white slavers, and other lurking scumbags who prey on rich Americans and young white girls. Since Steiger's granddaughter is both, she was irresistible.

Turns out, it's not just Maryanne we're trying to save. Richard's very expensive intelligence sources pointed to at least four, maybe five other girls who have gone missing around the south of France over the course of two days. They are now aboard a slave ship going back home to deposit its precious cargo of tender young American and European flesh into the meat markets of Africa and central Asia.

None of these girls will ever be seen by the Western world again.

I doubt any of them will live to see another year.

Twelve hours after Maryanne had been snatched from a cafe in Toulon, I was landing in Reykjavik. From there I wound up in London, then Lisbon, and finally on a forty-foot Portuguese trawler going well out of its way for the low low price of twenty thousand American dollars. When you're in my line of work, you travel in one of two ways; either fast and direct, usually in the belly of a cargo plane or sitting pretty on a Gulfstream V, or the most winding, oblique way possible, switching modes of transportation and direction multiple times for the sake of safety and security. It took me almost two days to get from my high-rise apartment in Boston to the deck of Steiger's Benetti, but all things considered, I'm just lucky I didn't get here via Rio de Janeiro. It wouldn't be the first time I've gotten to Europe from the States via South America.

I throw the last swallow of coffee down my throat before it goes cold and walk back along the railing. We're sailing south, and off the port side, over the horizon, lay Senegal's territorial waters. We're following the trail of the slave ship, a Liberian freighter steaming along just over the horizon in front of us. Every couple of hours we catch up long enough to ping her with the ship's radar, and we need to make our rescue attempt before we have to follow her into Liberian waters. I would much rather do this out in the open ocean, and Steiger agrees. He's desperate, but he's not an idiot.

The rest of the team is sitting in the main galley, right through the aft hatchway. The strike team consists of me and three other private operators, plus a French pilot named Andre who owns and operates the Eurocopter EC120B daintily perched on the aft deck of the Benetti. Andre isn't a mercenary; Steiger had hired him a few weeks ago to fly him around for fun along the French coastline. When Steiger's granddaughter went missing, he offered Andre a hundred thousand dollars to perch his bird on the tail of Steiger's yacht and bring us to the fight. The wiry Frenchman is sitting in a corner, smoking little brown cigarettes non-stop and watching the rest of the team prep their gear. I can't tell if Andre is enthralled or so paralyzed with fear he can't say a word. As long as he doesn't drop us in the middle of the Atlantic, I don't much care.

The guys are finishing their last weapons prep. James has the SAW, the light machine gun. He's young, a big beefy kid all of twenty-three years old, grown up on a diet of Grand Theft Auto and internet porn. He's complained the entire time he's been here that there was "no complimentary pussy provided". Definitely someone who's bought into their own self-projected stereotypes. All I got from Richard was that James found himself not so politely asked to resign from the airborne infantry at the age of 21, after three years in Iraq. I know the type; a gifted delinquent who's hooked on the real-life video game experience that war provides. It makes me a little nervous, but watching him strip, clean, and prep his SAW I can tell he doesn't fuck around when it comes to his wargear. As long as he doesn't try any Call of Duty bullshit while we're in the thick of it, I think he'll be fine.

Tommy is the complete opposite, the consummate professional. Career SAS until a roadside bomb took most of two fingers off his left hand, as well as a good deal of his face. Plastic surgery has left him merely ugly, but the fingers are long gone, so he was mustered out. I'm sure there's not a large job pool available to maimed horror-show career commandos, so he went back to doing what he'd been doing his whole life. The only difference now is that he gets paid better. Tommy's got the magazines for his Galil assault rifle fitted into quick-change clips so he can just pull the dry mag, turn it, and reinsert, easier for a guy missing some digits.

Kenneth is the last member of the team. He's tall and lean, with the rangy build of a cowboy. I know he was SWAT for some big southwestern city, maybe Phoenix or Tucson, and liked kicking down doors and shooting people just a little too much. He's got a week's stubble and a long ponytail tied back with a length of olive drab shoelace, and a fairly grubby baseball cap turned around on his head. He's feeding buckshot loads into the gate of his Benelli semi-automatic shotgun, and his tactical vest has filled cartridge loops down its entire length. There's also an honest to goodness six-gun riding in his thigh holster, a long-barreled Colt Python from what I can see. A couple of speed loaders are pouched on the opposite side of his belt, along with a fairly sizable Bowie knife. Kenneth's got himself kitted out like the hero of an 80's action movie, but word has it he is all business once the bell rings.

All these years working with Richard, and I'm still amazed at the company he keeps. We're misfits, all of us. Criminals, some of us. Sociopaths...well there's more than a few of them, too. But one and all, you better believe we know our way around a gunfight.

I walk through the ready room and further into the bow of the yacht. Steiger is there, holding his wife's hand. There's a pot of tea next to her, a highball next to him. Thankfully he's not taken on some manly pretense of wanting to go with us, or taking a gun out and keeping it handy as a show of bravado. The last thing we need is an accidental machismo discharge. Steiger looks me in the eye as I enter. It's his money that brought me here, he knows it, and he isn't the least bit sorry. His wife, a tiny little woman still vain enough to dye her hair, but classy enough to keep it a reasonable color, won't even look in my direction. I'm sure I look like something straight from the ugly part of the nightly news.

"We're ready to go," I tell Steiger.

He nods and stands up, giving his wife's hand a brief squeeze. She's daubing at the corners of her eyes with a handkerchief. Steiger gives me the once over with an odd look in his eye.

"I knew your uncle, you know. I met him the same time I met Richard, back in '73. You remind me of him. You have the same look about you, although I'm guessing he was younger than you are now."

I'm taken aback by this comment. "Uh, yeah. He

would have been twenty-three."

Steiger smiles at me. "I guess raising hell runs in the family. Your uncle would be proud that you're helping me. He seemed like a bit of a wild child, but I think he was a good man."

I can feel myself blushing, not knowing what to say. "Thank you, Mister Steiger," I gesture towards the hatchway, "I just came to tell you, we need to go now."

Steiger looks back at his wife for a moment and follows me out of the room. I put the coffee cup down delicately as I pass by an end table. The four other men are on their feet. Andre looks sadly out of place without being weighed down by guns, ammo, and body armor. He stands at attention in his trim navy blue flight suit, cigarette poised on his lower lip in the defiant angle only a Frenchman can manage. I know that of the five of us, he is the bravest. Not a mercenary or an assassin or an adrenaline junkie looking for another fix, he's just a working man who agreed to do what's right to save a young girl from a terrible fate.

I briefly look at each man in turn, and each gives me a quick nod. While I'm not technically in command of this team, the assault plan is my idea, and therefore the team is looking to me for the go-ahead. The feeling is a little strange, because I'm the second-youngest man in the team. Both Tommy and Kenneth are at least a decade older, somewhere in their early forties, and Andre is in his mid-thirties.

Steiger clears his throat behind me. We all turn

to look. The old man is doing his best to keep a tear out of his eye, but he's failing and he doesn't know what to say to us; action movie speech or something more heartfelt. Finally, he lifts his hand in a simple gesture.

"Boys, bring her back to me safe."

Even James feels the gravitas. I see him out of the corner of my eye, shifting his feet uncomfortably. He's probably done a lot of running and gunning over his short career, but this is one assignment that really counts. Bringing a young girl back to her family alive and well gives scoundrels like us a chance to feel genuinely good about what we do for a living.

Tommy gives Steiger a jaunty salute. Of all of us, he's probably the one most familiar with rescue operations, and he's trying to put the old man at ease.

"Never fear, guv. They won't know what hit 'em. Lads and me 'll have her back before morning tea time." His voice is like grinding two rocks together. Some of that shrapnel must have caught him in the throat. I honestly can't tell if he's exaggerating the stiff upper Brit lip or not, but I almost laugh in spite of the seriousness of it all.

Steiger follows us to the edge of the aft hatchway, but stays off the deck. Andre has the Eurocopter's turbines fired up, and the rotors are spinning as we buckle ourselves into the diminutive helicopter. The EC120B "Colibri" can hold five people, but when the manufacturers designed the passenger compartment, they clearly weren't considering that several of those men would be built like linebackers, carrying grenades and automatic weapons. We put James up front next to Andre, where he can lay down suppressive fire with his SAW and where his size, being the largest of the four team members, won't be such a hindrance. I sit behind him, being the lightest, with Kenneth riding bitch and Tommy covering us off the port side of the helo with his Galil.

Within moments of getting strapped in, Andre lifts us off the deck, then banks out and over the port side of the yacht before flying alongside the ship's hull, heading due south. I see Steiger on the deck now, watching us fly off into the night. I think for a moment he's looking straight at me.

Flight time to target is less than thirty minutes. Andre has the helo skimming the waves, no small feat for a guy who's never flown into combat. There's little light to fly by, and we're running dark to keep hidden. Thankfully, he's got an excellent pair of night vision goggles and he seems comfortable flying with them. The ocean is calm and although we're no more than ten feet off the deck, I'm not at all nervous. Well, okay, only a little bit nervous.

Before we make contact, I take a paint-stick from my pocket and blacken my hands, neck, and face. The other three painted up before we boarded, but I felt uneasy about walking around a multi-million dollar yacht drinking from a china cup while wearing my war-face. I make sure I don't miss a spot, even pulling my sleeves up and getting along my wrists and lower forearms. While the others darkened up as a matter of habit, and to make themselves less of an obvious target in the low light, I need to become invisible tonight.

"I see the ship," I hear Andre say over the helo's communications headsets. I look out past the open doorway of the helicopter and see a faint glimmer of light in the dark.

"Comms test," I say. We all tuck our earbuds in underneath the headphones, make sure our throat mics are sitting comfortably and the radios are on the right channels and frequencies.

"Kenny here," I hear Kenneth over his throat mic.

"Tommy here, Ken sounds good," Tommy replies.

"This is James, I'm hearing you guys." James is leaning out of the open doorway now, SAW tucked into his shoulder.

"Andre speaking, does everyone hear me?" Again, I can't tell if Andre is terrified or just excited.

I press my mic button. "William here. Everyone sounds good."

Twenty seconds out, and Andre has the Colibri screaming across the ocean. We're probably six feet off the deck now, and well over a hundred miles an hour. Five seconds out, Andre cuts the throttle back sharply and bounces high. We suddenly pop up out of nowhere off the ship's starboard bow, the tail rotor pushing the helicopter around a hundred and eighty degrees, bringing us to a full stop over the cargo ship's elevated foredeck.

"Here comes the whirlwind," I whisper to myself.

In the span of three heartbeats, I unclip myself from the safety harness, draw back the bolt on my Uzi, and jump out into the night.

There is a simple plan. I drop onto the foredeck of the freighter, hopefully unnoticed, while the rest of the team makes a balls-out assault against the ship's bridge only a few seconds later. Their job is to bring the ship to a halt, cut off communications, and draw as much attention to themselves as possible while holding the bridge against the ship's crew. Simple, certainly not easy, but to the point. If they aren't all dead in the next thirty seconds, chances are those three can handle themselves against the human trash sailing this bucket.

My job, on the other hand, requires a little more finesse.

I fall an easy three meters and drop-crouch onto the raised foredeck. Amazingly, I don't snap an ankle or impale myself on some sharp metal protrusion in the process. By the time I stand up, Andre has the Colibri hovering over the ship's bridge, a thrumming black shadow blocking out the stars. The freighter is operating with only the dim glow from the bridge windows to illuminate the ship. Above this, the helicopter is all but invisible.

Muzzle flare, on the other hand, is easy to see from this distance. The three mercenaries drop onto the roof of the bridge, then down onto the gangway that runs around the superstructure port and starboard. Automatic weapons fire and shotgun blasts light up the night. Even a hundred meters away, it drowns out the sound of the retreating helicopter.

"Moving to loitering position," I hear Andre say over the radio. He's climbing to two thousand feet and circling us half a mile out.

"William copies," I reply.

The foredeck hatchway below me slams open. This is what I've been waiting for, someone to leave the gate open so I can get to the chicken coop. Three guys with assault rifles are running across the main deck of the freighter, heading towards the bridge.

"William here, going below. Hold fire five seconds," I announce over the radio.

"James copies."

I drop down onto the main deck, tucking myself in behind the hatch. I wait a second, listening for the sounds of voices or pounding feet coming closer, and when I hear nothing, I slip around the hatch and down into the stairwell. Moments later, I hear the burp-roar of James' SAW, and I know the defense of the bridge is well underway. I glide down one level, my sneaker-shod feet making no noise on the rusted metal stairs. My Uzi is up and in front of me, pointing everywhere my head and eyes turn. I don't have any night-vision goggles or laser sights, nothing to restrict my senses or field of view, nothing to distract my attention from the task at hand. The dingy caged light bulb on each stairwell level provides just enough illumination to see down to the next level.

I'm two decks down, the level I need to reach, and I'm about to exit the stairwell when I hear the sound of booted feet coming down the corridor towards me in a hurry. I slip behind the hatch, let the Uzi sling back along my side, and I draw the Ruger .22 auto from its holster. The thigh rig is custom leather, molded to fit the gun, and holds it tight without need for a snap-catch that might be heard. The pistol has a round chambered, safety off, a little dangerous but it means there's no chance of a tell-tale "click" giving me away.

I love this gun. Richard acquired it for me seven years ago, after I got back from an extended stay in the Middle East, a "coming home" present of sorts. A heavily converted Ruger MK II .22 automatic, the five-inch barrel is completely shrouded with an integral suppressor, and when fired, the report doesn't make much more noise than dropping a paperback novel onto a desk, just a soft "thump" sound you won't even hear one room away.

I've seen similar models on the market, built by companies that sell to special military and law enforcement outfits, or private citizens who have all the appropriate permits and pay their fees to the federal government. I highly doubt the sale of this pistol ever made its way into anyone's accounting ledger. More likely, it wound up listed as a factory defect and marked down as destroyed, after a fat envelope of cash passed between hands with a wink and a nod. It's amazing what can be done through discreet back-channels under the guise of flag-waving, anti-fascist militant patriotism. These days, the whole "Don't Tread On Me, Big Brother" shtick is one of Richard's favorite ways of soliciting black market goods and services. Thank you, Patriot Act.

A man steps through the hatchway and into the stairwell, a battered AK-47 in his hands. He doesn't notice me lurking back behind the hatch, and he never will. I bring up the Ruger, take half a step forward, and fire three quick shots point-blank into the base of his skull, severing his spinal column in less than a second. Subsonic .22 ammunition doesn't always have the oomph needed to get through the skull at odd angles, so instead of killing the computer by trying to shoot through the case, I blow away the cable instead. Either way, it's lights-out for this guy. I catch him with my free hand as he rag-dolls to the floor.

Yup, that's how I do it. Not pretty, but it gets the job done.

After I drag the body behind the stairs, I unsling the Uzi and continue down the corridor running along the centerline of the ship. I've memorized the plans for this deck, and I know the hold is three bulkheads aft of the stairwell I just descended. It sounds like a fucking war zone up on the top-deck right now. I can hear the hard thumps of the occasional grenade going off, and if I press my fingers feather-light to the metal of the corridor, I swear I can even feel the irregular vibrations of small-arms fire ricocheting off the steel hull. I can't hear the comms from the team in the bridge - I'm tuned into another channel so that I don't have their constant chatter in my ear distracting me - but I can hear the occasional shout or scream coming from up above, and I only hope it's not my team getting wiped out. The whole point of the plan was for me to go in solo, nice and quiet-like, and secure the women while the rest of the team draws the crew away. However, that only works if a lucky grenade or opportune cross-fire doesn't wipe the three of them out, leaving me all alone on a ship filled with pissed-off sex slavers carrying smoking AK-47s.

I hear the rattle of a chain around the next dog-leg in the corridor. I glide up to the doorway, and take the tiniest peek around the corner of the open bulkhead hatch. Twenty feet down the corridor, three men stand around a hatch secured with a steel chain and a padlock the size of my fist. Two of them have AKs hanging at their chests, while the third - better dressed and, unlike the other two, not looking like he woke up in the gutter - has a slick-looking Steyr SMG in his hand. He's berating the other two, who are doing an admirable job of fumbling with the lock and the chain. It looks like I got here just in time, because I have the distinct feeling that the three of them are here to open up the hold containing the women and fill it with auto-fire.

I take all of this in with a one-second glance, before I slip back behind the hatch. I've got to kill them all without raising an alarm, because if anyone nearby hears something unusual, I'll find myself trying to get a half dozen scared, starving girls out of that hold while being shot at, and the thought doesn't appeal to me. With a soft click, I extend the Uzi's metal stock, and shift the fire-selector to automatic. Snugging the stock into my shoulder, cinching the sling in tight, I lock the weapon to me so it's an extension of my body, and I lean out into the hatchway about four inches, exposing my arm, shoulder, and just enough of my head so I can sight down the weapon.

And in three seconds, it's over. I cut down Steyr-man first with a burst through the skull. Before his body even hits the deck, one of the two other gunmen is spinning on his heel, blood gouting from his face and throat. The third man takes only half a step before he takes a five-round burst through the heart, knocking him flat on his back. I have to admit, killing that fast and with that kind of accuracy is a skill that takes a lot of practice and experience to achieve. That I've lived long enough to get so good always gives me a mixture of pride at my own prowess, tinged with an inkling of dull horror that it's been at the expense of more lives than I want to tally.

I don't want to give anyone a moment to squeeze a trigger for the last time, or pull a frag grenade from somewhere and make a mess, so I rush the twitching bodies, examining my handiwork as I cover the distance. One of the slobs and Mr. Steyr are both long gone. The slob looks like I cored out the center of his chest with a hand trowel, and his boss is missing most of his skull. But the third man, although choking on his own blood and missing an eye and part of his face, is trying to get his AK pulled around, so I line up the Uzi and fire a three-shot burst through his brainpan. His skull finishes coming apart, he twitches twice, then lies still.

I bring the Uzi up and cover the other end of the

hallway for a full five heartbeats, waiting for the pounding feet and the shouts and racking slides that would signal to me I'm seconds from death, but there's only silence. Convinced that no one was close enough to hear the suppressed growl of the Uzi, I do a fast magazine swap, then I turn to the hatch securing the hold, I see that the padlock's been opened and the chain is just hanging there, tangled around the hatch's locking wheel. I don't know what to expect, and I doubt there's a light on, so I pull the little tactical flashlight from my belt and clip it underneath the muzzle of the Uzi. I then take a deep breath, spin the hatch wheel and pull the door open quickly, getting the Uzi up as fast as I can as I sweep the muzzle of the SMG across the room, looking for a goon hiding in the corner somewhere with an AK or pump shotgun.

I needn't have bothered. Although the tactical light helped, there is a lone, dim bulb high up in the ceiling, protected by a rusting basket of steel wires. The room is hot and damp and reeking of piss and shit and sweaty fear, about twelve feet deep and twenty wide, with a ten-foot ceiling. The room is empty of furniture, just piles of what appear to be army surplus blankets here and there, each pile occupied by a young, filthy wretch trembling in utter, abject, mortal fear. There are a couple of plastic gallon jugs of water in one corner and a foul-looking bucket in the other corner, a half-used roll of toilet paper nearby. Otherwise, the room is devoid of any objects that could be hefted or pried loose or otherwise used as a weapon (or a means of suicide, depending).

Stepping to the side of the doorway, so I'm out of sight of anyone who might approach the hatch, I risk letting the Uzi hang from its sling, and I put a finger up to my lips, the other hand making a "get up" gesture to all the women on their makeshift beds. They all look at me like I've got a roaring, bloody chainsaw in my hands, and I'm sure they think I'm just another one of their captors. Looking around the room, I try to identify Maryanne, and even when I take the photo provided by Steiger out of my pocket to confirm what she looks like, it's tough to pick her out. The girl in the photo is laughing, blonde hair well-coiffed and clean, wearing a prom dress or some kind of evening wear. The best approximation I can find is a disheveled, battered girl in the far corner of the room, curled into a fetal position and wearing nothing more than a dingy, over-sized white t-shirt.

"Maryanne Steiger?" I call out softly to the girl in the corner. I see her stiffen, but she doesn't move.

"Maryanne, your grandfather sent us. We're here to get you and these other girls off the ship."

The girls are all looking at me now. No one is moving. I don't even know if they comprehend what I'm saying. I stand up a little taller, speak a little more loudly.

"Ladies, I'm part of a team sent to rescue you. We're going to get you all home. But you have to come with me now."

Maryanne is finally looking directly at me. I think it's beginning to come together in her mind that I'm not some horny asshole with an AK looking to drag one of them off as recreation. She sits up, brushes the hair out of her eyes. With a little confidence, she gets back some of her poise and looks a little more like the young woman in my photo.

I make eye contact with her and speak softly, but with purpose. "Maryanne, your grandfather is on his yacht, a few miles away. He's asked us to bring you home. I need your help to get these girls moving. Can you do that for me?"

Steiger had told me Maryanne wasn't your typical 19-year-old bubblehead; she had been third in her high school's graduating class of two hundred and sixty, now studying chemical engineering. She was an equestrian, played lacrosse, and preferred to drive stick. I doubt kidnapping her had been an easy task, and I banked on the kind of temperament she possessed to help me wrangle the rest of the girls.

Maryanne slowly gets to her feet and takes a few cautious steps forward. I resist tapping my foot with impatience. This was taking just a little too long.

"My grandfather hired you?" she asks.

I nod.

"Describe him to me," she says. "My grandmother too. What does the inside of the yacht look like?"

I give her the Cliff Notes version, a sentence or two apiece. When I mention the color of the china coffee cups, she accepts me as the real deal.

By the time I finish, Maryanne has come out of her shell. Back straight, shoulders squared. I've run into Serbian freedom fighters with less self-confidence than she is radiating right now. The other girls have picked up on her vibe as well. They see I am no longer a threat, but a chance to get off the ship and back to the real world.

I'm about to start giving the girls their marching orders when someone cuts in on my channel.

"William, this is Tommy. Kenny is dead."

Well shit, son. Them's the breaks.

"Tommy, I have the girls, everyone appears to be mobile. I am ready to make for the deck. Can you hold things together up there?"

"William, this is James. I've lost the SAW, grabbed an AK. We're attempting to hold the bridge on three fronts and it's getting hot."

"Roger that. Do you need me to secure the women and clear the deck?"

"This is Tommy. I am covering the deck. There are four assholes that need squaring away."

"I'm on it guys. Be there in two minutes."

"We'll hold, William. Just don't take your sweet bloody time getting here!"

I could hear the joke in Tommy's voice, but I know he isn't fooling around. I need to sweep the top deck and relieve the pressure on those guys, or between the port, starboard, and interior hatchways and the fire coming from the deck through the bridge windows, they'll slowly get torn apart.

And now to tell the girls. They've all been watching me, realizing I was talking over the radio, and a couple of them, Maryanne included, have figured out what was going on, that I had to leave.

Maryanne looks at me. "You've got to go?"

"One of my team was just killed. There's only two men left. I need to go up on deck and help, or they'll be overwhelmed on the bridge."

"You can't leave us here. If they come for us, we're all dead."

I jab my thumb over my shoulder, towards the hatchway leading to the corridor. "Someone already tried that. I took care of them before I came in."

Maryanne looks past my shoulder and out into the corridor for the first time. My auto-fire had knocked the three men away from the hatch, so I hoped all she might have seen was a sprawled limb or two and some blood, but it would be sure evidence that her freedom wasn't bought without bloodshed.

She isn't convinced. "That doesn't mean it won't happen again! What if someone runs past and just decides to finish us off?"

I begrudgingly admit she has a point. Especially after Kenneth bought it, going to all this trouble just to have some jackass waste them in a retreating drive-by wouldn't be cool. I raise a finger in the universal sign for "one moment, please" and step out of the hatchway. The AKs belonging to the dead thugs are too heavy, but their boss's Steyr SMG would work, and it was thankfully dropped clear of the blood and bone fragments. I pick it up, wipe clean a small splatter of gore with my sleeve, and then check to make sure its bolt is drawn back, ready to fire. I pull two spare mags out of the guy's pocket. It might be wishful thinking, but I'll give the girls every chance they can get.

Back inside, I hand the Steyr to Maryanne, "I'm going to shut the door and spin the handle closed. If anyone tries to open it and doesn't make it very clear they're one of us, put some lead into them the instant you have a clear shot. Tuck the stock into your shoulder tight, look over the top, aim at their bellies, and pull the trigger long enough to say the word 'apple'. You'll probably fire off four or five shots in that time. That gives you six, maybe seven trigger pulls. When it's empty, hold down this button, pull out the mag, push in a new mag until it clicks, then pull this knob back until it clicks hard. Then you're ready to fire again. You get all that?"

Maryanne looks up at me, SMG tucked into her shoulder, left hand on the foregrip. For a moment she reminds me of a photo I once saw, of a female French maquisard resistance fighter, and there is a similar, particularly lethal gleam in Maryanne's eye.

"Short trigger pulls, six or seven times before it is empty. This button. Pull out, push in, pull back. Got it."

The way she says it, I actually believe her.

Back out of the hatch, spin the wheel, one final glance, and then I'm gone. I eschew all pretense of stealth on my approach to the top deck, hoping that speed and an Uzi ready to rip and roar will do the trick in case I plow into anyone along the way. As I approach the hatch leading out onto the deck, I key the main channel.

"I'm about to step onto the deck. Can anyone point me to the shooters?"

"Tommy here. The fuckers are below the windows, trying to get in a lucky ricochet. Our angle isn't any good. Looks like we've secured the other vectors, so I think that's the last of them."

"Roger that, hold tight."

Uzi at the ready, I step out onto the ship's deck. Moving forward swiftly and silently in a combat crouch, I can see that the deck is littered with swaths of spent casings, splintered and shattered crates, and near to a dozen bodies strewn about in various degrees of brutal dismemberment. Up ahead, hiding down at the base of the bridge's superstructure, I can make out four figures in the shadows. Two of them are moving back and forth under the shattered windows of the bridge, occasionally leaning out and shooting while holding their AKs above their heads. They are attempting to send bursts of fire through the windows while keeping themselves under cover. The other two are split, each covering the metal staircases leading down off the sides of the bridge. These flankers are popping off the occasional shot and trying to ricochet a slug through the hatchway and into the compartment.

At this point, I'm fairly certain they don't know there's another attacker aboard the freighter. No one bothers to give so much as a backward glance towards the bow of the ship, and I bet I could have walked up and planted one behind the ear of each of the shooters from an arm's length away. But I decide to take the more prudent approach. I pull the single fragmentation grenade from my tactical harness, pull the pin, give it a three count, and then pitch it towards the two men below the bridge.

"Fire in the hole," I warn over the comms set.

I duck down behind a rusted winch bolted along the ship's starboard railing a moment before the grenade detonates with a sharp crack. I hear a voice cry out a moment later, and I peek around the corner of the winch, SMG at the ready. Both gunmen at the base of the superstructure are down, one of them twitching feebly while the other lies still, apparently tossed several feet backwards by the force of the blast. The remaining two men are frantically alternating between spraying auto-fire at the port and starboard bridge hatchways and back in my direction. Apparently they can't decide where the grenade came from, and might have figured out it was thrown at them from behind, not dropped down from above.

"William here. Two are down, remainder are firing blind. I'm going to make my play, so hold your fire on the deck."

"Tommy here, good luck."

I wait for a lull in the firing, and then eel out from behind the winch motor, already in a combat crouch with the Uzi ready to go. The shooter on the ship's starboard side isn't looking my way, but his buddy catches my movement out of the corner of his eye. It figures; the human eye sees better in the dark with its peripheral vision than it does looking straight ahead, and my motion attracts his attention. Unfortunately, the poor guy forgot one of tactical shooting's most important commandments; always keep your gun and your sight-line mated to each other, so wherever you look, you're pointing your gun. His AK is aimed up at the bridge windows, and in the half second it takes him to process that I'm not a buddy coming to join the party, I stitch him with two quick bursts of 9mm slugs. He stumbles back, arms out-flung, and tripping over a scattering of spent brass he slips and drops to the deck with a clatter and a loud gurgle.

The sound and motion draws the eye of the last remaining gunman, who spins in place, the AK already firing as it comes up to his shoulder. He is remarkably fast, at least as fast as I am, and I've had to draw quickly or die a few times in my life. Unfortunately the combination of spinning and firing his AK on full-auto means that by the time the shooter brings his weapon to bear in my direction, his shots snap harmlessly over my head.

Close, but no cigar. I put a long burst into him, ripping the shots across his left hip up to the opposite shoulder. The gunman spins and crumples to the deck without a sound.

I key my mic. "William here. The shooters are down, deck is secure."

"Roger that, we have no contact with any hostiles at this time." It was Tommy.

"Okay, I am moving to your position. Hold fire."

"Tommy copies, holding fire."

"James copies."

I advance towards the bridge, Uzi still up and

ready for action. I can't be sure either of the two gunmen I fragged isn't playing possum, so when I'm close enough I put a short burst through each of their skulls. Messy, but I'm not going to get butt-shot because I walk past some dirtbag with a pistol in his belt and enough blood in his veins to still draw on me. For good measure, I do the same to the two men I've just shot.

Climbing the port-side staircase, I give a holler before stepping onto the bridge. Tommy has me in the sights of his Galil all the same, in case someone's coming up with me, poking an AK into my back to ensure my good behavior. When he sees it's all clear, he moves the Galil away and continues to cover the deck through the shattered windows of the bridge. I turn and see James holding an AK, his beloved SAW abandoned in a corner with a massive, puckered dent in the receiver, probably the result of an AK round. James gives me a brief nod out of the corner of his eye while covering the hatchway that leads down into the ship directly from the bridge.

Or should I say, what's left of the bridge. You might as well have taken a wrecking ball to the place. There doesn't appear to be an intact pane of glass or a single intact, breakable display anywhere within sight. If it could be shot, smashed, fractured, or cracked, it's happened by now. The gray-painted steel deck under my feet is almost completely hidden by blood, broken glass, and hundreds of spent brass casings from multiple different weapons. Three Liberians are sprawled lifeless and bloody around the room. Two of them appear to have taken double-blasts of buckshot from Kenneth's Benelli 12-gauge. He must have been moving like greased lightning when he breached the room, solid evidence of his SWAT training.

But sadly, this bridge was the last room Kenneth would ever take down. His corpse has been dragged with little ceremony and shoved in a corner away from any dead enemies, his Benelli propped next to him. I can see he was done in by a single shot that caught him just above his right eye. I step over, and from a different angle, I see most of the back of Kenneth's head has been blown away.

James sees me looking at Kenneth. "He was trading shots with some asshole down in the hatch. Just a little too slow pulling back from the lip. Saw him go down out of the corner of my eye. Just dropped like a sack of beans."

"You get the fucker who smoked him?"

James nodded. "Dropped a frag down there, held it as long as I dared first, though. It went off before it even hit the ground. Heard the little bitch squeal for a bit afterward. I seen him dead down there later, and I put half a mag into him just to be sure. No good two-bit piece of shit motherfucker."

I can see James is visibly upset, and I wonder briefly if he's never lost a squadmate to enemy fire before, up close and personal, not some roadside bomb or a guy who's out on patrol while you're eating chow and comes back in a rubber bag.

I nodded to James and gave him an awkward atta-boy on his shoulder. "You did good, man. Kenny was one hardass dude, but I'm sure wherever he is, he appreciates you bagging that asshole."

"You think so, Will?" James asks me, dead serious.

"Sure kid, absolutely. That's how I'd feel."

When did I become the crusty old-timer comforting the new kid? I glance over at Tommy, but the Brit is ignoring us, if he's even paying attention to the exchange. Goddamn, that is one stone-cold operator. His face and arms are bleeding from a dozen small wounds, mostly broken glass. The man looks like he fell through a plate glass window, but the barrel of his assault rifle doesn't waver as he tracks it back and forth across the deck.

"Tommy, we lock up here, you going to be good if we sweep down to the girls' holding room to bring them topside?"

He doesn't even glance in my direction. "Go on then, I've got this old sow covered."

"C'mon, James. Let's introduce you to the ladies."

"Fuckin' A, Will! I bet getting rescued is a real panty-dropper."

"Easy, tiger. Those ladies are precious cargo."

Weapons at the ready, we descend into the bowels of the slave ship; a couple of guns for hire, coming to the rescue.

Several hours later, I find myself standing on the corpse-strewn deck, my sneakers soaked with gore, my clothes stinking of rust, diesel fumes, and gunsmoke. Andre is lifting the last of the freed women off of the freighter's deck. I look up, squinting against the rotor-wash and see Maryanne Steiger give me a shy wave as the Colibri helicopter flies away in the light of dawn.

I look around the battlefield of the top deck. James and Tommy stand nearby, keeping a wary eye on the deck hatches in the unlikely event that someone is still alive down in the bowels of the ship and looking for a fight. I've got my Uzi slung across my back, my gloved hands holding onto the railing, and I turn to look out over the ocean, staring north. The sea is mirror-calm this morning, and as far out as we are, there is nothing but glassy blue water around us as far as the eye can see. Even Steiger's yacht is over the horizon, far away from the freighter in case another ship appears and decides to investigate.

Tommy walks over to me, his Galil assault rifle still in hand, and motions behind him to a canvas-wrapped bundle on the deck.

"Will, I think it's time."

I nodded. Kenneth's body will be buried at sea. We have no easy way of getting his corpse back to the States, and Richard told me there would be no one willing to take possession of it anyhow. The three of us drag the bundle containing Kenneth's body, weapons, and wargear to the railing. We look at each other, unsure if we want to say any words before the final act. Finally, James clears his throat.

"He seemed like, a pretty hardcore guy. I would've worked with him again."

Tommy and I mutter agreement. On three, we heave the bundle into the ocean, where it disappears with a soft splash. Weighed down with weapons and ten yards of chain, the body sinks instantly, and within a heartbeat the sea is again mirror-calm.

We stand there for a moment, looking down into the water. This might be James' first loss on an assignment, but for Tommy and I, this is all too familiar. I think back to the men who bought it in Afghanistan, the guys who died in Mexico, then all the other losses over the years. Most were men I had only met a few times, if ever before. Men whose lives and backstories I barely knew, whose names were simply "Kenneth" or "Mikey" or sometimes just a nickname. Men who were often left to lay where they died, carrying no identification, no personal effects that could be traced back to their place of origin. Just broken meat.

Andre's helicopter has now disappeared over the horizon. Tommy is softly singing a hymn or lament to himself, and James has the streaks of tears running down his cheeks. I give him a soft smile and he wipes them away, not wanting to look weak, but I shake my head.

"Better to feel sad than feel nothing at all," I say to him.

James nods, returns my smile.

"Will, you going back to the States after this?" He asks.

I take a moment to glance at my watch; it's 6:02 AM. I do a little bit of mental arithmetic.

Well, what do you know? Happy 31st birthday to me.

The last ten years have passed by so fast. I guess time flies when you're killing for fun and profit.

I shake my head, looking north again, off to the horizon. Steiger will be returning to Europe now that this is all over.

"No. I think I'll visit Paris."

Chapter 2

The second semester of my junior year, I met Beth Callahan in my Global Economics class. I had seen her around campus here and there, and I considered her a real sexpot; ripe curves in all the right places, dark red hair, green eyes and a light dusting of freckles. Her smile was a mile wide and she had this way of laughing and sticking the tip of her tongue out between her teeth that just sent my hormones skyrocketing. Two weeks into the semester and we were fucking, that perfect storm of mutual sexual chemistry that just kicked us both into carnal overdrive whenever we were in proximity to each other. When a month went by and we were still enjoying each other's company, we allowed ourselves to consider it a relationship, and her present to me on my 21st birthday that February was letting me call her "my girlfriend".

Spring break was approaching, and I considered my parent's promise to send me to Paris for the week, all expenses paid, after the previous semester's A average. I brought Beth down from Boston to meet my family, arriving in Providence with a plan in place to get her included in my travel package. The dinner that evening went very well, and Beth was full-on charming. She talked about the possibility of law school with my dad, including internship possibilities. When she'd sufficiently charmed my old man, Beth brought up the other possibility of an MBA program with my mom, and the two of them discussed a future in banking. Beth even asked my sister about her plans after high school, mostly what colleges and degree programs looked the most appealing, and if she wanted to go to Boston or New York, or perhaps head out west?

I don't know how she managed to do it, but the bedroom animal who drove me crazy with lust was transformed into a polite and demure little thing, the very picture of modesty and decorum. I believe my mom wasn't fooled but accepted the polite fiction with a resigned understanding that her son was a red-blooded man away from home and would do what he wanted with whom he wanted. My father's only acknowledgment that the jig was up consisted of the slightest nod, a tumbler of scotch raised a couple of inches in salute, and the most nonchalant wink I'd ever seen. My sister, I could tell, was in a state of complete torment. My parents no doubt locked her down like Fort Knox so she wouldn't embarrass me, probably threatening a whole laundry list of punishments for even the slightest of comments. She strained at the bars of her verbal captivity the whole evening, but never once broke loose.

The entire evening I had been concocting and discarding a dozen different plans that I could hatch in order for Beth and I to screw while still under my parent's roof. But Beth was far smarter than I was. She could see the brass ring ready for the taking and knew that I'd try to do something to fuck it all up. As we were getting ready to head our separate ways for the night, she leaned in close and whispered in my ear.

"Keep it in your pants tonight, tiger, and I'll make it up to you in Paris."

I kept it in my pants, and the next morning, my Dad let slip to me in private that if things were still good with the two of us come mid-March, my parents would be glad to pay for Beth and I to go to Paris for spring break.

"Your mother feels that it would be cruel to break the two of you up and send you to Paris for a week while Beth was left behind. She told me 'Michael, Paris is for lovers, not loners'. So enjoy yourselves, okay?"

My parents were too fucking cool.

I don't remember much of Paris, all things considered. Little bistros and coffee shops, long walks down cobblestone streets. Kissing at the top of the Eiffel Tower and in the middle of the Louvre. Beth and I couldn't keep our hands off of each other, and she joked that we were missing all of Paris because we spent too much time in the hotel. I pled guilty to that charge, because I couldn't go for more than a few hours without dragging her back to our room and having at it. She was pure sexual adrenaline to me. What I do remember most of the first four days was Beth's face floating above mine, flushed and glowing with perspiration as she looked down, straddling me on the hotel bed. It was her favorite position, and I wasn't complaining, either.

The call came Wednesday morning around 9 AM. Beth and I had screwed maybe an hour before, showered, and then elected to go back to bed for an hour or two, no doubt meaning to go at it again before we finally left for the day. The hotel phone rang, and I wondered if someone complained about the noise. Beth would often tease me by being loud, real porno movie loud, just because she knew it embarrassed me thinking that some poor family next door might be subjected to our fornicating. I answered the phone with a fervent apology on my lips, only to be told in broken English that the front desk was transferring a call from a Jamie Lynch in America.

When I heard my uncle's voice on the other end of the line, coming from so very far away, my mind suddenly cleared from the fog of sex and sleep and I did a brief bit of mental math, realizing that it was three o'clock in the morning on the East Coast.

"William," Jamie said to me, his voice strangely detached and cold, "there's been an accident. A fire."

"Is everyone okay?" I asked.

It was the dumbest question I could have possibly come up with. If anyone was okay, it wouldn't be my estranged uncle calling from the backwoods of Maine at three in the morning. My uncle let out a long, tired sigh, the kind you only ever hear when it precedes the worst kind of news.

"No William. They're all gone. No one made it out alive. Your parents and sister, they're dead."

I don't recall much of the remaining conversation. Even now, years later, all I remember was sitting on the edge of the bed, with my head in one hand and the phone in the other, asking my uncle a series of senseless questions. Was he sure they were dead? Was he sure it was our house? It really was a fire? No one was left? He really was sure it was our family? Not the house next door?

Beth, dear Beth, slowly and with infinite care, wrapped herself around me on the bed. Her breasts pressed against my back, her chin rested gently on my shoulder, her temple against mine, her arms wrapped around my shoulders, her legs wrapped around my hips. I could feel her tears falling down my chest, and I thought how sweet she was to cry for me, because for no reason I could think of, I was not crying. Not one tear fell as I babbled away at my uncle on the phone.

Finally Jamie asked if there was anyone with me, and if so, could he speak to them? I handed the phone over my shoulder to Beth, and heard her voice, shaky and small next to my ear. There was a short conversation and then Beth hung up the phone. I noticed a change in her. She was no longer sobbing and grieving but instead, she was afraid, trembling even. She had the look of someone who was an arm's length away from a viper, trying to remain calm and failing miserably.

"Your uncle says he wants you to stay in Paris for a few more weeks."

"Why?" I asked. "I gotta go back...a funeral, there's going to be a funeral. I have to go back."

"He...he said it might not be safe," Beth replied. Her voice was quavering.

I didn't understand her. "But the fire will be out, they would have taken care of that. I don't understand."

Beth shook her head. "No, he meant, it's not safe for you to go back home. It might not have been an accident. Your family might have been killed because of your father's work. It might be because of a trial."

That was a moment of clarity for me. All the cobwebs that had been spun through my mind over the last few terrible minutes just blew away. I stood up and looked down at Beth, so beautiful and sorrowful and terrified. There must have been something dark and cold in my eyes now, because she drew the covers up to her chin and hid her nudity from me.

"Is that what he said? That they were killed? Is that what he told you?"

Beth buried her face in the covers and nodded frantically.

I walked over to my luggage, dug around and pulled out my little black leather address book. I looked up my uncle's number and called down to the front desk, asking them to put me back through to him.

"Jamie, I want to know what happened," I asked.

There was no sadness in my voice, no sorrow, no quaver. I might as well have been telling a classmate to go over an assignment again.

I heard my uncle make a strange sound on the other end of the line. It was a dry, humorless, evil sort of chuckle, the sound a man makes when he sees something bad about to happen that's going to bring him great satisfaction. It was the sort of laugh you made knowing your favorite prizefighter is about to destroy his unsuspecting opponent, and you've got a ringside seat. Jamie knew, although at the time I didn't, that I had just climbed over the ropes and stepped into the ring.

Chapter 3

I left Paris the day before Jamie buried my family. On his advice, I checked out of my hotel, put Beth on a plane back to the states, withdrew an absolutely ridiculous amount of money through the first bank I could find, and took a train out of Paris. I regretted not spending more time seeing the city, but it was dead to me now, and I needed to get out as soon as I could. I traveled instead to Calais, found myself a small coastal inn that had a room for rent, and settled in for the time being.

The first thing that surprised me was that I didn't drown myself in wine or brandy or something even harder. I spent most of my time walking the city, soaking up its architecture and history, eating in tiny cafés and watching the sun set over the Atlantic Ocean. I feasted on steamed mussels in garlic and butter, coc au vin, pot au feu, and many other French dishes with names I can't remember. I sampled a variety of amazing wines with my meals, but never more than a glass or two. I even tried to pick up a few words of French, although I utterly failed as I had no ear for that tongue and still don't today. It was actually the vacation I should have had, and even to this day I am still bitter at the fact that Beth and I wasted our time in Paris on something as transient as sex. While the coupling might have been incredible, we missed out on so many other memories, so many other moments that we could have carried with us as we moved on to our separate lives.

I stayed in Calais for two weeks before Jamie came to visit. He flew in to Paris and took the train like I did, and met me for lunch at a seaside bistro where I had picked an outdoor table with a great view of the English Channel. It was a beautiful day, warm but with a light breeze and not a cloud in the sky. Seagulls floated lazily in the air along the water's edge, and old French couples and young American tourists were scattered along the beach. I was having a lunch of steamed mussels in a garlic and wine sauce, a fresh baguette and butter, and a nice bottle of Semillon, decanted and breathing when I saw Jamie arrive, walking through the restaurant and emerging into the sunlight.

At least two years had passed since I'd seen Jamie last, and he didn't look much different. His hair, jet black laced liberally with grey, was cut short and neat, and I imagined he had it trimmed before the funeral. Clean shaven, his face was lean and handsome, and I knew that back when he was home from Vietnam, he had been something of a playboy during his years of wandering around the country.

Jamie was still strong and very fit, wearing a white linen shirt and khaki slacks with light brown top-siders. He looked positively upper class, perhaps an ad exec on vacation, not at all the backwoods recluse in the jeans and leather jacket I usually saw him wearing.

Uncle Jamie was my father's brother. He was a Vietnam vet, five years older than my dad. Jamie had volunteered to "go over" in 1968, joining the Army and immediately pushing to get into the Airborne Infantry. From there he made corporal, slugging it out through almost a full tour before being clipped by an NVA machine gun during the battle for Hamburger Hill, and going back to the States to recover. After his recovery Jamie pushed for, and was accepted into, the Green Berets.

Jamie went back into Vietnam in early 1970 as a buck sergeant, part of a four-man Studies and Observations Group "recon team". He spent the next year living and breathing jungle warfare, special operations, clandestine maneuvers, and who knows what other kinds of insane shit. He was one of those rare few men, that small percentage of a small percentage, who not only survive in a world of constant peril and violence, but blossom in it, thriving and growing like some kind of deadly jungle flower.

During one of the few occasions Jamie and I ever spoke of the war, when I was a senior in high school, he'd asked if the recruiters had been after me yet. He told me how, as he flew away from his last mission in the belly of a Huey transport chopper riddled with AK-47 fire, he found himself weeping. Not tears of joy at leaving the insanity of war behind after four long years, but rather tears of sorrow because the war was over, at least for him. It was that comment, more than anything else, that made me hang up on every recruiter who called, before they could even start their recruiting pitch.

After Vietnam, Jamie just sort of wandered off. He spent ten years or so working a variety of odd jobs from one end of the country to the other. I met him for the first time when I was seven years old, and by then, Jamie had settled down in Maine, working in a small sporting goods store up near Moosehead Lake. Every few years he would come down out of the wild and visit for one random holiday weekend or another, but it was never consistent and it always felt strange.

When I got older, I could begin to perceive that my father and mother didn't really want Jamie around, especially around and talking to me, and I once caught a fragment of whispered conversation between my parents the evening before Jamie arrived, something about dad not wanting his brother planting any ideas in my head about the glory of going off to war. My mother had always thought that I should make my own decisions, for good or ill, but on this point my father was adamant. He had seen what the war had done to his brother, how it had pulled him close and unlocked something in him that could never be put away again.

I never really knew what my dad was talking about, but I did know that sometimes, every once in a while, I would catch my uncle looking off into space, staring at nothing, with a secret smile on his face and the hint of tears in his eyes. I just knew he was thinking of the jungle again, not with sadness, but with a fond affection. It scared me like nothing had ever scared me before, because when he looked that way, I could see Death in my uncle's eyes, death dealt to more men than he could even count.

All of that went through my mind as I stood up from my chair and gave Jamie a warm hug. Despite the strained relationship he had with my mother and father, I had always thought well of my uncle. He might come across as damaged goods, but he was always friendly and warm with me, always speaking to me as an equal even when I was a child, never talking down, never coming across as condescending or babying in his manner or speech.

"How was your flight?" I asked.

He shrugged. "As good as could be expected. Landed in one piece and didn't blow up, didn't get shot at either."

I managed an awkward smile. "I'm glad you made the trip. The last couple of weeks have been rather peaceful. Healing, even. Although Beth went home, I think this was the sort of vacation my parents wanted me to enjoy."

Jamie nodded. "It might not have been an old fashioned Irish wake, but I think you did your family proud."

I could tell neither of us was willing to discuss the tragedy further at that moment, so we sat down to lunch. I gestured to the wine carafe, and Jamie poured himself a small glass. We tucked into the mussels with gusto; Jamie had landed in Paris hours ago, took the first train to Calais, and went to drop his luggage off at the hotel before taxiing over to meet me for lunch, so he was clearly famished. The waitress, a petite middle-aged woman who eyed my uncle very favorably, was back and forth to our table several times bringing more bread, butter, and mussels. We said little over lunch, mostly small talk about the food and the wine; a dry white that was paired well with our meal, no less that I would have expected.

By the time we had given up on stuffing ourselves and ordered cafe au lait to finish off the meal, Jamie turned back to the grim business we both knew had to be discussed.

"Before you left for spring break, did your father talk about the trial he was working on?"

"All I knew was that it was a high profile murder. A college girl raped and strangled in a hotel room in downtown Providence. The guy was some kind of small-time wannabe mobster."

Jamie shook his head. "There's no 'wannabe' about it. The Paggiano family is one of Boston's last true Italian crime families, although it's hardly living up to the glory days of La Cosa Nostra. Still, the family has been connected to racketeering, prostitution, blackmail, even some smuggling over the years."

"So why didn't they get scooped up with all the other crime families? Isn't the Mafia pretty much dead and gone?"

"Not so much dead and gone as playing it very, very smart. Organized crime is still alive and well in America, and certainly in Boston, although it's probably more Irish and Russian than Italian these days. Still, the Paggianos have played cat and mouse with the feds and the locals for ages. Thing is, being smaller and more low-profile than a lot of the other families, they have seen all the tricks and traps law enforcement's put out for their cousins. So, they always manage to adapt in time to avoid the worst of it. A few members of the family or their hired help have gone behind bars over the years, but the family is still very much intact. Hell, they've got a seaside mansion up in Swampscott, something right out of the roaring '20s, with a groundskeeper's cottage, a wrought-iron gate, cliffs down to the ocean, the whole works."

"So what happened?" I asked. "Why did they kill my family?"

Jamie shrugged and shook his head. "To send a message, William. This day and age, we all think the idea of strong-arming our way out of the courtroom is a joke, but all the evidence pinning Pauly Paggiano to the murder of that girl was based on eyewitnesses who would have testified against him, saying they saw him leave the nightclub with the girl, enter the hotel lobby with her, and leaving the room supposedly after the murder. Without those witnesses, there was no case."

"What about forensic evidence? Prints, hair, semen?"

"The killer wore a rubber, and they didn't find

any prints in the hotel room. As for hair, fibers, that sort of thing? Well, easy enough for the defense to say they were picked up from Pauly by casual contact in the nightclub. He never denied meeting the girl and dancing with her, he even admits that he left the same time she did. He just won't admit to leaving with her, or any other contact with the victim after that point."

"So what happens to the case now?"

"After your family was killed, the stories of the eyewitnesses started to become muddled. Suddenly it was 'might have been' rather than 'was', the usual bullshit. The case is completely falling apart. One of Michael's co-workers in the DA's office told me over dinner last night that he doubts the case is even still strong enough to go to trial; the judge might just throw out the charges and let Pauly walk."

"That's bullshit," I said.

"Of course it's bullshit, but that's how it works. No eyewitnesses to tie him to the murder, you can't put him at the scene of the crime. And of course, he's got alibis for where he was the rest of the night. Court cases cost money, and they take a long time. DA and the judge, they have to weigh that against the likelihood of a win."

"So that's that?" I asked, "He gets off on the charges now that everyone's seen what can happen if they testify?"

Jamie nodded. "It's one thing for a witness's family to get threatening phone calls and see a car parked across the street, making them nervous. They get told to expect that, talked through the rough patches if they start to panic. But having one of the prosecuting attorneys murdered in his own home, family beaten to death, house burned to the ground? That's not a message, or a threat, that's a fucking promise, William. That's telling those witnesses, 'you talk, we'll cut your goddamn heart out and make you eat it for lunch'. Better to play along and throw the fight, than to wake up one morning after you've done your civic duty to find you've been handcuffed to the bed while your house burns down around you."

I found myself staring out over the water for a minute or two. "And what about Mom and Dad and Danielle? What's happening with that case?"

I could see Jamie shaking his head out of the corner of my eye. "There isn't much to go on. The fire was reported around 2 AM. No one saw or heard anything before that. No discernible tire tracks. The fire destroyed most of the evidence, anyway. Not that these guys would leave much. Guns would have been throwaways, makeshift suppressor, wiped down so no prints. Accelerant was apparently kerosene, splashed all over the first floor of the house, probably two or three gallons. House was probably a fireball thirty seconds after the match was lit."

"And were they," I paused, unsure how to phrase it, "were they dead when the fire started?"

Jamie nodded. "Your dad died of gunshot wounds. Two to the head, at least two more to the body, as best as forensics can tell from the bone fragmentation patterns. Even that is hard to determine. The house burned to the ground, and the fire was...well anyhow, your mom and sister, both of them sustained blows to the skull that caused significant fractures. Blunt force trauma. If they weren't dead by the time the fire got to them, they were probably senseless or unconscious. Wouldn't have known what happened. Hell, they probably would have died from the smoke before..."

I waved my hand listlessly in front of me. "Okay. I get it."

Jamie frowned. "Sorry William, I know it's hard to take. Didn't mean to be so blunt about it."

"It's not about being blunt. It's just...I don't need the details. Dead is dead. Burned up or beaten or shot...they're in the ground now. They are gone. To prove a point, no less. To keep a murdering rapist out of jail."

"Pretty much sums it up, yes."

I stared off into the horizon some more, sipping my cafe au lait, my hands surprisingly steady. A couple of kids down on the beach were screaming and running around, parents chasing them without success. Two locals, an old couple wearing enormous sun hats, pointed and laughed without malice. This was how life should be, your greatest hardship trying to catch kids running around barefoot in the sand.

I thought to myself, I'm 21 years old and I'm an orphan. I have no siblings. My closest relative is an unstable vet who's holed up in the hills and sells ammunition and live bait for a living. I have no college degree, I have no girlfriend, I have no job, I don't know what I want to do with my life. I don't even like economics. I don't really like college, period. Or the idea of a real job.

I turned back to Jamie. "What happened with the insurance? Life, the house, stuff like that."

"Policies for your mom and dad were solid. So was the house. Your dad had a good government policy and your mom's policy wasn't anything to laugh at, either. And of course there's the house. Last estimate, it was worth over a million alone, never mind the homeowner's insurance on the possessions."

"So what are we looking at?" I asked.

Jamie gave me a strange look. "All told...maybe three million dollars."

"Do you want some?" I asked.

Jamie shook his head. "I have my own money. That's yours, all of it. I wasn't even mentioned in the will except as the legal guardian of you and your sister, at least while you were underage. Now that she's gone and you're an adult, it all falls to you."

I frowned. "Seems awfully harsh. I can't believe dad and mom wouldn't have included you."

Jamie shook his head. "I was included as long as one of you was a minor. But that's fine by me. Michael and your mother and I discussed all this when you two were little, and I told them I didn't want any of their money. I have my own nest egg set aside, and I live just fine within my own means and had no need of anything more. You were young and we didn't know what would happen in your lives, so we wanted the two of you to get it all. Now that it's just you...well the money is yours to do with as you see fit. On top of the payouts from the insurance claims, the assets in your family come in around another million, if you consider the savings accounts, CDs, bonds, and the stocks you'd be willing to part with."

"So all told, after taxes, around four million dollars?"

"Something like that yes. Young guy like you, smart, some of that economics degree under your belt, you take this semester off, since it's kinda blown right now anyway. Go back to school, ride out your last three semesters, you can put that cash someplace it'll do you good, invest it well, take a job you like rather than a job you need for the paycheck. You'll be able to live fairly well the rest of your days, as long as you don't do anything dumb with it."

I stared for a moment into the milky grey depths of my cafe au lait, imagining myself ten, twenty years from now. What kind of relationships to you build with people when your family gets taken away from you like this? I tried to picture the awkward revelation of what happened to my family, explaining it to some unknown future girlfriend. I could see the shock, the embarrassment when she realizes how she must look to me, the strained sympathy. The eventual disentanglement as she goes running, looking for someone without so much emotional baggage trailing behind.

I knew people could lead normal lives after family tragedies, despite the trauma and the grief.

Lots of counseling, forgiveness, channeling their emotions into making the world a better place, shit like that. But most of the time, what were we talking about? A bad fire? A drunk driver or other car accident? Plane crash, even? But how do you get past "my father was gunned down and my mother and sister were beaten to death, then my house was burned down. Why? Oh, an organized crime family slaughtered them in order to terrorize witnesses testifying against a murdering rapist".

See, that was the best part. There was no getting past this. It was 2001. Every major newspaper in the world put their stories on the Web. Even now, the whole awful business was probably a quick search-engine query away from any prospective girlfriends for the rest of my life, as well as classmates, faculty, employers, future friends and acquaintances, true crime writers...I had been immortalized to the world for the most terrible of reasons.

I can't place my finger on the exact moment the thought came to me. It seemed to worm itself into my mind, slipping in through some subconscious crawlspace, and before I knew it, the idea was right there before me. Not a possibility, not a half-considered urge, but a decision, a course of action fully formed before I knew I was even considering it.

I looked up and caught Jamie's gaze, saw his eyes change when they met mine.

"That look means nothing but trouble," he said.

I pondered for a moment. "My freshman year, to fulfill a humanities requirement, I took a survey course on ancient European history. One day the prof tells us how the Vikings were famous for blood-feuds, especially between families. A common but very extreme method of ending the blood feud involved surrounding the offending family's longhouse, usually at night when everyone is inside, and setting fire to the woven grass that made up the roof. If anyone came out to escape the smoke and the flames, they were killed with a bow or a thrown spear, or just cut down with a sword or axe. So, the family had two choices; come out fighting and die, or stay inside and die. Either way, the feud was over."

Jamie just stared at me.

"See, this is how I look at it. The Paggianos, they tried to do that to us. Burn the house down, kill everyone. Only you and I, we weren't in the family hall. Feud isn't over. Now it's our turn to do it to them. Go home, drive out to Swampscott, walk up to this place, throw a few Molotov cocktails through the windows, and anyone who comes running out, we just blow them away. Find ourselves a couple of black market machine guns or some hunting rifles out of that sporting goods store of yours up in Maine. We just burn those fuckers out and they either go quick with a bullet as they come out the door, or they go slow and cook in their fucking mansion."

Jamie kept staring at me. I couldn't believe how calmly it all came out. Even with the profanity, I found myself speaking in an almost conversational tone about burning a house to the ground and killing everyone inside. No one at any of the nearby tables even glanced my way, although I was glad for a moment that I was speaking English.

Our waitress walked by, and Jamie turned to catch her attention. I heard him ask for a bottle of cognac in passable French.

"I didn't know you spoke French."

"There's a lot you don't know."

"When did you learn it?"

"I was in Vietnam for almost four years, William. Before they kicked our asses, they beat up on these poor fuckers for a decade. Along with learning Vietnamese, we were encouraged to pick up a little French as well; it was easier for some of the guys, especially the college kids or the guys who went to good high schools; some of them had a little classroom French before they joined up."

The waitress brought us a bottle of Remy Martin XO and portioned out a fair measure into a pair of balloon snifters. Jamie picked his up, gave it a slow swirl, breathed in the aromas, and then imbibed half the glass in one long swallow.

"I think we're going to need the whole bottle, William."

I took a sip from my own snifter. It was like drinking smooth liquid flame. Fitting for our topic of conversation.

"So you agree with me."

"In principle, yes."

"What do you mean, 'in principle'? I would figure you'd be all over this idea. Hell, I'm amazed you aren't the one proposing it to me. Double hell, I'm actually amazed you aren't there right now, doing the deed, instead of here talking to me."

"Why is that?"

"You know why. You were in Vietnam. You've killed people before."

Jamie's face grew hard.

"Vietnam was war. I was eighteen when I signed up, and the world seemed a much simpler place when viewed through those eyes. I'm not the same guy I was back then, and I know the world isn't a simple place. In fact, it never was. You don't just go and burn people out of their own homes, not if you want to still think of yourself as the good guy."

"So you never did anything like that? Never burned 'Charlie' out of his hut and shot them dead as they tried to escape the flames?"

I realized I was beginning to sound like an asshole, but I didn't care. My blood was up and I was really beginning to feel the wine. The cognac wasn't helping matters.

Jamie finished his snifter, refilled it with a healthy pour. He picked the glass up, balloon cupped in his hand, and stared into the golden depths of the liquid like it was a crystal ball.

"The VC and NVA were experts at using the natural environment to their advantage. They would dig tunnel systems underground, vast networks, whole bases. You could walk a recon team right over their fucking heads and not have the foggiest clue there were two hundred guys right under your feet.

"Back in 1970, one of our recon teams provided us the location of this little hideaway, supposedly a whole company-sized body of NVA were entrenched in one of these underground bases, just over the Laotian border. My hatchet force, perhaps a hundred guys divvied up into a dozen Kingbee helicopters, we go out there, and sure enough, we find signs of these little fuckers buried in deep; ventilation tubes disguised as hollow tree trunks, hidden hatches, the works.

"So we all spread out, make sure we've got as many exits covered as we can, and we decide to tear gas these assholes out of their nest. Pop a dozen CS canisters down their ventilation tubes. Follow those with a couple of smokers, even a white phosphorous grenade or two. Those are incendiaries; burn so hot they can turn a tank to slag in minutes. We spent a good two hours just dumping grenades down those holes and waiting to see a whole mess of dinks boiling out of those hatches so we could cut them down; had a couple of M-60s set up to cover the most likely exits and everything.

"Problem was, none of those little fuckers came out. We waited, and waited, and finally the hatchet force leader, this lieutenant of ours, he gets all impatient and orders one of the Nung mercenaries we fought with to go on in and scout around. Gives him a Tokarev pistol and a flashlight and sends him in, tells him to be back out in ten minutes. Time passes, we don't see the guy. Ten turns to twenty, no show. We wait a whole half hour, then the LT sends in three more guys, down into different tunnel entrances. Same deal, no one comes back. The Nungs are starting to spook, and even us Berets are getting nervous.

"So I ask my best tunnel guy, little Hispanic fellow from Tucson, Javier. He's got his .45 auto, fighting knife, couple of frags if it's desperate, his flashlight. He's a stone-cold motherfucker, that little dude. I'd personally seen him kill two dozen men. I can see he's thinking the Nungs are pussies, they're lost or got caught by a booby trap, or ran into each other in the dark and bam bam bam, party's over. He's thinking this is going to be a piece of cake.

"So down into the hole Javier goes, pistol in one hand, flashlight in the other, and I'm at the entrance, got the hatch propped open, a flashlight on his ass in one hand, and my CAR-15 tucked into the crook of my elbow in the other, set to full-auto, ready to cover him if he comes squirming out of there in a hurry. I see his boots disappear around a corner, maybe fifteen feet in, and by now I'm halfway into the hole myself, so I can see in the dark better. I see his feet go around the bend, and not ten seconds later, I hear that .45 go wild, hear Javier empty those seven rounds so fast you think he'd had a submachine gun, not a pistol. I hear all those shots, and I give him a holler, ask if he's okay.

"I get no response. Nothing. Seconds go by. Minutes. I'm contemplating throwing a frag in there, but on the off chance that Javier is still alive, I hold back. But after twenty minutes, I know he's not coming out again. None of us have any idea how they were doing it, but those assholes down there; all the gas and smoke and fire we dumped down those holes, didn't stir them up one bit. They just waited it out, knew eventually we'd send someone in to take a look, and started making those guys disappear."

I sat there, almost numb. It was the most Jamie had ever revealed to me about Vietnam. I don't even know if he'd told that much to my dad before.

"So what did you do?" I asked.

Jamie smiled at me, gazed back into his glass. "Lieutenant called in a couple of our Kingbee helicopters. Had them chopper in as many artillery shells as they could get their hands on, a whole mess of demo charges, whole shit-ton of thermite incendiary charges. All in all probably a good five tons of explosives. We spent the rest of the day packing every entrance we could find with shells and explosives and thermite, and everything we had left, we just went around, dug a few feet into the ground, dropped a charge in, packed it down with earth. Wired the whole fucking place up like Bill Murray in Caddyshack, going after the gopher.

"Once we had all that in place, we pulled back, good two hundred meters or so, maintaining our perimeter best we could, and then we set that shit off. It was like seeing a football field just disappear in a shower of grass and dirt and trees. Once everything settled back to earth, it looked like one of those pictures you see of a newly-tilled field, just dark moist churned earth. But no bodies. No fragments of bodies, no bones or blood. There was some broken gear, some wooden supports, a few feet of electrical cable here or there, but no bodies at all, not even Javier or the Nungs."

"So what then?" I asked.

Jamie shrugged. "We said fuck it. Packed up, headed home. Wrote up in a report that we lost four Nungs and one SOG member and killed a hundred entrenched NVA, destroyed all their weapons and communications equipment, and sterilized their underground base of operations. That lieutenant of ours got a medal for it, too. As the highest-ranking man on the scene, it was technically his gig. We never did find out what was going on down in those tunnels though."

Jamie went quiet then, and took another long sip from his glass.

"Thank you for sharing that with me," I said. "I'd never heard anything like that from you before."

"William, there's a reason I don't talk about the war," Jamie replied. "I didn't spend all those years in another country; I was on another goddamn planet. In another solar system. Shit, another galaxy. Whole other fucking universe, even. There was a different kind of reality at work over there, so alien in how you thought about everything that when you come back to the Real World, this is the place that doesn't seem real anymore. It took me years, decades to work it out of my system enough that I felt I was fit to be around normal people again, and even now I don't feel quite right about it."

We were both silent for a few long minutes. I wondered what Jamie was trying to say, how I should ask him about his decision. Jamie refilled both our snifters, the bottle of cognac now half gone, and kept staring into his glass, possibly reliving the moment he saw Javier's boots go around that corner, seeing him for the last time over and over again. Maybe that's how he saw me, how I thought it was going to be a simple task, and Jamie knowing it'd be the end of me.

Finally I couldn't hold back any longer.

"Well, what's your answer?" I asked.

Jamie shook his head, the movement so small as to be almost unnoticeable.

"Doing what you ask, I'd be going back to that place, living in that alternate reality once more. I think it'd kill me to live like that a second time and then have to come back and readjust all over again. I'm too old, and finally at peace with myself. I'm sorry, I just can't do it."

I looked off into the distance, out to the edge of the horizon, west towards the States and the Paggianos and their shoreside mansion. I imagined I had a telescope that could look over the curvature of the earth and see their great house sitting up on its cliff, see the waves breaking white down below.

"I understand, Jamie," I said, not looking back at him. "But if you're not going to help me, I'm going to do it on my own. I owe it to mom and dad and Danielle."

I could hear Jamie let out a long breath, similar to the sound he made on the phone when he told me the news of what happened.

"Maybe I won't help you, William..."

I turned back and looked at my uncle, a small, sad smile on his face.

"But I know someone who can."

Chapter 4

We spent the rest of our time in Calais speaking of nothing consequential, and we were similarly quiet on the flight back to the States the next day. I spent most of it sleeping, and the few times I awoke Jamie was just staring out the window. When we landed in Bangor, the drive back to Jamie's cabin along Moosehead Lake was similarly silent. Only a few brief and meaningless comments were traded between the two of us, the ride interrupted just once by a quick stop at a small grocery store along the way.

I had never seen Jamie's cabin. It was tucked into a grove of large evergreens right on the edge of the water, a small natural cove with a short wooden dock leading out into deep water, an 18-foot Boston Whaler tied alongside. Jamie drove us back from the airport in his Jeep Cherokee, but there was a battered Ford Ranger pickup parked next to the cabin, probably used for hauling firewood or similarly rugged chores. The cabin was single-story with an enclosed porch facing the water, a carport for the Cherokee, and a large shed nearby.

Inside, the cabin was surprisingly light on all the stereotypical macho man woodsy bullshit I would have imagined; there were no trophy animal heads hanging from the walls, no paintings of wolves or snow-capped mountains, no bearskin rugs or chandeliers made of antlers. The inner walls were paneled, the floors hardwood, the ceiling low and open to the rafters, with a low sloping roof. There was a brick fireplace with a large pile of firewood taking up most of one living room wall.

There were a couple of small paintings hung here and there, but nothing garish or tacky. Instead, most of the wall decorations were photos set in small collections of two or four to a frame. Looking closer, I saw that they were all of young, lean men in fatigues with weapons, photos Jamie must have taken during the war. I found my uncle in a couple of photos, and his appearance was a little shocking, the way the war had made him so feral-looking. I'd seen photos of Jamie in high school, and you could have mistaken us for brothers. We had the same straight black hair, the bright blue eyes, fair skin, straight nose and boyish smile. Just a few years later, the same features were there, but the boy had been replaced by a two-legged predator in jungle fatigues.

There were other items framed and hung around the cabin, including a faded bit of unit insignia and a uniform patch, as well as a tattered military-style contour map. There were even a couple of what I assumed to be propaganda leaflets printed by the North Vietnamese, in broken and barely understandable English. The leaflets attempted to convince the American G.I.s that their government was throwing their lives away on a cause their families and loved ones would never approve. Guess the joke's on us, I figured, since those propaganda leaflets were just about spot-on.

I noticed that Jamie didn't have a television set, but he did have a very retro-70's high-fidelity stereo system with a turntable, 8-track deck and AM/FM tuner, big silver dials and all. In the corner next to the stereo there was a bookshelf filled top to bottom with dozens upon dozens of vinyl records.

"No television?" I asked.

"Television never tells me anything I want to hear anymore. 'Sides, the reception up here is shit, and I don't feel like paying for cable. I want news, I tune into the right station, or just pick up a paper on my way to the shop."

There were a few concessions to more modern living. I saw the bulbs in most of the lights were fluorescent, and although Jamie didn't have a microwave, his refrigerator and gas range were both very nice and very modern. A toaster oven and a little espresso machine occupied the polished granite counter top. I looked at Jamie with a raised eyebrow and gestured to the espresso maker.

"Vietnamese coffee gets brewed really strong, and I got used to it. Espresso machine makes it the way I like it," he replied.

"I might join you, then. I loved the coffee in

France. Americans can't brew a cup of beans to save their lives."

"The French introduced the Vietnamese to coffee."

"Cool."

Jamie didn't have a guest room, but one of his couches was long and comfy enough to suit me just fine. I didn't have much luggage to begin with. I just tucked my suitcase in a corner and threw my bookbag onto the couch.

I turned to Jamie. "It's weird. This is the only place left for me that I could technically call home anymore, and I've never seen it before today."

Jamie let out an indiscernible grunt. "Want a beer?"

"Thought you'd never ask."

Jamie produced a pair of bottles from the fridge, a couple of Sam Adams lagers. I took one from him gratefully and flopped down onto the couch. Jamie collapsed into a chair nearby. We both sat for a moment, staring off into space. Jamie raised his beer into the air.

"To family."

I raised mine. "To family."

I took a long pull off the bottle, then another. There is something strangely comforting in the simple act of two guys sitting and having a beer together, no need for idle chitchat, no attitude or posturing, just enjoying a cold beer and some friendly quiet.

Finally I turned to Jamie. "How long ago did you build this place?"

"Right around the time you were born. I don't think it had been finished when Michael called to tell me you had been delivered."

"I like it, it's simple and comfortable."

"That's all I want, and all I need."

"We pile a lot of unnecessary crap onto our plates these days, don't we?"

"Truer words, kid, were never spoken."

We sat for a few more minutes in quiet reverie, finishing our beers. Finally Jamie looked down at his empty bottle, over at mine, and stood up.

"You've never used a handgun before, have you?"

"I've never even held a gun, never mind used one."

"Wait here a minute."

Jamie set his bottle on the kitchen counter and walked off into another room. I heard him some distance away, moving things around. A quiet current began to hum through me, like the sound of a refrigerator running in the background that you noticed only when it turned on or off.

Jamie emerged a few minutes later with a cardboard shoebox in his hands. "Bring your beer bottle. Actually, throw yours and mine in the bottle bin next to the fridge, and bring 'em all with you."

I did as instructed and followed Jamie as he went out the front door. I saw him put the shoebox in the back of his Jeep. We drove for about five minutes, and then turned down a gravel road, heading away from the lake and off into the wilderness. I noticed there weren't any cabins or signs of habitation along the road, and after another two or three minutes of bumpy driving, we pulled into a horseshoe-shaped pit of earth and gravel.

"Although nothing would have come of us going into the backyard and shooting there, the sound would carry a little too well over the water. Easier to come back here so I don't annoy my neighbors."

We got out of the car. I went for the bin in the back seat, while Jamie picked up the shoebox. He dragged a bullet-riddled stump over and put it in the middle of the gravel pit. I could see this was a popular place for people to come and target shoot; there were spent casings all over the ground, in all shapes and sizes.

"Put three or four bottles on the stump," Jamie instructed.

When I walked back to the hood of the car, Jamie was taking a handgun out of the shoebox. It was a revolver of blued steel, not particularly large, with polished wooden grips.

"Watch what I do," he said.

Jamie pressed a button on the side and hinged out the cylinder. From inside the box he plucked six bullets, and one by one, slipped them into the cylinder, closing the revolver back up once it was loaded. He held the pistol up in front of me so I could see it clearly.

"Smith and Wesson Model Ten, thirty-eight special, four inch barrel, blued finish, walnut grips. Six shots, one hundred fifty-eight grain round-nosed lead bullets, muzzle velocity eight hundred feet per second, muzzle energy two hundred foot-pounds."

I didn't know what to say, so I just nodded.

Jamie gave me a commanding stare. "There are three rules you will abide by. First, this is a loaded weapon, even when it is unloaded - you get me?"

I nodded. "Always treat it as if it is loaded, yes."

"Second, only point this weapon at something you're willing to see destroyed."

"Only point at something I'm willing to destroy, got it."

"Third, your finger doesn't make contact with the trigger until you are committed to firing your weapon."

"Don't touch the trigger until I'm ready to fire."

Jamie held the revolver out to me butt-first. "This weapon might not be all that impressive, but you can snuff out a life in a heartbeat with one trigger pull. Just remember that every time you pick it up, and act accordingly."

I took the gun from his hand. I was surprised at how heavy it was; it felt like it weighed a couple of pounds. I carefully kept my finger held away from the trigger, and made sure the barrel was always pointed at the ground.

"Didn't think it'd be that heavy," I said.

"It's all wood and steel. More modern pistols use high grade polymers and ultralight metals, but that revolver's almost as old as I am, and still going strong."

I found myself trying to get a good grip on the butt of the revolver. Someone had taken a small knife or file and made a number of tiny grooves or notches along the back edge of each wooden grip.

"Is this to help get a better grip?" I asked Jamie,

pointing to the marks.

He grunted. "No, the previous owner, ah, wanted to add a personal touch, that's all."

"Okay, so how should I hold it?" I asked.

"Settle it in so the back-strap - that bit of blued steel between the grips - sits in the web of your hand so that it's aligned with your wrist. That way when the gun recoils, the force is translated right back into the bones of your forearm and it doesn't torque your hand left or right."

I did as he told me, and the gun settled into my hand.

"Now what?"

"Shooting a handgun is all about two things; sight picture and trigger control. If you have a proper sight picture and maintain trigger control, you'll hit your target every time."

"Okay..."

Jamie put his hand under mine, on the butt of the gun. He raised it up so it was pointing at the bottle in the middle of the stump.

"Focus on the front sight. You want it to appear clear and sharp in your vision. Once you focus on the front sight, feel yourself naturally aligning the rear sight so that it cradles the front sight, just like you're fitting a tab into a slot."

I held the pistol out and focused on the tiny blued steel blade at the end of the barrel. As I held my arm out straight and looked down the gun, the natural alignment of arm, wrist, and revolver placed the front sight almost perfectly within the V-shaped notch of the rear sight. A few adjustments and I had mated the sights together as best I could, but found that the gun kept wobbling.

"It's hard to keep it steady."

"Don't worry too much about that, you've got to train your muscles to hold a gun steady over time. Now, once you've got your sight picture, keep the front sight in focus, let it stay nestled in the rear sight, and bring the gun to bear on the target. Once you have those three points aligned - rear sight, front sight, and target - you draw the trigger back in one smooth, controlled motion. Don't pull or jerk the trigger, just draw back smooth and slow."

I lined up my sight picture as Jamie instructed, and in spite of the slight waver in my gun hand, I put my finger on the trigger, took a couple of calm breaths, and applied pressure to the trigger until suddenly it shifted back half an inch, and the revolver bucked in my hand. I felt the overpressure of the gunshot slap at my face and ears, and a tiny puff of gunsmoke appeared. The bottle I was aiming at didn't break, but I saw an eruption of rock dust behind the stump, perhaps thirty feet away.

"Not bad, "Jamie said. "Your pull was a little wobbly though, and you drifted to the right at the last moment. Go ahead and touch off the rest. Just focus on maintaining your sight picture and keep your trigger pull steady."

"I can't seem to find a comfortable position on the trigger."

Jamie reached over and adjusted my grip a bit. "You want your finger to sit so that the trigger is between the pad of your finger and the first joint. Too close to the fingertip and you don't have leverage. Too close to the joint and you lose trigger control."

With Jamie's help, I fired the remaining five shots, breaking two of the four bottles. I was pretty happy with myself, and even when I missed, I could tell that the shots came relatively close to the target. After Jamie showed me how to eject the spent casings and reload the cylinder, I replaced the broken bottles and asked Jamie to demonstrate for me how it's done.

Jamie shrugged. "Just remember, I've been doing this for over thirty years. I've got some practice under my belt."

I nodded and smiled. "Okay, so you're old and gray. I'll take that into account when you miss."

Jamie gave me a comical glare, then turned and fired the revolver six times as fast as he could pull the trigger. I actually missed seeing the first two shots hit; I only caught a glimpse of half a broken bottle disintegrating in mid-air before the next four bullets shattered the three remaining bottles. The second to last shot kicked the top half of a broken bottle into the air before the final bullet knocked it apart, just like the first bottle.

I looked from the stump, covered in broken glass, to the smoking revolver, to Jamie, who stood there gun in hand, calm and cool as a cucumber.

"Holy shit, that was amazing."

Jamie turned and reloaded the pistol.

"I can't believe you just did that."

Jamie smiled. "A lot of long hours and a lot of blood, sweat, and tears went into that. You don't serve on a SOG recon team without knowing how to shoot straight and fast."

I just shook my head. "That wasn't straight and fast, that was a whole other world of awesome. I wouldn't have believed someone could do that if I didn't see it."

Jamie just shrugged. "You could get that good someday, if you really worked at it. I've seen men with a real gift for pistol-craft who could have done that in half the time, and at twice the range. What you just saw was nine tenths practice."

"Can I try again?"

Jamie held the pistol out. "Hold on a second while I set up some more bottles."

It took us half an hour to exhaust Jamie's recycling bin. I fired several more cylinders' worth of cartridges with extensive coaching, but later on Jamie allowed me to cut loose and try firing as fast as I could. My batting average wasn't exactly major league, but by the end, Jamie reassured me that I had good reflexes and a sharp eye, and with practice and training I could someday get as good as he was.

By then it was getting dark, and we cleaned up our mess and drove back to the cabin. Before putting it away, Jamie demonstrated for me how to clean and oil the revolver after firing. I didn't see where the revolver had come from or gone off to, and I think that was deliberate. Jamie might trust me, but only so far, and I understood that perhaps he kept his guns someplace hidden that he preferred I not know about, so I respected his privacy and didn't inquire.

Jamie and I made sandwiches for dinner, washed them down with more beer, and just relaxed in the pleasant quiet of the evening. Eventually though, I could tell Jamie was growing somber, and he finally looked away from his view of the lake in twilight and turned to face me.

"So, you're still committed to your plan?"

"More than you can imagine," I said.

Jamie nodded. He got up and went into his bedroom, and when he returned a minute later he carried in his hand a battered leather address book. Jamie sat down next to the phone, propped his address book open on his knee, and dialed a long distance number. I heard the line ring twice, before a muffled female voice answered.

"I'm calling for Richard," Jamie said.

I couldn't make out the reply.

"Tell him it's the Hangman calling. Yes, he'll know who that means. Yes, I'll hold while you establish the connection."

There were perhaps two minutes of silence while Jamie waited. Then I heard a click from the handset.

"Richard, it's Lynch. Yup. I know, been awhile. No, I'm offering a contract instead. Not me, no. Someone else. Yes, he's solid. Yeah, I can vouch for the money, it's solid too."

Jamie listened for a moment.

"Yeah, if you can come up, that'd be easier. Can you fly into Bangor? We can meet you there. To-morrow? Oh, okay, sure. Didn't think you'd get here that fast. Chartered jet? Well, aren't you living the dream."

There was another brief pause.

"Yeah, we'll meet you at the airport. There's a place where we can grab some grub close by, nice little bar and grill. Yeah, I know. All right, I'll see you then."

Jamie hung up.

"He'll be coming in to Bangor tomorrow around five in the evening. We'll meet him at the airport and go someplace quiet to talk things over."

"What does 'Hangman' mean?" I asked.

Jamie grunted. "That was my nickname back in 'Nam. Hangman, Lynch, get it? Some gallows humor back in the day, literally. I met Richard not long after I got back to the States, so it was still kinda fresh and the nickname stuck."

"So...what exactly did you and Richard do together?"

Jamie glanced away. "I don't really want to get into it. Back then I was still a little ragged, just back from 'Nam. I did a little security work now and then. Couldn't find myself working a real job, you know? I went into the Army at eighteen. I never had a real job, and by the time I got back, the perception of the war, and especially of us Green Berets...it was pretty bleak. No one wanted to work with a baby killer back in those days."

"That's pretty awful."

Jamie nodded. "You ever see First Blood, the original Rambo movie? Not the one where he's got the bow and arrows, I mean the one where he gets run out of town."

"Yeah, a few years ago. That's where he breaks

down and cries because he can't get a job parking cars, right?"

"Yup. You think that movie was exaggerating, but it was really hard for us back then. We came back to the world with all this...experience, but they never taught us how to come home. It took me a long time to settle myself, got into a little trouble here and there. Richard and I had each other's back more than a few times."

"So he's also a vet?"

"I don't think so - I never really got where he learned what he knows. I kinda have my suspicions that he might have been a criminal who went mercenary after a while, or maybe he was a Fed. He's good. I mean, real good. Scary good. But he's a little...peculiar."

"Peculiar how?"

Jamie smiled. "You'll just have to meet him tomorrow and find out."

It had been a long day, so we turned in for the night, and I fell asleep on Jamie's couch in minutes.

Chapter 5

In the morning, after a quick breakfast and a double espresso, we took Jamie's boat out on the lake for a few hours, alternating between slashing across the water at twenty knots and quietly nosing around the little nooks and crannies of the lake's shoreline while Jamie attempted to fish.

While we didn't catch anything that morning it was a nice diversion, and I found that I really warmed up to my uncle. It was really too bad he didn't get along well with my parents, because once you moved beyond the occasional war reveries, he wasn't that strange a guy. In fact, I'd say he was downright easy-going. I guess after spending four years in a war zone, you learn to not sweat the little things.

After a lunch of sandwiches and iced tea, we drove into town and ran a few errands. I was introduced to a few of Jamie's local friends. Jamie explained that I was his nephew "from the big city" and I'd be staying with him for a while. Everyone seemed very laid back and friendly. I figured the sort of people who needed to go-go-go all the time didn't stay around very long.

We hit the road heading to Bangor around two in the afternoon. It had taken a little shy of two hours to make the drive from Bangor the day before, so we figured we'd get to the airport a little ahead of Richard's flight. Jamie told me that Richard would be coming in to a small private airport south of Bangor.

"The Brewer airport is a little private strip. The jet can come in, land, and he'll be able to just walk off and get in the car. It's a lot less hassle and a lot less paperwork, which is why he picked it."

We sat in the Jeep next to the airstrip with the windows rolled down, the late March breeze cool but still pleasant with the bright sunshine warming the car's interior.

Jamie turned to me. "Just so you know, Richard doesn't drink, so don't offer to buy him a beer. He'll probably just get a soda water with lime, or an iced tea. Also, you'll probably be getting the hairy eye-ball from him a lot. Don't let him intimidate you, just be honest with him. Believe me, your request isn't going to shock him. I've never met a more un-shockable person in my life."

"This is getting weirder by the minute."

Jamie smiled, then turned to look up at the sky. "Ah, here he comes."

I looked through the windshield and made out a white speck gradually approaching the airfield from the south. Within a minute the speck grew into a small twin-engined passenger jet, and soon it was taxiing around at the end of the runway, the pilot already aligning the jet so that it was ready for takeoff after refueling.

The passenger ramp lowered to the ground, and I had my first glimpse of Richard. He was tall, a little over six feet, with the lean, lanky frame of a cowboy. He was wearing a light gray suit and a white cowboy hat with a black band. As he approached the Jeep he kept his right hand down by his side, angled behind his leg, and it took me a moment to realize what he was doing.

"Jesus Christ, he's got a gun..." I whispered to Jamie.

"Just be cool. I told you, he's a bit paranoid. Once he scopes us out, he'll put it away. All the same though, keep your hands where he can see them."

"You're not comforting me much."

Richard walked up to the driver's side window and leaned down to peer inside.

"Howdy, Lynch. You're looking well."

Richard had a long, weathered face, clean-shaven with sandy brown hair and cold blue eyes surrounded by a surplus of crow's feet. He appeared to be around sixty, but he was obviously in good shape and carried himself with authority. He reminded me of a grizzled lawman, perhaps past his prime but still fast on the draw and more than a match for any two-bit criminal who might try their hand against him. But, when he looked past Jamie and made eye contact with me, I felt instead like I was looking into the eyes of a prairie lion a moment before it tore my face off with a casual flick of its paw.

"This can't be the client. When'd you take up babysitting? Times get that tough?"

Jamie glanced my way. "Richard, this is my nephew William. He wants to hire you."

Richard looked from Jamie back to me again, his eyes narrowing slightly in scrutiny. I felt myself flush, embarrassed.

"You don't say."

Jamie reached for the ignition with his right hand while pointing his left thumb towards the back seat. "Hop in, Richard. We've got a lot to talk about."

Richard took a step back, then a couple of steps to his right, eyeballing the back seat and the cargo bed of the Cherokee. Satisfied that there wasn't anyone lying in wait for him, Richard got in behind Jamie, but kept his pistol, a big stainless steel automatic, in hand.

"Alright Lynch, you've got three hours. Then the pilot's going to assume I'm dead."

"It's a five minute drive, Richard. I'll have you back before you're presumed KIA."

Jamie drove to a small bar and grill just outside of town. No one spoke during the course of the five minute car ride, and I didn't dare look back, not even using the rearview mirror. I kept imagining that big pistol pointing at my back, and just hoped we didn't hit any large bumps along the way.

We pulled into the restaurant's driveway and parked as far from the building as possible. I saw Jamie look at Richard in the rear view mirror.

"This will be a little less awkward if you put the gun away before we go inside."

Richard opened his door, stepped out and looked around, shielding his gun from view by keeping it inside the Jeep's cab. When he was satisfied nothing was awry, he holstered the pistol and adjusted his suit coat.

"Just being practical, Lynch. You've got to allow an old dog like me a few bad habits."

Jamie let out a small sigh and glanced at me sideways before getting out of the Jeep.

"Richard, I've given you many allowances over the years. Not because you're old, but because you're a weirdo."

"I'll give you that one, Lynch," Richard replied.

We entered the restaurant together, Jamie leading, me in the middle, with Richard bringing up the rear. Even then I couldn't tell if he actually suspected us of leading him into an ambush, or if this constant level of suspicion had become subconscious and second-nature to him after so many years.

The decor inside the restaurant was simple and subdued, a ubiquitous little blue-collar bar and grill where you could get a burger or a steak or a slice of meatloaf and mashed potatoes, and most of the beer was sold by the bottle. A jukebox played country music somewhere in the back of the bar. There was a pool table off to one side, a game seemingly half-finished, but no one was around. A handful of tables had seated patrons, and a couple of bar stools were occupied. Overall, it looked like it was going to be a slow evening.

We settled into a booth in a back corner. I noticed Jamie picked a spot close enough to the jukebox so that it would mask our conversation but far enough away that we didn't have to talk over the music. Jamie made sure we both sat facing inward so Richard could have the seat facing the door. Even after sitting down, Richard didn't remove his cowboy hat.

A waitress appeared shortly and took our drink orders. As Jamie had predicted, Richard just ordered a soda water with lime. I asked for a Sam Adams, while Jamie ordered a Coke. We waited in silence for the waitress to bring back our drinks, and we put in our dinner orders, not wishing to begin conversation until we knew we wouldn't be interrupted for a while. I ordered a chicken sandwich, while Jamie ordered fish and chips and Richard asked for a medium rare sirloin with a side of green beans and mashed potatoes.

After the waitress walked away, Richard took a long draw from his soda water straw and looked from Jamie to me and back again.

"So, what are we doing here?"

Jamie laid it all on the line. My family, the court case, the Paggianos, the murders and the arson, my time in Paris and his visit, and finally the decision I made to take matters into my own hands. I didn't comment during the exposition. Rather, I nursed my beer and watched Richard's reaction to the events as they were explained.

Just as Jamie had predicted, Richard didn't bat an eye.

Our dinners arrived shortly after Jamie completed his narrative. We all took a moment to dig in before continuing. Richard ate with a casual economy of motion, his fork and knife handled deftly, and one eye never leaving the front of the restaurant.

Once we hit a collective pause, I looked at Richard.

"What do you think?"

Richard shrugged. "Ain't for me to think anything one way or the other. You're the client, what exactly do you want done?"

"Well, what can be done, in your estimation? Given your resources?"

Richard chuckled. "Hell, son. I could probably find a way to get that mansion napalmed. But it's a question of balance, and a question of visibility. I could find someone who'd make sure the head honcho dropped dead of a heart attack within a month, but I don't think that's what you really want. I could contract a fire team, four or five guys, an hour's work. Drive up, tear the place apart, take off before the neighbors can pick up their phones. The choices are limitless, it's all about what you want, and what you're willing to spend."

I mulled that over for a few minutes as I finished my beer.

"When the idea first occurred to me, I thought Jamie and I could do it. Jamie refuses to go back into that part of his past, and I'll respect that."

There was a brief, cryptic look between Richard and Jamie.

"Now though, I still think I want to do it myself. If I just hire someone, that's meaningless. If I'm going to get revenge, I'm going to do it myself, not pay someone else to do my dirty work for me. That's what I want to differentiate me from the Paggianos."

Richard stared at me hard. I did my best to keep eye contact, but failure was inevitable. I chose to glance at Jamie instead.

"I know Jamie isn't willing to commit to helping me, but I think he understands where I'm coming from."

Jamie didn't respond. I couldn't tell if he was embarrassed or simply didn't know what to say.

Richard cleared his throat. "Y'know, maybe it's my Texan bias, but I still believe a man should never feel wrong taking the law into his own hands if he feels there isn't any other option, and blood needs to be answered with blood. So if you want to put them in the ground, you'll get no argument from me."

"All right, thank you. So where does that leave us?"

There was another awkward glance between Jamie and Richard that must have spoken volumes.

"I don't come cheap," Richard said, "but for a hundred large, I can teach you a few things. How to shoot, how to hunt men, how to do unto others before they do unto you. Maybe I can give you the tools and training you need to get the job done right."

"Tools...you mean guns, ammo, gear?"

Richard nodded. "I have enough backchannel resources that it won't be a problem."

"Jamie took me out to shoot a handgun for the first time yesterday," I said.

Richard looked at Jamie. "How'd he do?"

"Not bad, actually. He's got a good eye and his hand will steady up with some practice. I can see him shaping up just fine after a few thousand rounds."

"Fair enough, what'd he use? Your old slab-sides?"

"Nah," Jamie replied, "broke him in on an old Smith Model 10 I've had tucked away for a while."

I noticed a narrowing of Richard's eyes. "Some notches on it?"

Jamie nodded, smiling.

Richard let out an evil-sounding chuckle. "Don't imagine that piece of iron has seen daylight in a while."

Jamie shook his head. "It's been a long time, but it ran through some round-nosed lead just fine. It was kept cleaned and oiled, action was still smooth as glass."

Richard laughed his malicious laugh again. "Quite the souvenir piece, that one."

Jamie just smiled and nodded. Whatever they were talking about, I could see they weren't going to share it with me right now.

I decided to change the subject. "So, what other resources can you provide?"

Richard turned to me again. "I might be able to put a few intelligence assets into play. Grease a few palms, hire a few tails and spotters. Benign talent that won't get in your way, make up for the fact that you're only one man and can't be everywhere at once."

"Can you trust these people?" I asked.

Richard let out a frighteningly cold laugh. "Hell, son. There's no trust involved. They know that if they cross me, they better make sure I'm in the ground, or I'll bury them myself. Besides, I pay damn well, or rather, you will. That hundred grand doesn't cover expenses."

Richard was one disturbing motherfucker, but he wasn't going to flinch at the task, that much was certain. I looked at Jamie; he looked back at me with a level gaze. I turned back to Richard and stuck my hand out over the table.

"Looks like you have yourself a new student."

Richard accepted the handshake. His hand was bony but cool, his grip strong and measured.

"Classes start when the check clears, son."

Chapter 6

Three days after my meeting with Richard, I was flying into a tiny flyspeck on the ass-end of southern Texas known as the Terrell County Airport. I took a chartered jet from Bangor to Alexandria to San Antonio early that morning, and from there I hopped a taxi south across town to the smaller municipal airport. Richard had arranged for another quick charter flight, and within minutes of my arrival I was airborne once again, this time flying west in a twin-prop Cessna piloted by a man named Chuck, a former Air Force pilot and Vietnam vet. Although in his mid-sixties, Chuck was as spry as any man half his age.

Flying in over the Terrell airport and Route 90, I saw I was going to be out in the middle of nowhere, as isolated and remote a region of the United States as you can find in 2001. We flew over a tiny knot of dilapidated buildings that Chuck informed me was Dryden. The place was a real-life ghost town, with only a handful of people maintaining a post office and a convenience store for the few ranchers and other isolated people who didn't want to drive further on to Sanderson, the county seat and a booming metropolis of 861 people. Coming from southern New England, having spent most of my life around Providence, Boston, and New York, I could barely fathom living in so isolated an environment.

Even before we touched down, I could see Richard leaning against a white Chevy Suburban parked next to the airfield, a broad-brimmed straw hat pulled down low over his eyes, wearing a pair of faded blue jeans and a white cotton shirt. What surprised me for a moment, as we taxied up next to him, was the gun belt and holster hanging from his hip, the butt of a large automatic pistol clearly evident. If Chuck thought anything of it he didn't bat an eye. The Cessna rolled to a stop a few meters away, and Richard reached up and tugged the corner of his hat in greeting. The other hand was hooked to his gun belt by a thumb resting a mere inch or two from that big automatic. Here was a man who didn't take a damn thing in this world for granted.

I climbed out of the Cessna, and Chuck helped me unload my luggage. Pack over one shoulder and duffel strap over the other, I shook Chuck's hand and thanked him for the smooth flight.

"No problem at all, son. Happy to give Richard's nephew a lift out here. Me and him go way back. You take care now, and enjoy your time away from big city life."

"Way back, eh?" I asked. "Ever work with him, you know, before he retired?"

Chuck gave me a grin as wide as the Texas panhandle. "Don't know what you're talking about, son. Besides, Richard is about as retired as an old rattlesnake. He might be a little slower with his bite, but he'll still put you down, you ain't careful."

"I'll keep it in mind, Chuck. You take care of yourself."

We shook hands again and two minutes later, Chuck's Cessna was turned around and rising back up into the west Texas sky.

"Chuck and I met several times back in the mid 70's," Richard explained. "After he got out of the Air Force. He flew spotter planes in Vietnam, buzzing the treetops and calling in air strikes, artillery, and naval gunfire while little men in black pajamas riddled his plane with AK-47s."

"That's got to take some nerve, putting yourself out there as a target while still concentrating on doing your job," I said.

"The kind of nerves that earn you the big bucks once you get out from under the thumb of Uncle Sam and start working for people who pay you what you're worth. Chuck banked himself a nice little nest egg over in Africa after the war, then came back here to live the slow life."

"Still can't keep himself out of the cockpit, though," I said.

"Man's gotta find himself ways to stay young," Richard replied.

We drove northwest along Route 90, passing

through Sanderson in a matter of moments. A small, quiet throwback to the world circa twenty or thirty years ago. We turned north onto Route 285 just outside of town and followed a worn stretch of two-lane blacktop through battered-looking scrubland and rocky desert. The road followed a small river, fed from the endless number of little tributaries snaking out from between the countless low desert hills we were driving past.

After a few minutes of silence I turned to Richard. "What's with the gun? You're not exactly hiding the fact you're wearing one."

Richard didn't turn his head, he just glanced sideways at me through the corner of his eye, a small smile appearing on his lips. "Son, don't you know where you are? This is Texas. Older fellow such as myself would look out of place without a firearm on my hip. Why do you think I moved here, so many years ago? Most everyone in these parts still feels Texas should be its own sovereign nation, and in that nation, under God, the Almighty has made the right to bear arms a divine right, one that most people hold as near and dear to their hearts as that best-selling book of fiction they all love, the Bible."

Jamie had hinted at Richard's infamously flagrant atheism, but such comments didn't bother me one way or another.

"Well that's all well and good," I said, "but aside from just hanging off your belt and looking pretty, why would someone bother? This isn't exactly Tombstone."

"Oh, there's reasons. Plenty of folks around here carry them in case of snakes, or mountain lions, or in case coyotes get to close to the henhouse. Better to have a gun and not need it in those situations, than need a gun and not have it. Never mind that we're only a little distance from the border, and you never know if you're going to run into trouble. Or at least, that's what the locals think."

"Why, are the illegals violent?" I asked.

Richard laughed. "Of course not. Honest, hard-working people trying to make their lives better. But a lot of folks don't want them passing through here, harmless or not, so there's a lot of posturing. And truth be told, the two-legged coyotes they hire to get them over the border, some of them are pretty bad hombres. If they run into trouble with the border patrol and you're in between them and getting away, they'll turn you into buzzard meat sure as a skunk can stink."

"So we're that close to the border?" I asked.

Richard looked at me sideways. "Didn't you look at a map before you flew down here?"

I shrugged. "For a minute or two, I just saw we're in southern Texas."

Richard shook his head. "Not good at all, kid. You flew into unknown territory in the hands of a man you've never met before, to meet me in the middle of nowhere so we can go and drive off even further into the middle of nowhere, so you can live out here for a month?"

I didn't know what to say. "Well, you told me all the arrangements had been made. I figured you were good at this sort of thing."

Richard laughed at this. "I'm the best there is, but that doesn't mean I can't get my ticket to Dead City punched at any time. I've made more enemies than I can count, and one day someone's going to catch me in the right place at the right time and I'll be shaking Death's bony hand, wondering where my head went. What would you have done if you had shown up at that little airfield and I wasn't there?"

"I don't have a number to contact you, so I guess I'd have just hunkered down and waited."

Richard shook his head. "Tell me, why would I have been late? Ain't got anything better to do today, so I was there two hours early just to make sure if I got a flat or some other problem along the road, I'd still have time. I'll tell you now, if I am ever late to meet you, don't wait around like a dummy. I'm either dead in a ditch or trying my best to keep that from happening, so you do the same. Now, knowing that, if I hadn't been there, what would you have done? How much money did you bring with you?"

"Ten thousand dollars in twenties, just like you said. Two thousand on me, four in my backpack, four in the duffel, all of it well hidden."

Richard nodded. "All right, what are your options? Plane touches down, I'm not there."

I considered the problem while looking out over the rugged landscape as it passed by. "Either someone's gotten to you, or has tried to get to you. Either way, I have to write you off as a means of support. I also have to wonder if Chuck is in on the deal, as he'd be the only person other than myself who'd know where you were going to be that day."

Richard nodded again. "Good, go on."

"I don't know if I can trust Chuck, so I have to take him down quick. Knock him down with my pack or something else handy. Try to get him to talk. Regardless, I can't trust him to get me home. Assuming he's in on it, he'll probably have a gun in the plane. I'll get my hands on that."

"What next? How do you get away from the airport?" Richard asked.

"The airport attendant. I saw a truck parked over by one of those hangers as we drove by. There's probably someone around there during the day. I take the truck by gunpoint, tie up the owner in a broom closet somewhere so he won't get out any time soon, and start driving."

"Where are you going? You didn't do your job and study the territory before you got here. How are you getting back?"

I thought for a moment. "Between Chuck's plane and the truck I'll steal, someone's got to have a decent map of the area. I'll use that to figure out where I'm going next. I'll want to get back to San Antonio; it's the only territory I'm familiar with now."

Richard reached under the seat of the Suburban and handed me a battered state atlas. I flipped through it until I found where we were.

"All right, I'd avoid taking Route 90, since that's the most obvious way back and has the least traffic, meaning if someone wants to make a move on me there's less chance of witnesses. I want to be in public, so I'll drive up and hit Interstate 10, and then gun it for San Antonio. Looks like a five hour drive, six considering I've been sitting on planes all day and need to move around a little, but I could probably get back there by late tonight if I had to. Ditch the car somewhere secluded, get a taxi to the airport, and then get myself out on the next flight to wherever I can. From there I make my way back home."

Richard drove on in silence for a few moments, digesting what I'd said.

"Not bad for an amateur. Now here's the problem. You're assuming six hours on the road, then a taxi and a ticket at the airport. If you leave Chuck and that airfield attendant alive, especially if one or both of them are in on the deal, whoever went after me is going to eventually find them. Then they are going to figure out how you got away, and they'll either try to catch up with you, knowing what you're driving, or they'll just pass the information along to the police, who'll do the hard work for them. Easy enough to find you and kill you in some two-bit sheriff's station than run all over southern Texas looking to find you."

I looked at Richard. "So I'd have to kill them both?"

Richard shrugged. "It's all about weighing choices. If you figure Chuck was in on it, you'd want to punch his ticket for sure. If you think the attendant is innocent, you might not want that blood on your hands, but you also don't want him blabbing to anyone, so your best bet might be to bring him with you. Eventually you'll also want to dump the truck you took from the airport and steal another. One of the good things about these rural areas is that everyone's nice and trusting and many folks leave the keys in their cars, making a getaway swap simple. Ditch the attendant and his vehicle someplace where he won't be found for a bit, grab another car somewhere away from where you ditch the first vehicle, and maybe make a second swap further along just in case. When you're on the run, often you're not only trying to dodge your hunters, you're dodging the law as well."

I contemplated all this for a while. "Still, my chances would be pretty slim, wouldn't they?"

Richard smiled at me, one eye on the road. "Slim to none, but you can't ever let that fact get to you. I've had to roll a hard eight more times than I can count, but I'm still here. The key is to be prepared, to never think about giving up, and to make sure they are more afraid of you then you are of them."

"I'm guessing that's easier said than done."

"Don't worry, you'll get used to it," Richard assured me.

After another fifteen minutes of driving down a series of ever-worsening desert roads, Richard motored the Suburban up a broad, low hill towards a dilapidated shack sitting on the summit. As we drew closer, I could see that while the small wooden building was pretty run-down, it was far from falling apart. Sturdy wooden shutters protected the windows, and the door looked like it was solid and well-fitted to the frame, without the usual warping and separating that comes from long exposure to the elements.

Richard pulled the Suburban up near the front door, killed the ignition, and drew his pistol, the heavy stainless-steel automatic steady in his hand. "Stay in the car until I call for you. If I go down, get into the driver's seat and get the hell out of here."

I looked from the cabin to Richard, nervous. "You think there's going to be trouble?" I asked.

"I always think there's going to be trouble. That's why I'm still alive."

Richard slipped out of the Suburban and slithered over to the cabin, moving quickly and smoothly. I was incredibly unnerved by how he was able to move from the vehicle to the corner of the building without seeming to cover the intervening distance.

Richard moved around back behind the cabin, and a few moments later, emerged from around the other side. Further scrutiny of the steps and the front door took a few more moments. Finally, Richard waved me out of the Suburban. I gave the whole area a final look-over, then climbed out of the Suburban and walked over to Richard. The entire time, I felt like there was a target painted on my back.

"The dust and sand around here is so fine, it's impossible to enter or exit a building without leaving signs you've been there. No one's been inside or skulking around," Richard explained.

Getting the Suburban unloaded and the cabin returned to a habitable condition took the better part of two hours. Richard went inside first, disarming a series of "surprises" in various locations throughout the small structure. He assured me he only armed them when he was gone for long periods of time, but the thought of a neglected booby-trap blowing me to pieces set my teeth on edge.

Although he lived a few hundred miles away, Richard had bought this cabin several years ago as a "bolt-hole" to use if his own residence was ever compromised. The cabin was simple and rugged, with a main room right inside the door containing a cast iron, wood-burning stove that served as heat source and kitchen range. There were a couple of chairs, a table, and a cot in this front room, along with a pair of large locked steamer trunks. Although the room was without decoration, there was a pair of glass-chimney oil lamps mounted on the walls, as well as a more modern gas lantern hanging from a peg inside the doorway.

In the back of the cabin there was a short hallway with a room on each side. One of these was Richard's bedroom. It consisted of a cot, a chair, and a wooden chest in the corner, with a candle sitting in a wrought-iron candle-holder mounted to the wall. The third and final room was a storage pantry, containing shelves of canned and dried goods, lamp oil, medical supplies, a five-gallon gas can filled with gasoline in case a vehicle needed to be refueled. There were also several five-gallon cans of potable water and a number of sundries such as large containers of matches and boxes of tools. Several larger implements hung from hooks, such as axes and spades.

All in all, the cabin was clean, well-stocked, and suited to our purposes. I was sure a man such as Richard, who had little qualms about living without the luxury of power or modern amenities, could have set himself up here for a week or three without any trouble. But there was one minor detail missing.

"Here, give me a hand with this." Richard gestured towards the water cans.

We dragged them across the floor and out into the hallway. Stepping back into the room, Richard proceeded to carefully lever up several of the floorboards in the far corner of the storage room. In a few moments, he exposed a hole in the floor nearly a yard square, revealing a small pit underneath the cabin. Richard climbed down into the pit. I could see the excavation was deeper than he was tall, and at six feet Richard wasn't a short man. This was some hidden storage area for those things Richard couldn't afford to lose if someone successfully broke into the cabin.

I could hear Richard rummaging around, and soon he was placing a number of cases and boxes on the storage room floor.

"Take these and put them in the main room. We're going to need this stuff over the next month," he said to me from down inside his cache.

The cases and boxes were fairly heavy, and it didn't take a genius to figure out most of them contained weapons and ammunition. Some of them were actually old army surplus ammunition cases, scuffed olive-drab sheet metal containers with orange stenciling saying things like "5.56MM NATO". Others were plastic, aluminum, or even wooden cases that no doubt held firearms. There were smaller cases the size of a lunchbox, probably containing handguns, while others were long and flat and thin, no doubt for longer guns.

Once we had unloaded all the weapons and ammunition from Richard's underground cache, we began organizing the supplies he had brought with him in the Suburban. Several new gun cases and ammo boxes went down into the cache before we covered it back up. More water cans, cases of bottled sports rehydration drinks and packages of energy bars, dried meat and fruit and canned goods, as well as more fuel and other living amenities such as toilet paper.

"There's no running water, but there's an outhouse around back. It's simple, but it's also in good shape and with the right amount of lye and other chemicals, fairly odorless," Richard explained.

I realized why we had so much water. There wasn't even a well here, up on this low, gently sloping hill, and I knew we were going to try to remain isolated as much as possible over the next month.

"The water we brought with us, along with the bottled drinks and the water here at the cabin should get us through the first week," Richard explained. "We'll take a drive into town now and then to resupply, but the less contact with the locals, the better. They've seen me off and on enough to not ask any questions, but you're new around here. Explaining your presence is just another complication."

By the time we unloaded, unpacked, shelved, stored, and settled in, it was well into the evening, with perhaps only an hour of daylight left. Richard assigned me the relatively simple task of preparing dinner, but I didn't mind. I had already seen this was going to be a mentor and apprentice dynamic like you see in the movies. Trying to argue that "I'm here to learn how to seek vengeance on my enemies, not sweep the floor and cook dinner!" wasn't going to get me anywhere, so why bother with the drama? I knew I needed hardening. My life until this moment had been that of a soft, wealthy, white-collar kid living on easy street. If I was going to dish out what the Paggianos deserved, I needed to turn myself into something much, much rougher around the edges, and be quick about it.

I dug around the pantry and acquired the necessary kitchenware. In moments like this, I was thankful that my family wasn't in love with the typical "meat and potatoes" Irish diet. My parents were a pair of epicures, and my sister and I were taught the basics of preparing meals at an early age. I boiled some rice and dried beef, then added cans of black beans and tomatoes, along with a little chili powder. Finally, I heated a package of soft flour tortillas on a flat cast-iron skillet.

Richard and I helped ourselves to the meal of simple burritos while sitting on the front porch of the cabin, watching the sun set off in the west. Coming from the urban east coast, you never understand what all the fuss is about until you go to Texas and watch a real sunset in the desert. Sitting on the porch of an old log cabin, next to a grizzled local wearing blue jeans, cowboy boots, and a battered straw hat was just added gravy. Richard even brought along three bottles of Tecate for me, still cool after their long voyage next to some cold packs inside an insulated cooler.

"That's the only alcohol you're going to have for the next month," Richard warned me, "so enjoy it tonight. Starting tomorrow, you're going to need to stay sharp and avoid anything that's going to throw your system out of whack, because you're not going to be very gentle to your body over the next few weeks."

After dinner, Richard and I got down to business. One by one, we opened his gun cases and unpacked the ammunition and weapon magazines, laying everything out in neat and concise groupings by weapon type and category, ammunition and magazines next to their respective firearms. When we were done, Richard began to talk me through an introduction to each weapon.

Richard started with the pistols, working from smallest to largest. The first handgun he showed me was a little revolver, a blued steel Smith & Wesson with a two-inch barrel and substantial rubber grips.

"This isn't a fire-fight gun by any means; it's strictly for backup and close-in work. A lot of people dismiss the snub thirty-eight as a useless gun, but within five feet, a good trigger-man can get all five slugs center mass within two seconds. Get in close and empty it into your target, and I can guarantee you he won't be getting back up. Plus, no hot brass bouncing up into your face in the middle of a tussle, and without empties lying around, there's less forensic evidence."

"What happens," I asked, "if I need more than five bullets?"

"If you can't punch the ticket on some knuckle-dragging goombah with five shots after I'm done with you, I'll eat my cowboy boots."

The second handgun was a sexy-looking little Beretta automatic, matte black, with several fat magazines and what I assumed was a suppressor about half a foot long.

"The Beretta .32 auto is a good balance between stealth and firepower. It's got a twelve-round magazine and it's accurate enough for most handgun shooting. When you fit it with the suppressor, it's quiet enough that anyone nearby, who isn't familiar with the sound of a suppressed handgun, won't know what they're hearing. You could probably shoot a man in one room of an apartment, and someone in the next room would hear a noise like a fist punching a pillow. It's a good gun to have when you're not sure whether you need a combat handgun or an assassination piece."

"The bullets look kinda small," I said.

"It's not the size of the bullet, it's where you put it in a man that counts."

"I feel a little uncomfortable with you saying that to me," I replied, earning myself a stern look from Richard.

The third pistol wasn't much larger than the

Beretta, but aside from being a compact handgun, the similarities ended. Where the Beretta was sleek and sophisticated looking, this pistol looked like a child's representation of what a gun might look like, molded from a block of plastic putty. Richard had a suppressor for it as well, although the tube was both wider and longer than the suppressor for the Beretta.

"This is going to be your primary fighting pistol, the Glock 19 nine-millimeter automatic. The magazine holds fifteen rounds, so you've got sufficient firepower, and the nine millimeter cartridge is plenty of punch for a new shooter like yourself. There's no safety catch for you to forget in the middle of a firefight, and the short trigger pull means the muzzle doesn't wander too far while you're taking your shot. It's simple, effective, accurate and reliable. It's also lightweight and compact, so it's easy to carry and easy to hide. You're going to make this little gun an extension of your own hand by the time I'm done with you."

"Won't that make going to the bathroom a little dangerous?" I asked.

"Don't come crying to me if you shoot your pecker off, dummy."

We moved on to the three long guns. The first was a stubby-barreled shotgun with a folding stock. At first I thought it was some kind of pump shotgun, but Richard informed me it was actually semi-automatic.

"This is a Remington 1100 auto-loading shotgun. Four twelve-gauge shells in the tube under the barrel, plus a fifth you can load right into the chamber. With some practice, you can get all five shots into a target in less than two seconds, just like the thirty-eight. But, with a man-killing load like double-ought buckshot, that's forty-five pellets. Probably more lead down range than any submachine gun in the same amount of time. This brute will kick like a mule, especially if you're just using the pistol grip and not the stock, but you're not looking for precision. This is the gun you want when you need to walk into a room and tear everything apart in a couple of heartbeats."

"I suppose the same caveat that applied to the little revolver applies to the shotgun," I said.

"If you can't do the deed with five loads of buckshot, I'll eat my boots and my hat."

The second long gun was a rifle with a short, overly thick barrel, a folding stock, and a small, sophisticated-looking telescopic sight. A small lever with a round knob reminded me of a deer rifle, but the overall impression was something a lot more menacing and dangerous.

"This is a custom-built weapon based on a little-known beauty called the DeLisle Commando Carbine. It's a bolt-action rifle that fires subsonic forty-five caliber pistol ammunition, and the barrel is actually fitted with an integrated suppressor that's second to none. British Commando units during World War Two would use the originals to silently kill German sentries and perform other clandestine assignments. While it's not completely silent, within an urban sniping environment like you're likely to work in, you'll be able to take shots out to a hundred meters and your targets won't hear a thing except their brains hitting the sidewalk."

"I'm assuming you mean that figuratively?" I joked.

"Kid, I'd clock you with this thing, but I don't want to damage it."

The last weapon was something I finally recognized from countless '80s action movies; the Uzi. Although my parents had never approved of mindless violence on television, they were gone from the house so often that as a teenager I absorbed more than my fill of Chuck Norris, Arnold Schwarzenegger, and Sylvester Stallone mowing down bad guys by the dozens with Uzis. My recognition of the gun was immediately obvious to Richard.

"I'm guessing you already know what this is; the Uzi nine-millimeter submachine gun. This weapon is blowback operated, fires from an open bolt, with a thirty-two round magazine and a folding stock. The design may be fifty years old, but this little chatterbox can still be found all over the world, burning brass and filling graves."

"Not that I care, but isn't illegal to own one of those?" I asked.

Richard shook his head. "It's not illegal as long as you've got the right paperwork filled out and you meet all the other requirements and pay the proper fees. Of course, this beauty has never been seen by a U.S. government official; she was smuggled into the States probably twenty or thirty years ago. Been living in a crate ever since."

I pointed at the suppressors for the two pistols, as well as the DeLisle and the foot-long suppressor for the Uzi.

"All of those, they're also illegal, aren't they?" I asked.

Richard shook his head again. "They can be owned legally, with the right forms. They're almost impossible to regulate, anyway. Any half-decent machinist with the necessary tools could make the parts needed to construct a suppressor. There's dozens of little garage businesses around the country that could make one with a little work. That's how I got these," he explained.

"Those people can't get away with it, can they?" I asked.

Richard shrugged. "It's a big country and the sorts of people who do this for a living have a dim view of Big Brother and its habit of covering everything in red tape. Besides, these guys are the same sorts who take pride in living off the grid if possible, folks whose granddaddies ran their own backwoods moonshine stills and fought it out with the revenue bureau. Mostly a law-abiding sort, but the law they abide by isn't always the same law as the government wants them adhering to, and that's when you get into some sticky situations."

"So there's a whole black market being supplied by backwoods gun factories building these things?" I asked.

"You got it. God bless capitalism and free-market enterprise."

Chapter 7

The next morning, I was up at five o'clock. It was pitch black outside, and I dressed swiftly in just a tee shirt and a pair of running shorts. I ate a few pieces of dried apple and drank some water, and then we went outside in the first murky light of dawn. Richard wore a pair of running shorts as well, and led me through a series of stretches and cardio exercises. I had been on the track and field team in high school, but since going to college I hadn't engaged in more than the occasional jogging stint or a little basketball at the athletics center. Now, I knew I would pay the price.

"You're in half-decent shape, but you don't have any real tone. Working alone like you're planning, you absolutely have to be in better shape than the opposition. Going up against a bunch of easy-living mobsters, that's not too hard, but if they ever decide to bring in contract muscle to sniff you out, you might fight yourself having to outrun some ex-Army ranger who jogs ten miles a day out of habit."

"What about strength training? I'm never going to get all that strong, I'm just not built for it," I said.

"That's what guns and judo are for, to make up the difference. But I don't have time to teach you both guns and judo, so we're going to work on the guns and make sure you can run like hell when the devil starts chasing you, because trust me, in this line of work he surely will. Besides, as you become more toned and build your endurance, you're going to develop strength anyhow; your body is going to learn how to use everything it's got more efficiently than ever before, including your muscles. More importantly, in an urban environment the fast man on foot can get away from almost anything; the key is winning the race early on, before they close the net with the black and whites and the helicopters. If you can get three blocks away before the cops arrive on scene, you're home free."

While we warmed up, I got my first good look at what a life of hard violence had done to Richard's body. Although he was in excellent shape for a man of his years, seemingly without an ounce of fat on him, and ropes of corded muscle evident in his arms and legs, he was a roadmap of scars from his ankles on up. Light lines of scar tissue ran criss-cross patterns here and there, little nicks and gashes that didn't heal without leaving a mark. Other scars told of burns, bullets, bomb fragments, even bite marks, both human and animal. It was the clearest evidence you could face that no matter how good you are - and I was confident Richard was one of the best - it didn't mean you weren't going to bleed in order to get the job done and survive afterward.

Richard saw me looking at his old war wounds and chuckled. "That's forty years of abuse, but it's been a long and interesting road."

"Looks like the road had its fair share of bumps," I said.

"Bumps and more. But I'd have hanged myself in the sort of life most Americans lead, stuck in a nine-to-five job, going from cookie-cutter condo or white picket jailhouse to a small office box inside a bigger office box. And once you're there, someone tells you every day they can hire some poor schmuck in India to do your job for a tenth of what you earn. I might have lived through four decades of hell to get here, but by god I was my own man, earning my own way, and beholden to no one who didn't pay for it in the end."

"So it was worth all the blood and pain?" I asked.

Richard paused in the middle of sitting and stretching out to touch his toes, leaning with his elbows on his knees and looking out into the brightening skyline.

"The only worth a life has, is what you accomplish during your time here. If it wasn't for me, and the guys I fought and bled with over the years, the world would be a much meaner place, and I'm not just speaking in hyperbole! That, at least, makes it all worthwhile."

After we completed our stretching routine, Richard and I went through a full complement of gymnastic exercises. Push-ups, sit-ups, pull-ups, jumping jacks, back-bridges, leg-lifts, an extensive routine that had me breathing hard and feeling my muscles burn as the sun peeked over the horizon.

And that's before we started running.

"We're going to keep the runs short this week, but we'll be extending the distances over the course of the month. Your body needs to be toughened. We have to burn away the fat and leave just the rawhide and steel springs behind."

Richard's "short run" took us across the desert rocks and sands, over three dunes and through two valleys separated by long stretches of blasted nothing. Finally, at the top of the third dune, we looked back. The cabin was a fleck of dust on a small flat bump far out by the horizon. I stood there, sucking wind and soaked in sweat, bent over with my hands braced against my thighs. Richard wasn't even breathing hard. We had covered perhaps two miles.

"I never run any further than this," Richard explained, "I always want to keep an eye on the cabin. I won't get lost out here - you can always backtrack if you need to - but I never want to let the cabin out of my sight long enough for someone to deliver a hit-squad and depart."

"So what would you do if that happened? You're not exactly ready for a gunfight right now."

"Follow me and learn, Grasshopper," Richard said with a sly smile.

We walked down the back slope of the low hill we stood on, cutting to the right and running along the shallow valley. After ten minutes, we came across a small gnarled bush clinging to the side of the hill. Richard stopped next to the bush, looked at me, and then crouched down, digging into the rocky, sandy soil next to the bush. In a couple of minutes, he had dug free a white PVC plastic tube about four feet long and about nine inches in diameter.

Unscrewing one end, Richard slowly removed the contents one by one; a tightly-folded backpack, two plastic one-quart bottles of water, several packages of dried meat, fruits, and nuts, a long-barreled Colt .45 automatic with a box of fifty cartridges and three magazines, a compact pair of binoculars, a set of lightweight desert cammies, a long-bladed knife, and a partially disassembled bolt-action rifle, with two boxes of twenty cartridges and a scope.

"Food and water, long-range rifle, mid-range handgun, fighting knife, camouflage, observation equipment. If I can't deal with some armed squatters with this goodie bag, I've grown too soft anyhow."

I looked at Richard in near-wonderment. "Is this really how you live your life?" I asked.

Richard nodded. "Keeping two moves ahead in the game, just like chess."

"Remind me never to play against you," I said.

"I shouldn't have to remind you. There's a reason you hired me."

We alternated between running, jogging, and walking back to the cabin, because at that point I was utterly winded. After some water and a set of light stretches to keep from tightening up, Richard and I began the business of getting to know my newly-acquired arsenal.

"You're going to start with the long guns first. You need to know them better than you know the handguns, because a novice like yourself should make up for a lack of skill by using superior fire-power, against targets who will almost exclusively be using handguns," Richard explained.

"Do you really think Paggiano's goons will be that good?"

"Of course not. Do you think these guys belong to a rod and gun club, go shooting after brunch on Sundays and then retire for cocktails? These idiots don't know the first thing about real pistol-craft."

"So a few weeks of training from you and I should be able to shoot circles around these guys. Where's the problem?"

"The problem is, these are stone-cold murderous thugs who think beating two women to death and riddling daddy dearest with slugs, then burning down the scene of the crime, is of no more difficulty than you or I changing a flat tire. Behind the slick suits and the gold watches and the Italian sports cars, these guys are all bloodthirsty savages. What they lack in skill, they make up in their willingness to inflict extreme violence without the slightest provocation.

"When you draw down on one of these guys for the first time, no matter what you do, there are going to be lingering moral doubts floating around in your mind - is this the right thing to do, should I turn the other cheek, am I lowering myself to their level - all things that don't even occur to these dummies. Until you can purge yourself of these

109

concerns, they will always have the advantage because they won't hesitate to blow you into corpseland the moment they realize you're coming for them."

"So what you're saying is, I should make up for the fact that I'm really a bleeding heart pussy by bringing a machine-gun to a pistol fight."

Richard grinned. "I believe the term is, 'peace through superior firepower'."

The first weapon of the day was the Uzi. We went through the basics of operating the weapon; a loaded magazine goes into the receiver, the bolt gets cocked back, trigger pull lets bolt move forward, stripping a cartridge from the magazine, pushing it into the chamber, and as the bolt hits home, the firing pin strikes the primer, and the gun goes bang. Once the cartridge is fired, the recoil pushes the bolt back, the extractor pulls the shell casing free, the recoil spring pushes the bolt forward again, and the whole process repeats itself until the trigger is released or the Uzi runs out of ammunition.

"The blowback-operated submachine gun is one of man's greatest military achievements," Richard said. "The process is utter simplicity, and it gives a single man an immense amount of close-range firepower in an extremely small package. You could carry enough ammunition to kill a hundred people stacked in a few magazines and tucked into your back pockets. Ten men could turn a Greek phalanx into a corpse-pile in seconds."

"So much for man's other achievements, like the Mona Lisa," I said.

"Da Vinci would've been better off getting his tank to work," Richard replied.

Richard handed me seven empty magazines for the Uzi, each capable of holding 32 bullets. We sat and talked about how the weapon worked as we loaded each mag, and by the end, the tips of my thumb and forefingers were raw and sore.

"By the end of the month, you'll have calluses just from loading magazines," Richard told me.

Once all the magazines were loaded, Richard and I drove the Suburban down the hill a short distance from the cabin to where the desert flattened out. From the back of the Suburban we unloaded six five-gallon white buckets Richard had packed full of loose sand. Each bucket had a foot-tall number painted on it, from 1 to 6. Walking away from the vehicle, we placed them in a deep semi-circle, an inverted U twenty feet wide and thirty deep, with the opening facing us. I stood ten feet from the opening of the U.

"We're on a timetable, and don't have the luxury of having you fire at paper targets for weeks at a time. The point of this exercise is, to teach you to engage multiple random targets at different ranges. When you're ready, I'm going to call out a number. You fire on that bucket in bursts of two to four shots until I call out another bucket, at which time you shift fire to that target, and so on. When you run dry, reload and keep firing on that target until I say otherwise. Understood?"

I nodded and slapped a magazine of thirty-two cartridges into the receiver of the Uzi. I pulled back the cocking lever, felt it catch, and then brought the weapon to my shoulder. It was such a crude weapon, all stamped steel and flat black finish, but I felt a sudden love for the thing. It was all fucking business. No engraved walnut stock, no nickel plating, no pearl handles, just a bare minimum of parts and lots of bullets ready to go down the barrel. I pictured Chuck Norris in Delta Force or Arnold Schwarzenegger in Commando blazing away with an Uzi in hand, killing terrorists or pissant soldiers, and suddenly all my nerves and anxiety melted away. I straightened up, leaned into the target a bit, and snugged the extended stock against my shoulder.

"Ready when you are, Richard."

"Three!" Richard shouted, and I started killing nameless Hollywood extras.

We stayed out most of the morning. It was amazing how fast the Uzi could go through seven magazines, and since reloading took far longer than shooting, there was ample time for Richard to critique my work while we loaded.

"Working with a chatter-box like the Uzi, trying too hard to use the sights will get you killed as you muddle about lining up the perfect shot. Best to sight over the weapon at these ranges and watch where the bullets strike, then correct your aim accordingly.

"I can see you're trying to count exactly how many shots you're firing. Don't do that. Get good at firing in short bursts, and then practice not necessarily counting the bursts, but knowing how many you've fired instinctively. The more you practice, the more it'll become second nature.

"Don't put a death grip on the gun, even in full-auto. Trying to keep the gun from jumping from the recoil by holding tighter is just going to tire you out even faster. Instead, use the recoil to your benefit. Aim low with your first shot, then ride the recoil up through the target, like you're closing a zipper starting at his navel and ending at his chin."

"Only I'm not zippering him up, I'm zippering him open." I add.

"That's the ticket," Richard nodded. Our conversations always left me in awe of how casually Richard discussed an automatic weapon's ability to tear a person apart.

We ate lunch back at the cabin, and in the afternoon, we walked back to the well-ventilated white buckets, bandaged their burst bellies with a roll of duct tape, and topped them off with spilled sand and desert dirt. By now, the sun was a white-hot hammer beating at me from the sky, the desert floor serving as the anvil. We weren't sweating so much as simply evaporating water directly through our pores, and we hydrated constantly. We guzzled warm water from plastic bottles, left in the shade of the Suburban's cargo bed to keep them at a drinkable temperature, but the water left our bodies almost as quickly as we drank it. Even though I had been drinking water all day, I found by one in the afternoon I had yet to pee.

I did protect my light skin from the sun, wearing

a pair of sunglasses and a wide-brimmed straw hat like Richard, with a bandanna tied around my neck kept soaked with water, the evaporation helping to keep me cool. I made sure to regularly coat exposed skin in sunblock, although Richard had me use a low SPF so that in time I would develop a healthy tan.

"If you baby your skin out here too much, that one day you forget to protect it, you'll pay. Better to build up a good tan over time and let it do some of the work for you."

During the afternoon, Richard had me begin working with the little Beretta automatic.

"Shooting with a handgun in close combat is all about making sure the gun is pointing in the right direction when you pull the trigger."

"My uncle said much the same thing when we shot that revolver," I said.

"Jamie certainly knows what he's talking about. Problem with a pistol is, it's a very short and light object being held out from the body unbraced and subject to many gross motor functions being applied in the simple act of pulling the trigger. Your body's natural action in pulling the trigger, if unchecked, will cause that barrel to wander all over hell and back. The only thing that prevents that mess, especially when the pucker factor is high, is training and muscle memory."

So, unlike shooting the Uzi, with the Beretta we took things slow. Richard showed me how to hold the pistol correctly, how it should sit in my hand and where my finger should rest on the trigger, repeating the instructions I received from Jamie a few days before. Once my grip was correct, I began to fire slow, sure, steady shots at the buckets, one shot every few seconds, focusing on keeping the movements consistent and smooth, not worrying about putting every bullet as close to the "bulls-eye" as possible, just keeping all my shots consistently center mass.

"It's cliché to say it," Richard explained, "but you don't pull a trigger, you squeeze it. Of course, it's not a slow squeeze, not in a firefight, but it is a smooth squeeze. There's a difference between doing something slowly and doing something smoothly. It's a subtlety that you'll learn over time and it's going to give you an advantage over all those other dummies. When they draw and fire, their guns are never pointing in the right direction when the hammer drops. If your gun points true when theirs isn't, you might just walk away intact."

"I thought you said this morning that marksmanship isn't as important as having the right kind of killing instincts," I said.

Richard gave me an ominous smile. "Don't worry, we'll work on that too."

As the afternoon shifted to evening and the air began to cool down a little, we collected most of the spent brass from the day's shooting before returning to the cabin.

"Even though we're in a state that discharges more firearms per capita than anywhere else in the country, I don't want someone wandering through when we aren't around and finding hundreds of new, shiny, spent pistol casings. At best, it might draw unwanted curiosity to what we're doing. At worst, someone might think I'm stashing guns in the cabin and try to break in, which would result in a very bad accident on their part, and me needing a new cabin."

Before doing anything else that evening, Richard taught me how to break down, clean, and reassemble the Uzi and the Beretta.

"For a soldier, there is no more important skill than being able to quickly and proficiently service their weapon in any condition; rain, sleet, snow, desert, swamp, jungle, whatever. Guns in the field get dirty, and dirty guns fail to work, which gets you killed. You, on the other hand, will be working for only short periods of time in a mostly clean urban environment, and can break down and service your guns at your leisure, so we're not going to do the whole field-strip and clean blindfolded routine like you see in the army movies."

After cleaning the guns, Richard put me through another set of stretches, loosening up those muscles that had tightened during a day of range work like my neck, shoulders, arms, and back. Stretches were followed by more calisthenics, which were in turn followed by another run. This time Richard required me to run out to the hidden cache so I knew where it was if I needed to find it, and after a little confusion, I was able to locate the gnarled bush on the back slope of the hill. We then half-ran, half walked back to the cabin, Richard looking none the worse for wear, while I was utterly spent.

After dinner, it was time to do my homework. Richard had prepared several binders for me filled with photocopied or scanned articles from a number of combat-related periodicals, some geared towards civilian sport shooting and personal defense, some geared towards law enforcement, and some purely for military or "armchair commando" types.

"This is going to be a crash course in the world of the private sector gun-for-hire, so you need to get your head into that world, and fast. I'm going to be using terms and talking about concepts that I need to express without taking the time to explain them to you, so this is going to be your required reading."

That evening I read articles on the history of the Uzi, about point shooting and trigger control, on concealed handgun carry, self-defense laws in various states and the overall perception of self-defense as it pertained to handguns in America.

"Richard, I suppose this is all relevant, but I'm not looking to engineer my revenge killings into a series of legally justifiable self-defense shootings. Why am I reading this?"

Richard sat down at the table next to me. "First things first, it's all about cultural immersion. Illicit or not, you're entering a niche with its own lingo and its own viewpoint on the world. Second, if you ever find yourself caught in the web of Johnny Law, you're going to want to know what to expect. I hope to teach you what you need in order to avoid getting caught, but there aren't any guarantees in life, except for death."

"So this is hoping for the best, but preparing for the worst."

"Got it in one," Richard said.

I finished my reading by ten and rolled into my cot ten minutes later, after brushing my teeth and a quick wash-towel bath. I don't think I'd ever been so tired in my life. Oddly, I don't think I'd ever felt so satisfied in a day's hard work, either.

I was probably asleep before my eyes closed.

The rest of the week, we continued what had I started. Every morning Richard and I would start with stretching and calisthenics, followed by a four-mile round trip run. We'd then have a light breakfast and follow that by loading magazines, then spend the morning shooting the Uzi. After a couple days playing "pick a number", Richard had me try shooting at a distance, learning control and technique, as well as firing at a walk and even at a run. I must have fired ten thousand rounds of ammunition by the end of the week.

Afternoons were dedicated to handgun shooting, and after the third day, Richard had me working on rapid firing two or three shots at a time. I also expanded my practices to include all three pistols, switching between the Beretta and the Glock, sometimes even emptying one, then drawing the snub-nose revolver from a back pocket and emptying it as a follow-up. Richard explained that often, the fastest reload was simply to draw another firearm and keep shooting.

For most of the pistol drills, Richard's emphasis

was on close range, center of mass targets, engaging quickly with several shots at a time.

"Don't fire once and pause to see if you hit or not. Handguns aren't reliable man-killers, especially something small like the Beretta. You want to shoot until you put your target on the ground, then maybe a couple more for good measure. Remember, you're not a cop or a law-abiding citizen. For you, there's no such thing as excessive force when it comes to dealing with these slobs, just kill or be killed."

In the evenings we would conclude the physical training with more exercises and another run, followed by a quick dinner and more homework. There was an unbelievable amount of information to take in, and Richard was an expert in all of it, from guns to explosives to disguises to logistics and finances.

"Your first week, we are going to focus on shooting. Using a firearm is something that, once upon a time, any young American male living in a rural area learned as a perfectly normal part of becoming a man. Certainly around here, marksmanship would have been learned alongside riding a horse, building a fire, and navigating the wilderness by the sun and the stars. All of America's wars, even back before we were Americans at all, were fought and won by young men who had learned to lead a moving target and put a round in a vital place long before they entered military service."

"So what you're saying is, I've got a long way to go."

"I've got a lot of later twentieth-century poppy-cock to drum out of you, kid. We've got a long way to go before you're anywhere close to your average turn of the century rabbit-sniping hillbilly."

"In happier times, I'd consider that a compliment."

One of Richard's homework assignments was to memorize a deck of one hundred index cards, each with the picture of a gun on one side and a handful of relevant facts on the other. The cards listed caliber, capacity, basic method of operation, whether it had a safety or not, and any other notable features. About half of the guns were pistols of some sort, while the other half were split between rifles, shotguns, and submachine guns. Their designs and intended uses were myriad, and they came in all shapes, sizes, and styles.

Richard insisted on the importance of this knowledge. "Sooner or later, you will find yourself in a situation where the only working gun you can use is the one in the hands of the guy you just killed. You're going to need a basic familiarity in how the gun operates, where the safety is, if you need to cock it before it can fire, how to check the magazine, even how many bullets it can hold. Having that knowledge in your head and ready to be recalled is going to save you precious seconds and keep you alive."

By the end of the first week even Richard admitted that, within urban firefight ranges - perhaps thirty or forty feet - I was able to point and hit my target with acceptable reliability. Richard reminded me again and again that lining up for the perfect bull's-eye wasn't what won a gunfight; it was hitting your target and putting him down.

"The only scorecard that ever gets tallied in the real world is how many times you walk away from the fight and leave your opponent dead in the dust. I can shoot damn straight when the occasion calls for it, but I'm not a bulls-eye expert. The difference is, I can hit a man on the other side of the street while I'm running, ducking, and dodging automatic weapons fire. Sacrificing pinpoint accuracy for shooting fast and on the move may mean you burn a little more ammo, but in the end, it's going to keep you alive a lot longer. Gunfighting isn't a biathlon. It's an ugly business that rewards dirty tricks and being faster and meaner and more ruthless than the other guy. It's the only way you're going to win."

Little did I know, I was about to learn exactly what Richard meant.

Chapter 8

I awoke to Richard's boot lightly nudging my cot. Sitting up, I rubbed my eyes and looked around. It was still dark out, and a sleepy voice in the back of my head told me I hadn't been asleep for more than a couple of hours. Richard held a lantern in his hand. He was fully dressed, and a heavy black automatic fitted with a suppressor hung under his armpit in a shoulder holster.

"What's up?" I asked, running a hand through my hair.

"Time for a field exercise," he said to me, little humor in his voice.

I dressed quickly, the fog of sleep in my brain evaporating fast. Black boots, dark blue jeans, black t-shirt, a dark grey pullover, black knit watch cap, and thin black neoprene glove liners. Southern Texas in the spring can be positively frigid when the sun is down, and I could almost see my breath outside. Before we got into the Suburban, Richard handed me a gunbelt with my holstered Glock, two extra magazines, and a small tactical flashlight. No sooner did I buckle it on, when Richard then handed me a Kevlar-lined tactical vest with six SMG magazines, three to each side. I could tell just by looking at them that they were magazines for the Uzi.

"This is a lot of firepower," I said.

"Trust me, always better to have too much than not enough," Richard replied.

I got into the cab of the Suburban, and propped against the seat between me and Richard was the suppressed Uzi submachine gun. A black gusset bag, contents unknown, also lay on the seat between us.

"Where are we going?" I asked.

"You'll see," Richard answered.

We drove in silence for perhaps half an hour. Soon after pulling away from the cabin, Richard slipped what appeared to be night-vision goggles over his eyes and killed the headlights. We were driving through the darkness of the Texas desert, and a thin crescent moon illuminated the countryside in the dimmest of shadows. I felt certain that wherever we were going, it wasn't for the purposes of a "field exercise", and I was filled with a deep sense of foreboding.

Richard turned off the road and drove the Suburban down a rutted gravel trail at the bottom of a low, narrow gulch, going slow with the windows down, stopping and listening every so often for anything unnatural or out of the ordinary. Eventually we arrived at the end of the gulch, surrounded on three sides by steep hardscrabble rock and tough brush. Richard killed the engine and we sat in silence, listening to the motor tick and ping as it cooled down, the only sounds that reached our ears. I checked my watch; it was 2:30 in the morning.

After a short while, Richard took off the night-vision goggles and put them in the bag. He slipped out of the Suburban, taking the gusset bag with him. He motioned for me to take the Uzi, and put his finger to his lips, indicating we move silently. I opened the door to the Suburban as quietly as I could, taking the submachine gun with me as I climbed out and gently pressed the door shut until I heard it click. Turning from the door, I discovered Richard had silently made his way around to my side, and without saying a word he motioned for me to follow him up the side of the gulch.

We walked through the desert night, silent and careful but making good progress. With my eyes fully adjusted to the moonlight, and with my senses strung taut, I had little trouble avoiding a misstep or finding a dry branch underfoot. Richard was positively a ghost; he made no sound and was constantly having to slow down to wait for me. I was sure he could have doubled his pace while moving just as quietly.

Finally, Richard fell back alongside me, and put a hand on my shoulder to indicate caution. We slowed down almost to a crawl. I soon realized we were coming to the edge of a wide valley, easily half a mile across. I could see, perhaps three or four hundred meters away, a couple of lights, maybe cabins close by each other. I looked to Richard and saw him pull a pair of heavy-looking binoculars out of his gusset bag and peer through them at the lights down below. It was a few minutes before he took the binoculars away from his eyes. Richard then turned and handed them to me.

I brought the binoculars to my eyes and looked down into the valley. The binoculars were night-vision, and what I thought to be a pair of cabins was actually a couple of trailers and three parked automobiles, two trucks and a van. One of the trailers was boxy and rectangular, with several windows and a small chimney at one end, sending a lazy curl of smoke up into the air. It looked like the mobile field offices you'd see at a construction site. A set of rough wooden stairs was placed in front of the door, and the windows had a dim light glowing from within, partially hidden as if behind thin sets of blinds. The other trailer was a towable campground-style family camper. The three windows I could see from this angle were lit with a flicker that I assumed meant someone was watching television. Next to each of these trailers there was a heavy-duty pickup truck. Each truck was more than capable of towing either of the two trailers out of the valley. The van was large, capable of seating at least eight men, and nearby I saw a portable gasoline generator. I could detect the faintest growl on the wind when the breeze blew right, and cables snaked from the generator through the rocks and dirt to both trailers.

Richard touched my shoulder, and when I glanced his way, I saw his finger pointing to the left of the trailers. Bringing the binoculars up and slowly panning to the left, I came across a man, walking along the valley floor, holding what I guessed was an AK. I watched the man for several minutes, and it became evident that he was a guard or sentry, slowly circling the encampment on a perimeter patrol. I brought the binoculars away from my face and turned again to Richard. He motioned with a nod of his head that we should begin to walk back the way we came.

As we moved back away from the valley, knowing there was an armed man, certainly a criminal, not too far away added an extra dose of caution to every step I took. When we were perhaps another five hundred meters away from the edge of the valley, Richard stopped us and stepped in close to me so he could whisper and be heard.

"What did you see? Tell me all the details."

I told him everything: what I saw, and what I surmised. My best guess, it was a temporary camp set up by an unknown criminal element, smugglers or drug dealers or other criminals who needed a base out in the desert.

"You're pretty close. Those aren't exactly drug dealers, they are drug makers. Cookers, actually. They're cooking chemicals together to make methamphetamine. The boxy trailer is their lab, the chimney is their ventilation, the generator is providing power. The camper is their bunkhouse. Chemicals and generator came out here in the van, they set up the trailer and get to work. In a single night they can cook up a hundred grand worth of drugs."

"How did you know where to look?" I asked.

"I've had my eye on them for the last couple of months. They move around some, but tend to use the same few remote locations over and over again. I planted a little seismic transmitter along the road leading into this valley a couple of weeks ago, been checking every night to see if it's noticed movement. Tonight it picked up the right sort of ground vibrations; three large, multi-wheeled vehicles and two towed bodies without engines. It's the only traffic - other than the occasional dirt bike or jeep - that ever gets out here, so I knew it was these dummies."

"Okay, but how did you find out about these guys in the first place?"

"Was out hiking around here a while back, just getting out into the desert to keep myself sharp and familiar with the land. I came across some tire tracks and signs of spilled chemicals, a fire pit, recent trash. These boys aren't exactly the "carry in, carry out" types. Didn't take a detective to figure illicit activity was going on, so curiosity got the best of me and I started checking this valley regularly. Found them one night, so I decided to take a look. Worked my way right into the middle of their camp, scoped out the cooking trailer, the camper, the whole operation."

"Why didn't you do anything about it? Least you could have done was report it."

Richard gave a small shrug. "Curiosity, mostly. Nobody pays me to be a law enforcement official, so I wasn't about to do the job for them. Also, if I was going to report anything, anonymously of course, I'd want more information and a bigger fish to snag on the hook than just some armed tweakers cooking up ice out in the middle of the desert. There's probably a hundred cooking camps scattered throughout Texas this very moment."

"So what are we doing?" I asked.

Richard gave me his grimmest smile, barely illuminated in the moonlight. "We're here for a little target practice. You need some seasoning, son."

It took me a moment to understand what Richard meant. "Wait, hold on. You want me to go down there and kill a bunch of drug dealers?"

"Like I said, they're probably just the cookers and their guards, not the actual dealers. Although if their operation is small enough, they might sell directly to the street vendors, which would then make them dealers."

I waved my hands in front of my face. "Whatever, who cares. I'm not going to just walk down there and kill a bunch of guys cooking up drugs out in the desert. That's just nuts."

"Why?"

"Why what?"

"Why is it nuts? They're brewing up pure poison. They sell that garbage to moms, dads, kids, everyone. These criminal delinquents ruin lives. Their poison ends lives. Taxpayer money gets wasted fighting a losing battle against drugs because we don't have the stomach to do what really needs to be done in order to win, and that's to hunt the slimeballs down and blow them away. What's wrong with that?"

I looked at Richard in disbelief. "What do you mean, what's wrong with that? Everything! We can't just throw aside the legal system and go around shooting every drug dealer or dope grower in the country. There has to be some kind of order."

Richard had to keep himself from laughing out loud. "Listen to yourself. What are you paying me to help you accomplish? Step outside that 'legal system' of yours and blow away some greaseballs who managed to dance through some hoops and get away with murder, literally. Why is it okay for you to consider shooting up the Paggiano family, but not these turkeys?"

Before Richard began to chastise me I was already cringing inside, because I recognized the hypocrisy of what I was saying as it was coming out of my mouth. Organized crime family, meth cooking trailer trash. Two categories of people in this world that were both deserving of some extremely capital punishment. So why did I consider taking my revenge on the Paggianos to be acceptable, while the thought of killing people who directly contribute to the misery of innocent lives was somehow anathema to me?

Richard could see me working it out in my head, and he knew the answer before I did. "It's because the revenge is personal to you; that's how you can justify it. You don't know the rednecks down in that valley, and you don't know the people who deal their drugs, or the people buying and using, either. So you can't work up that righteous indignation, you can't make it a crime of passion."

I shrugged and looked a little embarrassed. "You're right. I just can't justify it to myself."

Suddenly, Richard stepped in close and gripped my shoulder. I looked down and almost shouted in surprise when I realized that he had drawn the heavy black automatic without me even seeing it. The muzzle hovered an inch from my gut.

"That's real gosh-darn unfortunate, because if you need to 'justify your actions' before dropping the hammer every time you've got some jerk in your sights, I might as well spare you the trouble of going on this little crusade of yours and blow your kidneys all over the desert right here and now. Killing isn't about weighing the morality of every trigger pull, it's about putting people who deserve to die in the ground so the people who don't deserve death can go on living their benign, meaningless lives a little while longer. That's it. Do you think you can shoot Pauly Paggiano in the face for what he did, but you can't go down and cap the filth brewing up poison going to some single mother in need of a fix? Well, what makes you think you can shoot Paggiano's bodyguard, who never did anything to you? I mean, he just works for the family, right? Once you start letting that nonsense corrode the wiring between your brain and your trigger finger, you might as well put one in your own brainpan, because you're done."

"So you'd go down there and kill everyone just because you think they deserve to die?"

"Just because I think they deserve a bullet doesn't mean I'm going to go down there and give 'em one. I'm a retired mercenary, not a serial killer, and I'm not a vigilante, either. I kill when there's something in it for me: money, information, self-preservation. If I started making it my life's work to bump off every jerk who needed burying, I wouldn't be able to enjoy any of the retirement nest egg I've set aside!"

"So if it's a for-profit venture, where's my profit? Or, for that matter, where's yours? You could've taken my money and never bothered to bring me out here. What's the angle for you?"

Richard still hadn't taken away his automatic, but he let out a little grunt and his arm lowered a fraction. "What's in it for you? You need to get your dipstick wet, son. You've got to pop your combat cherry while I mother hen, before you go out on your own and take your vengeance. On-the-job training in this line of work is a recipe for an early and permanent retirement, but if I can guide you through your first firefight, watch your back a little so you don't make any rookie mistakes, help you Monday-morning quarterback a little afterward, maybe you won't get dead the first time you run into some of Paggiano's hired goombahs."

"You still didn't answer me. What's in it for you? There's no guarantee one of those guys isn't going to get lucky and end you too."

"Two reasons. First, you paid me to teach you to kill, and I'm going to make sure you get your money's worth. You don't learn to kill without doing some killing, so here we are. Anything less and I won't have fulfilled the spirit of my contract with you, and believe it or not, I'm a man of my word. I'm not sending you away without doing my best to make sure you can do the job."

"And the second reason?" I asked.

Richard grunted and holstered his pistol, then turned and started walking back towards the valley. "I made your uncle Jamie a promise to prepare you the best I could, because I owe him a debt from a long time ago. That means even more to me than the money you paid. I can always return my fee to you. I can't repay Jamie what I owe him."

I watched Richard walk away, and a sudden resolution came over me. I had been given a peek, a sliver of understanding and insight into the sort of world Richard came from. I knew now that he was right. I made an oath of vengeance to pay the Paggianos back, believing they deserved to die and thinking I would be able to kill them, while at the same time thinking there was no way I could kill men I didn't know, who ruined lives every day with the drugs they created. Not only was it naive, but the self-rationalization would get me killed long before my task was completed.

With my mind finally clear of doubt, I turned and followed Richard back into the desert night.

In vengeance, there are no half-measures.

Chapter 9

It took us an hour to get into position, moving only when the night-vision binoculars told us no one was moving around the encampment, and the sentry was on the far side, with the vehicles and trailers between us. We had skirted the camp until Richard found a good point for our ambush; a bit of scrub brush that would provide some concealment. Richard draped us with a thin camouflage net he had taken from his gusset bag. It would break up our outline enough that hopefully, as long as we were still and silent, we wouldn't be noticed in the dim moonlight.

There, we hunkered down and waited for the sentry to make his final pass, as he came around the trailers and circled back in our direction. I was lying on my stomach, the Uzi aimed out in front of me, a magazine loaded and the bolt cocked and ready to fire, my finger well away from the trigger.

Richard leaned in close and whispered in my ear. "Here he comes now. We are going to let him go by. Once he gets about twenty feet away, I will pull away the net and you are to fire. Put at least three bursts into him, even if he goes down with the first one. We can't let him get off a shot, so use at least half a magazine to make sure he's down and dead. Then, we'll get close and examine him."

In the moonlight, I could barely make out the sentry as he came closer and closer. I could hear his booted feet crunching through the loose sand and rock more clearly than I could see him. Richard spotted for me with the night vision goggles now. We were too close for the binoculars and Richard wanted his hands free in case he needed to bring his pistol into play. I could see his gun clearly now, held in his hand as he lay in the dirt next to me. It was a big black Heckler & Koch .45 automatic, and from my reading I knew it was designed with special forces types in mind, useful for eliminating sentries and guard dogs. A long, fat suppressor was screwed to the muzzle, and a small laser sight was attached to the trigger guard underneath the barrel. That a firearms manufacturer could justify designing a pistol for the explicit purpose of shooting unsuspecting men in the dark of night was both fascinating and terrible to me.

Richard placed his hand on my shoulder and brought me back to the here and now. The sentry walked past us, slow measured footsteps unhurried and without any pretense of stealth or caution. No doubt this guy had walked a patrol duty here dozens of times without encountering so much as a curious coyote or jackrabbit. He probably thinks there's as much chance of getting into a shoot-out tonight as some sleepy small-town sheriff thinks he'll be getting into a gunfight with a gang of professional bank robbers. Unfortunately for the sheriff, and for this guy, sometimes the day just doesn't turn out like you planned.

The guard was walking away now, just a few feet to go. I felt Richard lift the netting from the barrel of my Uzi and over my head. My mind raced. I could feel panic overtaking me, and for a terrible, awful moment I almost started to cry. I was going to shoot a man in the back, for fuck's sake. It was one of the lowest, vilest, most uncivilized things you could do to another human being, and I was -

Richard tapped my shoulder with a single finger. I fired.

The first burst was three, maybe four shots; just a soft, stuttering cough thanks to the suppressor. The Uzi spat brass into the dirt a few feet away, and I saw the dim shape of the guard stumble and lurch, heard him gasp. I fired again, a longer, raking burst that started near his thighs and rode up his body, perhaps half a dozen slugs. He toppled over and sprawled onto the ground, his rifle making a soft clatter as it tumbled from his hands.

"Up! Hit him again, one more burst!" Richard hissed in my ear.

I scrambled to my feet, almost firing the Uzi into the ground in my haste. I took half a dozen hurried steps forward, just enough to get a better view of the target, and then I brought the Uzi up to my shoulder and raked the dim shape from hip to head with another half-dozen rounds. I could see the body jerk and twitch a bit as each of the shots struck home, but I knew at that moment he was dead before he hit the ground; the last fusillade was just me punching holes in dead meat.

Richard walked up next to me, putting his hand across the top of my Uzi and gently pointing the weapon down at the ground. "You've got him, William. Come on, quick. Let's check the body, confirm the kill. Can't leave him behind unchecked even if you're sure he's done."

As we approached the body, I could smell the blood. It was an awful, foreign smell. Modern, first-world types rarely know what a large volume of hot, freshly spilled blood smells like, and we're better off not knowing. I found myself choking back against it.

Richard leaned in close. "Breathe it in, get used to it quick. Breathe through your mouth if you have to, it won't hit you as hard. Get past it as fast as you can."

I opened my mouth wide and pumped air into my lungs in quick, quiet breaths, trying not to gasp or gulp but rather just inhale and exhale as much air as possible. It helped clear my mind and kept me from feeling so queasy and faint as we reached the body and crouched down. I could see the guard's back was riddled with bullet wounds, at least eight or ten, and at least one bullet had struck him in the back of the head. The diagonal shot had torn through the skull at an angle and blown away a chunk of bone and scalp as big around as the palm of my hand. In the night, the colors were all washed out to shades of grey, but the ragged circle of dark, glistening flesh surrounded by blood-spattered blonde hair was unmistakable.

Richard reached under the body and felt the guard's throat for a few seconds, then withdrew his hand and nodded. "He's gone. The hit to the head flipped his switch for sure, but at least three of those body shots would have been terminal. Still, best to have made sure. Check his gun, but be careful. Don't make any noise, and make sure it won't go off."

I turned from the body, grateful to have something to do even for a few seconds, and I carefully picked up the AK. I saw one of my bullets had punched a massive dent in the stamped sheet steel receiver, and a second bullet had glanced off of the magazine a third of the way down its length, warping it badly. I showed it to Richard.

"Leave it, it's useless now. Come on, time to move. We don't know when someone's going to come looking for this dummy."

I stood up, took another few deep breaths, and tried to compose myself. Surprisingly, I found I was holding it together better than had I imagined. I wasn't shutting down, I wasn't bawling or cursing my lost innocence. Truth be told, the adrenaline was coursing through my body at a hundred miles an hour, every nerve singing and on full alert. You hear about such a thing as a "combat high", but now I understood what people meant by it. I pulled the half-spent magazine from the Uzi, put it between my teeth, and then pulled a fresh "stick" from my vest, reloading the submachine gun and tucking the half-empty mag into the empty pocket.

"Now what?" I whispered to Richard.

Without answering, Richard motioned for me to follow. We moved twenty meters back along the guard's route, heading towards the meth cooking trailer at an oblique angle. When we came within thirty meters, Richard stopped me and dropped down to one knee. I did the same, tucking the Uzi into my shoulder and propping its warm suppressor on my knee.

Richard pointed to the trailer. "I want you to empty a magazine into the meth lab. Walk the shots back and forth the length of the trailer about four feet off the floor. Hopefully we'll upset something delicate and start a fire. When your mag runs dry, reload as fast as you can. We want to draw these dummies out of their camper without them knowing what's going on, and then cut them down before their eyes adjust to the dark. Got that?"

I nodded. All hesitation was gone now. I was positively thrumming with the excitement of the moment. I brought the Uzi up, sighted down the weapon towards one end of the trailer, and squeezed the trigger. The submachine gun snarled deep and low thanks to the suppressor, brass spinning out into space and tinkling across the ground to my side, the slugs rattling and thumping into the wooden siding of the lab trailer like the frenzied, staccato hammering of a mad woodpecker. Near the end of the magazine I heard a brief, strangled cry from within the trailer. I realized I'd just killed, or at least wounded, another person inside the lab. About the same time, I saw a brief flash light up the curtained windows, and I knew I must have ignited something inside the trailer.

The magazine emptied, and just as I'd practiced while shooting on the range, I unfastened the empty mag, tossed it to the side, and pulled a fresh one from my vest. I slid it home smoothly and gave it a sharp rap on the base with my open palm to make sure it was seated tight, all in one fluid movement. I drew back the bolt, ready to fire; the reload took all of three seconds.

"Here comes the whirlwind..." I heard Richard whisper next to me.

I saw out of the corner of my eye he had the night vision goggles propped up on his forehead, the H&K .45 held out in front of him in a two-handed grip, elbow propped on his knee. He might as well be waiting for a traffic light to turn green, for all the lack of concern in his features.

Two heartbeats later, the door to the meth lab trailer slammed open, and silhouetted in smoke and flame a man in blue jeans and a white t-shirt stained red, a respirator and goggles on his face, stumbled down the stairs and half-sprawled in the dirt. He was hollering something incomprehensible, but it was obviously heard by someone in the camper, because a moment later the flickering blue-white glow of the television ceased.

"Take him, take him!" Richard hissed.

I shifted my aim slightly from the camper to

the foot of the lab's stairs and raked a burst into the wounded man. The shots jerked him to the side and rolled him into the dirt, but I couldn't see where I hit him from this distance. We were too far away from the trailer, sacrificing accuracy for the concealment of the desert night, well out of the illumination coming from the trailers.

I heard a deep cough from my side, and a fat brass casing spun past me. Richard grunted in satisfaction and I realized he must have finished off the "cook".

A moment later, the screen door of the camper flew open, and a tall, lanky man in shorts and a wife-beater came out, a pump shotgun in his hands, stock tucked into his shoulder. The man was looking down the barrel but not aiming, sweeping the muzzle of the shotgun side to side, always pointing it where he looked. I sensed he knew what he was doing, and I had to put him down quick. I took a breath, let it half out, made sure to use the sights on the Uzi, and squeezed off a single aimed round at the man, hoping for a head shot. By the firelight coming from the open trailer door, I saw the dark blossom of red suddenly appear high on the right side of his chest. The man staggered back half a step, then brought up the shotgun and fired.

I quailed at the sound. Up until this moment, everything had been relatively quiet. All my gunfire and Richard's single shot were suppressed, the loudest sounds had been the bullets hammering through the lab trailer and the muffled shout of the cook. Compared to that, the shotgun sounded like an atomic bomb going off. I didn't notice where the pellets struck, but I heard a faint whispering off to my right, the sound of the shot pellets cutting through the air. I lined up and fired again, this time a short burst of three slugs, and the shooter pitched back into the dust, arms and legs splayed out.

"Now, move!" Richard growled.

We shifted just in time. One of the camper's windows shattered outwards, and a foot-long tongue of flame lit up the night as someone inside sprayed the desert with an automatic weapon. The ground near where we had been kneeling exploded in dust and small stones catapulting into the air. We dropped to a low crouch to the left of our original position, the burning trailer eclipsing most of the camper.

"Light automatic rifle fire, five fifty-six mil, probably an M-4. He just burned through a thirty-round mag. He's reloading. Hose either side of the window, now!"

I brought up the Uzi and put a long burst through both sides of the window. When I switched to the right side and fired, I saw something fall into view inside the camper door. The shooter, right-handed, had been hiding behind the thin trailer wall as he reloaded. The Uzi ran dry as I finished my right-hand burst, and as I pulled the mag free and reached for my reload, I heard two men shouting, not from inside the camper, but from back behind it.

Richard pointed towards the back of the camper. "The windows, they crawled out. We need to move. We have to outflank them before it happens to us!"

With that we got to our feet and turned to run,

only to be knocked flat when the world split in half with fire and thunder. Something nasty inside the lab had finally caught fire. The entire trailer, filled with vapors and gases and god knew what else, maybe propane tanks or bottles of volatile chemicals, blew out and up in a great rolling fireball.

I sensed Richard rolling to his feet, uncoiling into a combat crouch, the H&K in that steady two-handed grip, tracking back and forth looking for a target. But we were lit up almost like it was daylight, and I knew the advantage we gained staying hidden in the dark was long gone. I scrambled around in the dirt, trying to get to my feet, but my head felt like it was filled with cotton and I couldn't find the Uzi.

"Your pistol! Stop looking for the chatterbox and draw your sidearm!" Richard shouted, all pretense of stealth gone.

I stumbled to my feet and pulled the blocky automatic from my belt. I mimicked Richard's combat grip and scanned the area, looking for the two men who had escaped from the camper. I could see the truck nearest to the lab was covered in flaming debris, and the paint was beginning to peel and burn. Bits of burning wood siding and other flaming or smoldering debris were scattered all over the place, a score of little campfires in a twenty meter radius. The smoke had an awful, acrid, chemical reek to it and I dreaded thinking of what I might be inhaling.

"Fall back and circle to the left - we need to find those jerkweeds!" Richard shouted.

Richard began to walk with a crabbing,

side-stepping motion that kept him facing the camper but moving to his left. I had practiced this sort of walk before on the range, but I was too disoriented. Instead I just held my pistol in my right hand pointed towards the camper and walked in a crouch as we circled around.

The first shots almost took me in the face. I heard the report of a pistol, and felt the snap-crack of the bullet as it passed an inch or two from my head. I saw the muzzle flash from more shots a moment later, coming from the right side of the camper. The shooter was obscured by the flames and smoke of the ruined trailer, and I sensed another pair of shots passing by me. I swung about to face the shooter, pulling the Glock into a two-handed grip, and fired five times as fast as I could work the trigger. I didn't see the shooter go down, or if I hit him, but there was no return fire.

We continued to circle, slowly shifting back and to the left, the back of the camper and the dented white van coming into view. I was more terrified than I had ever been in my entire life, certain that, at any moment, a shot would ring out and I'd find myself tumbling into the dirt. I saw Richard out of the corner of my eye, calm and sure on the surface, but I could tell that underneath he was a tense as a drum skin. Beads of perspiration were running down his face, drawing channels in the coating of dust across his features. It struck me that despite his long, long history of service and slaughter, Richard was keenly aware of his own mortality at this moment.

"Could they have run off into the desert?" I whispered.

"Maybe, but we can't take the chance. Besides, they have to know it's just one or two men. Better to wait until we show ourselves and cut us down."

"So what do we do?" I asked.

"Make sure we shoot faster and straighter."

The moment was broken as the headlights of a pickup truck cut two paths of light out into the desert off to our left. The engine roared to life, and the tires spun in the loose desert dirt as the truck lurched forward, spraying a fantail of dust and pebbles. The driver must have slipped into the cab from the opposite side of the truck, and as he pulled away, an arm extended out of the cab and a two-foot jet of flame blazed at us. A line of bullet impacts raced towards Richard and me, and we threw our bodies to either side in an effort to get away from the barrage. Then the driver's gun ran dry, some sort of little submachine gun that ate through its ammunition in a second or two, and the driver raced the engine again, attempting to make his escape.

"Stop him!" Richard yelled as he came to his feet, moving so fast I could only marvel at how quickly he got his legs back under him.

Richard aimed the H&K and emptied it as fast as he could pull the trigger, running the pistol dry and beginning his reload before I even fired my first shot. I brought up the Glock and fired off the remaining ten rounds, and halfway through Richard had finished reloading and started firing again.

The truck swerved once, twice, and finally skidded to a stop perhaps a hundred meters away. Richard broke into a run, reloading again as he ran, sprinting at a slight angle to the left of the truck. I stood and reloaded as fast as I could, then dashed after Richard, and as I ran I saw the driver's door slam open. The driver stumbled free of the cab, silhouetted by the glow of the headlights in the dust cloud around the truck. The driver brought up his submachine gun and fired an erratic burst, ripping up the ground to my right.

Without slowing down, pistol out straight and level in front of him, Richard fired twice while at a dead run, and I saw the driver flop against the open door of the truck and drop to the ground. I couldn't believe the shot, at least thirty meters and in the dark, after running flat out for over twice that distance. By the time I caught up to Richard, I was already trembling with adrenaline and exertion, the pistol unsteady in my hands. Richard kept his pistol motionless, walking towards the driver at a quick combat crouch. I followed behind and to his right, my own pistol raised but certainly shaking.

We needn't have bothered. The driver had been shot at least five times; twice in his left arm, once through the back, then Richard's last two shots, one low in the throat, the other creasing the skull at the hairline. He was a young Hispanic man, probably around my age. He was propped up against the open door of the truck, short bubbling breaths coming through clenched teeth dark with blood. His right hand stirred listlessly through the dirt, hunting for the gun he had lost. His eyes were locked on mine, and I could see nothing but hate.

Richard covered him with his pistol, but didn't shoot. "You need to do one up close. Finish him. Put one in his head."

The young man's eyes flicked to Richard, and then back to me. He saw me hesitate for a moment.

"C'mon, cabron," he choked out between clenched teeth, "do it, you little bitch."

I brought up the Glock in one hand and squeezed the trigger. The man's head snapped back against the truck door, then sagged until his chin rested on his chest, a neat dark hole in the bridge of his nose. The back of his head ran down the door in gobbets and streaks.

"We need to go back and account for the last man, the shooter near the camper," Richard said, reloading his pistol with another fresh magazine.

We didn't have to look for long. It took a few minutes to circle counter-clockwise back the way we had come and move to the right of the encampment. Approaching the camper, we immediately saw the body of a man lying by the corner, sprawled on his back. Up close, I could see I'd only hit him once, but the shot had torn open the side of his throat, and he had bled out thrashing in the dirt, gleaming sprays of drying crimson fanned across the corner of the camper.

"He didn't die easy, but at least he died quietly," Richard noted, staring down at the body.

I turned and looked at Richard. He was filthy from head to toe, night vision goggles askew on his forehead, sweat streaking the dust covering his face. Richard was back to looking calm and composed, no more concerned about the dead man lying in an enormous puddle of blood at his feet than if he was looking down at a broken lawn ornament.

"Small consolation, don't you think?" I asked.

Richard looked up and gave a small shrug, then turned and started walking towards where we had first begin the firefight, off to the side of the meth trailer. "Come on, let's police our gear and get moving. It's going to be light soon, and someone's going to come looking when they see the smoke plume."

I let out a long, slow breath and moved to follow him, emotionally and physically exhausted. As I caught up to him, Richard turned his head my way just a bit.

"We'll go over the details after we get some shut-eye," he said. "All in all though, not bad for your first time."

And then, incredibly, Richard winked at me.

Chapter 10

I dreamed that night I stood outside the camp after the gun battle. I was looking at Richard, his face glowing in the firelight. Suddenly, he was no longer merely Richard, but a murderous, demonic warrior. The flickering light twisted Richard's features and made them savage and bestial. The twin lenses of the night-vision goggles on his forehead morphed into a pair of grotesque, barrel-like horns growing from his skull. Instead of black denim and wool, he was clothed in shadows and dried blood. Instead of the southern Texas desert, I was standing in a desolate expanse of Hell, the ground barren and featureless as far as I could see, dusted with fragments of bleached bone. I realized I had been tricked into descending into the underworld by a monster looking to corrupt another soul for his own devilish schemes.

Richard sensed by gaze and turned to me, his own pistol holstered but with captured weapons in both hands. I saw the fire wasn't actually reflected in his eyes; it burned from deep within two empty, smoking sockets.

Richard smiled, a hideous, rictus-like grin that stretched to impossible proportions, and he said to me, "Welcome to the brotherhood, William."

Richard turned and walked away into the night.

I had no choice but to follow.

I didn't wake up the next day until almost ten. The cabin was hot and stuffy by then, heated by the desert sun for almost four hours, and I was too uncomfortable to stay asleep. I awoke feeling utterly drained, my eyes crusted with sleep, my mouth gummy and dried out. My body ached all over, I was ravenously hungry, and I felt like I needed to drink a gallon of water, I was so parched.

But I was alive. Despite all my enervation and discomfort, that thought alone made it the best morning of my life.

I vaguely recalled that I had fallen asleep around five that morning. After Richard and I found our spent and discarded magazines, we dragged the bodies of the two men I had killed in the camp into the camper, along with the lone sentry. The driver who tried to get away, we tossed inside the cab of his truck. Richard had me collect any weapons we could find in serviceable condition; the long-barreled pump shotgun, the assault rifle, a stainless steel .45 caliber automatic that the throat-shot man had fired at me, and the Ingram machine pistol used by the driver. There was also a scoped .30-06 bolt-action hunting rifle in the camper, and a .357 magnum revolver lying in the passenger seat of the white van.

"We'll take the guns, cache them under the cabin. Never hurts to have a few disposable stolen guns on hand for a rainy day. If they have a criminal ballistics profile already, it might help throw an investigation off-track and onto someone else, even for a short while."

In addition to the guns, we found a lock-box in the camper. Richard blew the flimsy lock out with a single shot from his H&K. Inside we found about ten grand in various denominations of used bills.

"Don't ever feel bad about taking a dead man's money, especially scumbags like these. They can't take it with them, it wouldn't go back to anyone who'd make better use of it, and you never know when a nice wad of untraceable cash can come in handy. Otherwise, it'd just end up in an evidence locker, or buried in some crooked cop's backyard."

The last thing we did before leaving was to burn everything. Richard produced a number of small incendiaries from his gusset bag, tossing one into the camper and one into the cab of each vehicle. Each of the grenades burst with a soft "whump", and sprayed out burning fragments of what Richard called white phosphorous. It burned at an extremely high temperature, capable of melting through glass and steel. In a few moments, the three vehicles and the camper were completely engulfed in flames, the white-hot fires lighting up the desert night for a hundred meters all around us.

Once everything was well on its way to being completely incinerated, Richard and I hiked back to the Suburban. Before we drove away, Richard unlimbered a makeshift contraption from the trunk; a long, heavy wooden beam studded with a number of thick iron spikes, with a length of chain attached to either end. Richard fastened the middle of the chain to the trailer hitch.

"We'll drag this behind us as we drive out, and it'll obscure our tracks so no one can get an identification on the kind of vehicle we drove based on tire treads or the width and length of the chassis. This way, even if they track us back to this point with dogs, they'll have no idea which way we came or what kind of vehicle we used."

I assisted Richard in getting the makeshift "rake" back into the Suburban once we got to the road. When we hit the pavement, I slumped back in my seat, exhausted, and I dozed until we returned to the cabin. I took a few minutes to strip down, splash a little water on my face, and wipe my body down with a damp rag. I passed out the moment I hit my cot.

This morning, I dressed quickly, t-shirt and shorts and sneakers as usual, straw hat on my head. I picked up a lukewarm mug of tea Richard had left me on the table next to the stove, along with a tin plate of dried apricots, beef jerky, some salted table crackers, and a wedge of cheese. Caffeine, sugar, protein, carbohydrates, and some fat; the breakfast of champions. I also took a handful of vitamins left in a small plastic cup, dietary supplements provided by Richard to make sure that I wasn't missing out on anything important.

I stepped out onto the porch. Richard sat in

his customary wooden rocker, faded jeans, check shirt, straw hat, cowboy boots, a wet bandana tied around his neck. He looked the picture-perfect grizzled cowboy resting in the shade of the covered porch, except for the brick of nine-millimeter cartridges balanced on one thigh, and a half-dozen long black magazines balanced on the other. He had one magazine in his hands, popping shiny brass cartridges into the end with such speed and efficiency he might as well be feeding quarters into a laundromat dryer. He looked up at me, peering from the side of his eye out from under the corner of his hat.

"Howdy," he said to me. "Sleep well?"

"Like the dead."

Richard gave me one of his trademark mirthless smiles. "The dead don't sleep, they rot. Best to keep that in mind."

"After last night, I won't forget that any time soon."

Richard turned away for a moment and went back to feeding cartridges into the magazine in his hand. "Do we need to talk about your feelings? Need a hug, perhaps?"

I sat in the other chair, propped my mug and my plate on the railing in front of me. I chewed a bit of jerky for a moment, swallowed.

"No need to be an asshole about it, Richard."

"You want to think I'm being an asshole about it, that's your prerogative. I just want to know how you feel about last night."

I thought for a minute, drank some tea, ate a

couple of dried apricots. Despite the relatively early hour, it was already in the 80s. If it wasn't for the roof over the porch, I'm sure I'd already be sweating.

"Last night I had a dream. You were a demon covered in blood, and you tricked me into following you down into Hell, where I killed those men and gave up my soul so you could corrupt me for your own diabolical schemes."

"Sounds about right to me."

"The best part," I said, "was that at the end, you welcomed me into your brotherhood, and I followed you off into the darkness."

Richard nodded, not even looking at me. "Still sounds about right."

"Me dreaming you're demon from Hell and corrupting my soul sounds about right to you?"

Richard finished loading the magazine in his hand, laid it across his leg, picked up another empty magazine, and continued loading. "I've been on the warpath for forty years. I've probably put a thousand men in the ground. Women too. Hell, probably some kids mixed in along the way, although I can't say for sure. And I know some good guys got caught in the crossfire, too; cops, security guards, watchmen, even your run of the mill innocent bystanders. Wrong place at the wrong time and all that."

I stared off into space. "Why are you telling me this?"

"Because you need to remember I'm not a nice guy. I'm not far removed from that thing in your dream. Call me a war criminal and you'd probably be more right than wrong. I always thought at the time I was working for the good guys, fighting for the right reasons. But the Cold War was still a bloody business and I was always there at its bloodiest. Afghanistan, Burma, Egypt, Iran, India, Brazil, Russia...I've been all over, always where the fighting was the dirtiest. Tore up some places here in the States as well. Things the press was threatened to keep quiet about, or bribed into silence, or worse."

"Just keeps getting better and better," I said.

"And just remember, I'm one of the good guys. Some of the animals I worked with, they make your run of the mill concentration camp guard look like he's gentle enough to run a daycare center. Some of those older guys, they probably were concentration camp guards back in the day. Plenty of the grey-hairs I went into the field with, those were the war addicts, the guys who couldn't go back home. Saw it after 'Nam, too; men who lived for death, lived for the blood and the thrill of the kill. They weren't much better than the dummies we were gunning after. Matter of fact, most of them were probably worse. At least the guys at the end of my gun usually died for a cause: communism, Islam, even plain old fashioned world domination. Some of the savages I fought with, they killed simply for the fun of it. The money? That was just gravy."

I turned to look at Richard, slouched in his rocker, hat pulled down low over his blue eyes. "So what about you? Killing for a cause, or was it the fun?"

Richard finally turned and looked me square in the eye. "You ain't figured that out yet? I killed for profit, kid. And back in the day, business was good. Business was really good."

I finished my meal in silence.

Although it was mid-morning, and the sun was already setting the sand on fire, Richard and I did our stretching, calisthenics and run. Neither of us said anything; we just worked through our routine in silence with the occasional gesture, nod, or inarticulate grunt. It was perhaps the closest I'd seen Richard get to being embarrassed, although I didn't think that was necessarily the problem. I think he had to remind himself now and then I was struggling to come to grips with a great deal in a short amount of time, and he needed to throttle back sometimes or risk burning me out.

After we finished our exercise, Richard called me back into the cabin. He had laid out the DeLisle carbine on the table top, broken down into its constituent parts.

"We've spent a week working on the basics of submachine guns and pistols. Last night you proved you know how to use those tools effectively. Now it's time to move to something a little more exacting."

"The sniper rifle," I replied.

"Not exactly a rifle, a carbine. It's a longarm firing a pistol round, but that's just being pedantic."

I stepped closer and took a good look. The wooden stock had a folded aluminum butt, spray-painted black. The magazine was removed, and a box of pistol ammunition sat next to it. The scope was removed, and set next to the DeLisle's receiver. The bolt had been pulled free, and sat next to the receiver as well. A small black collapsible bipod lay folded underneath the barrel.

Richard gestured to the parts. "I want you to put it together for me."

It took a couple of minutes for me to figure out, but eventually I locked the bolt in place, reattached the scope and the bipod, loaded and inserted the magazine. The parts were meticulously machined and well-oiled, and the weapon clicked and snapped together effortlessly.

"Take it apart, unload the mag, and do it again," Richard stated.

I reversed the process, and put the gun back together again. This time I assembled and loaded it within a minute.

"How was that?" I asked.

"Well, this isn't the Marine Corps. As long as you can put it together quickly, and then break it back down, that's good enough for me."

"Glad to hear it. I'm no Forrest Gump."

Richard cracked a ghost of a smile. "Now, let's go shoot."

We went back outside, me with the carbine, Richard with several boxes of ammunition and two sandbags draped over his shoulders. We walked out to our makeshift shooting range, and I saw Richard had set up some bulls-eye targets earlier this morning, perhaps a hundred meters away from our normal shooting position.

"The .45 ACP can fly hundreds of meters, but you're going to want to keep your distances short, a hundred meters or less. That puts you within a good-sized city block of your target, maybe a little more or a little less."

"But bullets drop as they fly, and a pistol bullet is going to drop faster than a rifle bullet."

"Correct. The key is to know that drop, anticipate it, and compensate for it by altering the windage and elevation of the scope."

Extending the bipod legs, I laid down on the ground, propping my elbows on one sandbag and the bipod on the other, so there was a steady surface underneath me and the carbine. I worked the bolt to chamber a bullet, then hit the button to pop open the scope cover. Peering through the optics, I could see the target a hundred meters away, concentric rings of black and white perhaps a foot across at its widest point. The scope used a simple set of crosshairs, and I slowly settled myself in, watching the crosshairs wobble around on the target.

"Whenever you're ready, just go through the seven round magazine and get a feel for it. Keep the crosshairs settled on the center of the target, breathe in, let it out a little, and then squeeze off the shot. Don't drop the hammer until you feel you're ready. It's all about patience and timing."

I took perhaps four minutes to fire the whole magazine. When I was done, we walked over to take a look at the target. All my shots were clustered in a space as big as the palm of my hand, right at the bottom of the target.

"Subsonic 230-grain hollowpoint loads like these are going to strike six or seven inches low at this range," Richard told me. "Adjust the elevation and try again."

We changed out the targets, marked the old target with the date and time, ammunition and weapon used, range and firing position.

"A sniper is like any precision craftsman; he wants to look back at his body of work and be able to remember when and how he accomplished that particular task. By keeping these notes, you'll begin to build a body of knowledge you can refer to in your own mind in order to adjust the scope or correct for windage."

After reloading the carbine, I adjusted the scope several clicks and emptied the magazine downrange again, this time taking all seven shots in two minutes. Checking the target, the grouping had tightened up a little, and was only halfway below the bulls-eye.

"What you've got dialed in now would be a good general-purpose adjustment. Too fine-tuned, and you'll shoot too high up close, say within 20 meters or so. Better to aim a little low at a distance so you're not aiming too high if you have to use it quick and can't adjust the scope. But for good measure, let's pin down the range."

Two more magazines' worth, and I worked out the range so all my shots clustered around the bullseye. My grouping tightened up a little more, but Richard explained to me that pistol ballistics at this range just wouldn't lend themselves well to precision shooting.

Once we had zeroed-in at one hundred meters,

we pushed the targets back in 25-meter intervals, all the way out to two hundred meters. At this distance, I was aiming over a foot above the target itself, but I felt confident I could hit a man at that range, given a little preparation time.

The carbine was a pleasure to shoot; there was almost no recoil, just a slight jump, and with the suppressor, we weren't wearing hearing protection. All that emerged from the DeLisle was a muffled "foomph". After the thrill of firing a submachine gun on full automatic, or rapid-firing a pistol as fast as I could acquire the target's center of mass, I found this kind of shooting - relaxed, methodical, precise, studied - to be far more enjoyable than I thought it would be.

After I adjusted to shooting at various ranges, and knew what to expect in terms of trajectory and groupings, Richard shifted me from more stable to less stable firing positions. Instead of firing prone, I fired sitting up with my elbow resting on my knee, then kneeling, and then finally standing upright and firing unsupported. My accuracy was pro-gressively worse with each position, but Richard assured me that with time, I would get better.

"Your uncle was right; you've got a good eye and you're a fast learner. Over the course of the day you've improved significantly, and now it'll be a matter of refining technique."

We returned to the cabin by mid-afternoon, and Richard showed me what needed to be done to clean the carbine, making sure all traces of dust and fouling were removed and the gun was carefully lubricated. After the previous week, the ritual of stripping and cleaning weapons had gone from a puzzle and a chore to a familiar activity I used to reflect on what I had learned that day, and more importantly, what it would mean once I went back to Boston.

After I finished cleaning the carbine, Richard set me to the task of reading and learning a number of ballistics tables and other data pertaining to using pistol-caliber weapons at long ranges. I could hear him in his room, and assumed he was using the communications gear he kept stored in a foot locker inside the room. He had shown it to me a couple of days after I arrived; a secure satellite cellular phone hooked up to a laptop computer, with a heavy-duty battery power supply. By spending a month with me here in the desert, Richard was taking a lot of time out of his usual schedule, and like any businessman, he needed to keep in contact with clients, vendors, and information sources.

Although he had pointed it out to me, so I didn't grow suspicious or curious when he disappeared into his room for extended periods of time, Richard forbade me from opening the foot locker and "playing around" with his communications rig.

"The foot locker is booby-trapped, and if the laptop isn't given the right password, it'll self-destruct. I don't mind letting you know I've got this rig, but you gotta know right now, this is confidential; I catch you snooping around in here, I may just have to tell Jamie you suffered an accident with your gun and shot yourself in the back of the head."

Richard's expression was all I needed to know he wasn't joking.

When Richard emerged, I could tell he had something to share with me, "We're going to head into town. Going to pick up a few necessities, and we've also got a plane to meet. Some items are being flown in."

"What time is the meet?" I asked, glancing at my watch; it was two in the afternoon.

"Flight's coming in at eight. We want to be there ahead of schedule, before it gets dark, so let's get going."

We drove into town in order to stock our larder, buy water, and pick up a few other supplies. Driving down the quiet streets, passing pedestrians minding their own business, I began to idly imagine lining them up in the sights of my Uzi and riddling them with bullets. A man walking towards us, newspaper tucked under his arm, cowboy hat pulled down tight; I saw him jerked backwards in my mind's eye, riddled with slugs and thrown against the wall of a nearby store. A mother with two small children, holding their hands and walking away from us as we drove by; I saw myself empty half a magazine into her back, spinning her around before she tumbled to the sidewalk.

The daydreaming disturbed me, because it wasn't anything I'd done before. Sure, when pissed off I sometimes saw myself kicking some douchebag in the crotch or giving a really bitchy classmate a slap across the face, but I couldn't recall ever imagining killing anyone, certainly not random strangers in an imaginary drive-by.

"What's the count so far?" Richard suddenly asked me.

"What do you mean?"

He pointed a thumb towards my side of the street. "Body count. I've been watching you track 'em with your eyes as they go past. Your trigger finger spasms occasionally. Having a little imaginary fun?"

Jesus, it was weird, the things he noticed.

I turned away from the side window and felt myself blush with embarrassment. "It just sorta happened. Never thought like that before today."

Richard smiled as he glanced at me from the corner of his eye. "Nothing to get too worked up about, it comes with the change. You'll get used to it."

I frowned at him. "'Change?' I'm not a goddamn werewolf, Richard."

This time he laughed out loud. "Sure you are! Maybe you ain't got claws and fangs and overdeveloped facial hair, but believe me son, you've changed. You didn't piss your pants or throw up or toss away your gun and run like you were yellow. You stood fast and cut yourself some scalps last night. That's not something just any ordinary person can do, even after a week on the firing line. There's a switch inside you gotta flip that says 'killing people that deserve to die is something I can do'. Son, that switch is now 'on' inside you. There's no going back after that."

I had nothing to say after Richard's comment. I

turned away and continued to look out the window of the Suburban.

Eventually we finished our shopping errands. Richard bought several cases of water, more perishable foodstuffs, and most notably, several large sacks of big round red apples.

"Targets," Richard explained.

"I'll be shooting at apples?"

"If you can hit an apple, you can hit someone in the vital part of the brain. Also, it's easy to spot one out in the desert."

"Out in the desert..." I said, cautiously.

"Yep. We're going on a little hiking trip tomorrow."

Richard and I ate dinner in a small roadside diner on the edge of town. Oddly enough, it reminded me of the bar and grill in Bangor where we first talked about my offer. A radio back in the kitchen played oldies country music, a ragged-looking steer head was mounted next to the bar, and a battered dart board hung from the wall near the bathroom. There were a couple of patrons, definitely locals, and although a couple sets of eyes followed us as we found a seat, no one seemed particularly interested, even with Richard's big stainless steel pistol out in plain view.

"What model of pistol is that?" I asked him. "It's pretty fancy for a .45 automatic."

"That's because it's not a .45 auto, it's a ten-millimeter automatic. Colt Delta Elite, to be exact."

"That's quite the badass name for a handgun."

"It's quite the badass handgun. Eight rounds plus

one in the chamber. Ballistic profile somewhere near a .41 Magnum but in a 1911-sized frame. The gun kicks like a mule, but gives me a good mix of ammunition capacity, range, penetration, and stopping power."

"It's scary how much you think about these things."

"Thinking about it now keeps me alive later."

We made it to the tiny airfield twenty minutes early. Richard parked well away from the runway, killing the lights on the Suburban. By now only the slimmest edge of sunlight was still coming over the western horizon, and the temperature was already dropping. Nevertheless, we rolled down the windows, listening for the approach of the plane. Richard reached underneath the seat and produced my Glock and two spare magazines.

"Chuck is flying in, and he should be alone. But remember, I never leave anything to chance. Keep your eyes open and make sure there's one in the chamber."

I took the pistol from Richard and performed a "brass check", then tucked the two spare magazines in my pocket.

"You live in a fucked-up world, Richard. How long have you known Chuck? Thirty years?"

"Thirty years or thirty seconds, you don't trust anyone any more than you have to."

"And you don't trust anyone at all."

"Can't tell Jamie you haven't been paying attention, kid."

In a moment we heard the faint drone of an

approaching prop plane, and Richard reached into the glove box, removing a single-lens night sight. Scanning the purple-black sky to the east, he finally stopped and pointed into the night.

"He's right up there, flying without lights."

"Isn't that dangerous?" I asked.

"It is, but he's running covert tonight. He wouldn't even have flown out of an official airfield to get here."

After a minute's wait I could finally see the plane, a black shadow in the darkness. Flying with remarkable skill, the pilot touched down and taxied to a stop with room to spare.

"That was a really smooth landing," I remarked.

"He's probably using night-vision goggles, but yes, he's got a lot of night-flying hours under his belt."

The pilot's door opened up, barely visible in the dim twilight, and a man who appeared to be Chuck stepped out of the aircraft. I saw a brief red light wink twice, then three times, and then once more. Richard raised a penlight in his hand and flashed another sequence back. The pilot replied with two brief flashes.

"We should be good. Step out on your side and keep the engine block between you and the plane until I call you over."

We got out of the Suburban, and Richard walked over to the pilot. I could see Richard carried his Delta Elite behind his leg, as he had while getting off the plane back in Bangor. I kept the majority of the Suburban between me and the plane, with my Glock in hand just below the edge of the hood. After a few moments, Richard gave me a wave. I tucked the pistol into the back of my waistband and walked over.

Chuck held a fat manila envelope, which Richard took from him and handed to me.

"Take a look."

I opened up the envelope while Richard held his penlight for me, shielding the light from the highway. Inside, I found a Massachusetts driver's license, a Maine driver's license, two US passports, two bank cards, four credit cards, and two smaller envelopes containing an assortment of different papers. Looking closely at the identifications, I saw they both had my photo, but neither of the names were mine.

"Fake IDs?" I asked.

"They aren't fakes," Richard said. "They're alternate identities."

"I don't understand."

"A fake ID is made by a forger. Even the best fakes have tells that an expert can spot. These aren't fake, they're just made using false identities."

I looked at him quizzically. "Wait...you mean these are real? Made by the government?"

Richard and Chuck both smiled at me. "The best fake ID isn't a fake at all," Richard replied.

I was incredulous. "How on earth did you manage that? These are the photos from my Rhode Island driver's license and my passport. How could you possibly get them?"

Richard laughed. "The same people who make

IDs and passports are the same people we use to make our false identities. You go to the source, where the information and photo is already available. Just a matter of putting your image into a new ID and generating it as a legitimate record. Now not only is it a genuine piece of identification, but you're in the system as well."

"So why do I need two sets of alternate ID?"

"One of them is going to be your 'White' identity. That's what your apartment will be rented under, you'll use buy your groceries, pay your utility bills, all that clean stuff. When you operate though, you work under your 'Black' ID, which means no one can trace you back to your civilian activities."

"Which should be which? The IDs I mean."

"Your Mass ID is already set up for your apartment and your utilities. The Maine ID is also set up with a residence, but since you'll be living in Boston, use the Mass identification for your White activities."

I dug through the smaller envelopes. They contained a number of receipts, utility bills, and pieces of junk mail. All of it associated with my false identities.

"I take it this is to make everything look good?"

Richard nodded. "One of the easiest tells of a false identity is lack of evidence that the identity is real. Real people have bills, they buy things with credit cards, they rent movies, they get junk mail. The more details you add to the picture, the more believable it becomes."

I turned to Chuck, who had been silent for the

whole conversation. I stuck out my hand, and he shook it.

"Thank you for doing this. Your support means a lot to me," I said.

Chuck just smiled. "Hell kid, I'm not doing it for free. But you're welcome all the same. Always glad to help a new player find his way around the game board."

I didn't quite know what to say to that.

After shaking Richard's hand, Chuck climbed back into the cockpit of his plane. We walked back to the Suburban as Chuck taxied around, and in moments, he was roaring into the night air. We were on the road back to the cabin before Chuck climbed past a thousand feet.

"So, how much did these cost me?" I asked.

"Twenty thousand apiece."

"Holy shit, that's a lot of money. So much for buying a fake ID off of someone's older brother's best friend."

"Remember, these aren't fake. People in very sensitive positions take great risks to generate those IDs. That's the bulk of the money. Then, you've got to pay the gardeners."

"Gardeners?"

"The identity gardeners, the cultivators of the background information. They are the people who maintain and prepare false identifications once they go active. Rent the apartments, set up the utilities, go out and make the purchases, furnish the apartments, make sure the lights are turned on and such. They're like the theater technicians who prepare the costumes and set dressing for the actors."

"Also analogous to the real gardener who tends your flowers, making sure they have the proper water, sunlight, no weeds, fertilizer, all of that."

"Exactly. They help your false identity grow in a more organic fashion."

"So let me get this straight; there are people whose whole purpose is to make sure false identities seem believable?"

Richard smiled. "You'd be amazed at the size of the infrastructure running in the background that supports our operations. Organizations like the CIA, the FSB, MI6? For every field agent they deploy, you've got dozens of analysts, costumers, support technicians, computer experts, weapon-smiths; it's no different for the private sector market, we just have to keep much of it underground."

"So there are people who make a living supporting what you do?"

"For most it's not their day job, because you've got to claim something on your taxes, but yes, for many of these people, the work is a full-time job. Some of those identity gardeners have to move around within a large city or a whole state, in order to support multiple identities. You can't just set up a cover residence and then never use it. Someone has to make sure the mail gets collected, the home hasn't been broken into, the lawn gets mowed if it's a home. Making sure there's a strong backstop on these IDs is critical if anyone takes a hard look. Who doesn't have and use a credit card these days? Who doesn't get junk mail? There needs to be a veneer of authenticity on even the simplest false identification if it's going to stand up to a cursory sweep."

"I had no idea it was all so complex. I figured some guy in the back room of a photo lab or a basement somewhere just created fake IDs and that was that."

Richard nodded. "Oh, those people exist, but they are there for expediency's sake. The sort of people you can visit with a strip of drugstore photos and leave with a driver's license that might let you buy a six pack of beer or get into a club. Nowadays, any cursory traffic stop by a police officer will unravel a backroom fake in seconds. You need a real identity behind you in order to move through the system, and for that, you have to go to the source."

Back at the cabin, we unpacked and repacked the supplies Richard and I had bought. It was clear we were going to be driving someplace.

"I thought we were going out into the desert?" I asked.

"We are. The Suburban will get us anywhere we need to go. We'll be gone a few days, and there's no easy way for us to carry the water we need. Don't think you're going to be too comfortable, though. You're going to eat up some serious shoe-leather."

"Gee, I can't wait." I said.

That night, I didn't dream at all.

Chapter 11

In the morning, we got up at our usual hour, did our stretches and exercises, and went for our run. By now, I felt like not only had I lost every ounce of fat, but I had become stronger, quicker, and more limber. I could cover the distance of our run with a lot less difficulty, and even though I was still breathing hard by the time we got back to the cabin, I was able to pick up my pistol, then load and fire at a target twenty-five feet away and keep everything in the kill-zone.

"You're picking this up a lot quicker than I had hoped," Richard said.

"If I don't, I'll have some serious problems this summer."

"Glad to see you're well motivated."

We climbed into the Suburban with five days of food and water, plus our handguns, the DeLisle, a heavy-barreled AR-15 with a detachable scope taken from the basement cache, and a small mountain of ammunition. Before leaving, Richard moved the trunk with his communications gear into the cabin's underground cache, keeping only the satellite phone. He also activated the cabin's booby traps.

The sun was well into the sky by the time we pulled off the road and started down some nameless rocky desert trail. We had driven mostly north and west, and we hadn't seen a town of any appreciable size the entire trip.

"I take it you've been here before," I said.

"Like I said the other day, I take little excursions into the wild to keep myself sharp. Texas is a great place for a man to wander into the middle of nowhere with a loaded gun and not be bothered by anyone, even if he's noticed. People around here see a white guy in a cowboy hat with a rifle, you might as well be in Boston walking down the street with a cell phone and a cup of coffee, for all anyone's going to care."

Eventually we drove into a small gulch, similar in appearance to where we parked two nights ago. One side of the small, narrow valley was sheer enough to put the Suburban into complete shadow.

"This will be our base of operations for the next couple of days," Richard said. "Then, we'll move on to another spot."

We got out of the Suburban and dropped the tailgate. We removed our packs and our guns, along with a healthy amount of ammunition. We also changed into sets of lightweight desert camouflage and military-style desert boots. Our gear, a mix of military, paramilitary, and civilian, was intended to give us the look of militiamen or even tactical law enforcement types on a training exercise.

"If we run into any nosy locals or pestering cops, you leave things to me. Do not try anything clever, just follow my lead completely," Richard said.

"Understood."

We climbed out of our little gulch and walked into the rocky, broken ground to the north of where we parked. The terrain was an endless panorama of hardscrabble rocks, ground fissures, hills, buttes, and valleys. As we walked, Richard began to explain to me why we're here.

"You're going to be operating a lot in the city, and when you look at the modern urban landscape from a structural perspective, it has a lot in common with a rocky desert like this. The terrain is broken, the shadows are sharp and deep, and there isn't a lot of soft cover or concealment. Any target in line of sight is probably a clear shot, while if you can't see the target, the obstruction is impenetrable, most likely a building, a solid car body, or some other hard object. In addition, when it comes to sniping, you have to be aware of how cross winds coming out of alleys and intersecting streets are going to affect the bullet's flight path. The best way to simulate this behavior away from the city is out here, where there's plenty of wind moving through these valleys and gulches."

"All right, all of that seems sensible," I replied.

"Because of this, learning how to find cover, lines of sight, and how to maneuver out here among the hills and valleys is as good a simulation of working in the city as you're going to get."

"That also makes sense to me," I said. "The ridges and buttes are buildings, the valleys and fissures are streets and alleyways. Boulders are like cars, the dips and rises here and there are similar to curbs and other city features."

"Right. You silhouette yourself along the top of a ridge trying to make a shot down into a valley, ain't no different from silhouetting yourself on the rooftop of some apartment building, trying to get a shot down into the street. Instead of seeing the desert here, you need to train your mind to see a city instead."

And so, that's what we did. For the next few days, I trained myself to see not a rocky desert landscape, but an urban cityscape. Richard taught me how to approach a cliff edge in order to peer down below while presenting the smallest possible silhouette. We practiced how to fire and maneuver from one position to the next, picking our shooting locations ahead of time to make best use of the available fields of fire and the cover they provided.

For targets, Richard would bring along a bag of those red apples he bought, and while I looked away, Richard would hurl one down into the valley floor. I would then have to spot the "target" and then "kill" it with a single shot. The hardest part was actually finding the apple. Sometimes, Richard would throw it into a spot where it wasn't visible unless I moved to the other side of the valley, at which point we would work on techniques for rappelling down off the side of a rock face to the ground below and then climbing back up on the other side of the valley.

In order to make sure I didn't grow too familiar with any one location, we would often pack up and hike down a valley or cross-country to another valley entirely. During these transitions, Richard would move ahead of me and I would have to stalk him, staying within a distance of about two hundred meters. Richard would move in an erratic fashion, stopping and starting suddenly, speeding up to a jog or slowing to a crawl. Often, Richard would turn with little or no notice to see if he could spot me, and I had to try and get into cover before I was seen, while still being able to follow after him. Whenever he spotted me, Richard would give a short blast on a plastic whistle he had brought with him to let me know I was seen.

When we would get to our destination, Richard often made me move up onto the valley's ridge to one side or the other, and instruct me to circle around him at a set distance, again without being spotted or heard. Whenever I had to get myself down off the rocky ledges and cross the valley floor, then make my way back up onto the opposite side, Richard would inevitably see me, and give me a blast from his whistle.

That damn whistle would taunt me in my dreams for a long time to come.

By the end of every day, I was completely exhausted. The previous week, while we would run, exercise, and shoot out in the open, we would eat our meals in the shade of the cabin, and breaks were plentiful. While there was a certain level of exertion, especially later in the first week when I would fire while on the move, I didn't go terribly far.

But out in the desert, we were constantly on the move; hiking, climbing, crawling, lying down, getting up, crouching, jumping, rappelling, jogging, sprinting, and hiking some more. We were also carrying our weapons, ammunition, food, water, climbing gear, and other supplies with us all day long, only returning to the Suburban's hiding place as the sun started to go down. Once back at our base camp, Richard and I would make our evening meal using a small gas camping stove rather than a real fire, to prevent the risk of any tell-tale smoke or firelight being noticed by someone from a distance, even down in the gulch where we were largely hidden from view. Furthermore, with the little gas stove, there were no ashes or burnt wood to hide when breaking camp.

"The best operators are like pro-environment hikers," Richard explained. "You carry out of the field everything you bring in, so there is as little evidence of your presence as possible. The more you leave for the forensics team after an operation, the more information they will gain about you, and the easier it becomes for the authorities to tie you to other operations. It might be bad to get busted for one operation, but you don't want to get linked to them all."

The afternoon of the third day, while moving to a new location, Richard suddenly stopped ahead of me. Thinking he was going to turn around, I hid myself and waited. After a few moments, poking my head out from behind the rock I was using for cover, I saw that Richard was standing on a small boulder, waving me up. I presumed he wanted to show me something, but as I began to walk ahead, he motioned for me to approach with stealth.

It took me several minutes to make my way to his position. Richard had slipped down off the boulder, and he pointed ahead of us.

"Take a peek around the boulder, get your carbine up, and look for some movement."

The DeLisle at the ready, I eased myself around the boulder and looked down the narrow valley through the scope, breaking the terrain down into segments and scanning each individually for movement or a tell-tale target like Richard had taught me.

After a few moments, I saw what he must have meant. A big, lean desert hare was tucked next to a large slab of rock, perhaps twenty five meters away, nibbling at something.

"It's a big jackrabbit," I said.

"I caught him out of the corner of my eye," Richard said, "and so I tossed him a piece of apple to keep him occupied. Take him."

I looked back at Richard, frowning. "You want me to shoot the rabbit?"

"Yup. Blow his little bunny brains out."

"You're fucking with me."

"I am not, in fact, fucking with you. Waste the damn rabbit."

"I don't want to kill the poor guy; you just fed him an apple. That seems cruel."

Richard pulled me aside behind the boulder and leaned in close. He seemed almost as angry with me now as he did the night we attacked the meth lab.

"Look here, son. That's just a dumb rabbit out there. It is not a struggling single mother raising a family, nor is it going to go on and cure cancer someday. The most important thing that rabbit will ever do it its life is possibly make a few more rabbits, and then eventually fill the belly of some lucky coyote. As sad as it might make you feel because you've been raised in a world where no one kills what they eat anymore, that creature only exists to be killed and eaten so that the lucky predator can go on to live another day. Do you hear what I am saying?"

I nodded.

Richard gently pushed me back towards the edge of the boulder. "You need to get over the hurdle of killing something with that carbine. Take the shot. If that rabbit possessed the power of understanding human speech, and you explained to it why you're out here and what you hope to accomplish, I think the rabbit would understand, even if it didn't like going into tonight's cook pot."

I peeked around the edge of the boulder. The rabbit had finished eating the piece of apple Richard had thrown, and was sitting under the edge of the rock slab, ears up, nose wiggling as it sniffed the air for predators. Leaning into the boulder for support, I settled the crosshairs on the rabbit's center mass, and with all possible care and patience, squeezed the trigger until it gave.

The rabbit tumbled across the ground in a tangle of slack limbs and a puff of dusty gray fur.

Walking over to the rabbit's corpse, I saw it was killed instantly. The bullet had caught it in the torso right behind its foreleg, destroying the rabbit's heart and lungs before blowing out the other side.

Looking at the sky and then checking his watch, Richard jerked his thumb back in the direction we had come from.

"Let's head back to the truck and get this fellow in the pot."

Richard made me carry the carcass by its legs the entire way.

Once back at camp, Richard drew a knife from his belt. "Have you ever skinned an animal before?" he asked.

"Nope."

"Of course you haven't, how stupid of me. Time for you to learn."

The deed only took a few minutes. The rabbit weighed just a couple of pounds, and Richard walked me through the process of gutting and skinning the rabbit with a few cuts of his knife. The task of pulling away the rabbit's pelt was something akin to pulling a furry sock off a boiled chicken.

I promptly turned and threw up in the dirt.

"Last week you shot a man in the face and didn't so much as blink," Richard said.

"Yeah, but I didn't skin his corpse afterward."

Nevertheless, the rabbit stew was delicious.

Two days later, we found ourselves on the edge

of a ridge, preparing to move to another location. Suddenly, Richard brought up his AR-15 and scanned the next ridge over, some four hundred meters away.

"What is it?" I asked.

"Hiker. Male, looks young, probably around your age. Civilian dress, no weapon visible. Probably just out for a day trip. There's a road a few miles to the west. That might be where he's coming from."

I looked through my carbine's scope, and could make out the tiny figure striding along the next ridge.

Richard put his hand out for the carbine and offered me the AR, with its better scope. "Here, take a better look."

The subject jumped into view. I could see he was a young man, fit, with a backpack and baseball cap. He definitely had the look of a casual hiker enjoying the late spring weather before it got unreasonably hot later in the season.

"Yeah, I see him," I said. "You're right, probably just a hiker."

"Take him."

I brought down the rifle and looked at Richard. "Now you really have to be fucking kidding me."

Richard shook his head. "You need some experience taking shots from this range. You haven't used the AR yet, but it shoots like a dream. Just adjust the scope and put one in him. The round is still lethal out to that range. If you just clip him, you can finish him off quick with a follow-up."

"Richard, you're insane. I'm not shooting some

guy just hiking out in the desert."

Richard slung the DeLisle and crossed his arms over his chest, leaning in close like he always did when trying to prove a point.

"How do you know that's just 'some guy'? What if he beats his girlfriend? What if he molests his baby brother? What if he sells meth out of his dorm room? None of us are as innocent as we'd like to think. I'm willing to bet that dummy's done something in his life that warrants sixty grains of copper-jacketed lead through the ten-ring."

I was disgusted. "I see where you're heading, and that bullshit isn't going to work this time. It shouldn't have worked last time, but I am willing to admit that what we did was, if not necessary...well I can live with it. Those were definitely bad guys. But this is just some stranger out for a hike. Maybe he deserves a bullet and maybe he doesn't, but I have no evidence to support your theory."

I held out the AR to Richard.

"You're so eager to see him drop, you take the shot," I said.

Richard stared daggers at me for a moment, then snatched the AR from my hand in a blur. Bringing the rifle up in one smooth motion, Richard lined up the shot and squeezed the trigger.

The rifle clicked.

Richard looked at me out of the corner of his eye.

"You asshole," I said. "There's nothing in the chamber."

Richard brought the rifle down from his shoulder, held it up so I could see the receiver, and drew back the bolt. A gleaming 5.56mm NATO cartridge jumped from the chamber and tumbled at me. I caught the cartridge out of the air and looked at it. The primer was dented, and a quick shake let me know there was powder in the case.

"Must have been a dud round," Richard said.

"Dud round my ass. We've been shooting for two weeks, and we've never once had a dud round. I think you doctored the bullet."

Richard shrugged and snapped the AR-15's bolt back into place. "That ammo's been sitting down in my cache a long while. There's always the first time for a dud."

I stared incredulously at Richard. "And if it wasn't? What would you have done if I'd shot that guy? Would it have been another 'life lesson' for me to learn? How to deal with killing innocent people?"

Richard gave me one of his hard looks. "The 'life lesson' here is that killing's a slippery slope. I've seen men, good men, tumble down that slope. First you kill out of self-preservation, then you're killing for God and country, and before you know it, you're killing out of fun and amusement. Maybe you come up with some kind of cockamamie story like I was feeding you just now in order to justify the killing to yourself, at least at first. But as time goes on, even that charade falls away. Eventually, you're just a rabid dog in need of a bullet."

I pointed at the AR-15 in Richard's hands. "And if I'd pulled the trigger? Then what?"

Richard narrowed his eyes and put his hand on

the butt of his Delta Elite. "Like I said. A rabid dog in need of a bullet."

"And what about you?" I asked. "You pulled the fucking trigger yourself. What am I supposed to think of you?"

Richard slung the rifle over his shoulder and began walking again.

"I've done a lot worse," he said.

I looked down at the cartridge in my hand, and threw it into the desert.

Chapter 12

Before dawn the next morning we policed our campsite one more time, hung Richard's "road rake" from the trailer hitch of the Suburban, and drove out of the desert. I hadn't slept all that well during the night. Several times I had woken up after dreams that ended in either the rabbit or the lone hiker being blown away by yours truly. The dreams ending with the rabbit bothered more because I knew it wasn't a fantasy.

Why did it bother me so much? Mankind had hunted for food since before you could call us "Mankind". We were omnivores, we ate meat. All acknowledgments towards the beneficent path of vegetarianism aside, Man had grown big and strong on a diet high in protein and fat derived from animal meat. Some of our earliest tools doubled as weapons used for hunting, and some of our earliest technological achievements had revolved around how to kill game, be it with spears, clubs, darts, knives, nets, or some other method to arm our relatively weak primate bodies and give us a predatory edge.

But Richard had been right; those of us living in the 21st century never had a need to kill and eat our own food. How many Americans had seen a dead animal that wasn't a deceased family pet or some anonymous smear of roadkill? How many Americans had seen an animal die in front of their eyes, or done the deed themselves, and then gutted, skinned, butchered, prepared, and eaten that animal mere hours later? I knew hunting was still alive and well, but to the average white-collar urbanite such as myself, the activity bordered on the grotesque. Who needs to do such a thing? If I wanted to eat a wild animal, I could order wild game meat from my local butcher.

I remembered coming across a passage in one of my western civilization textbooks about why certain cultures came more easily to "real" violence, as opposed to the ritualized "show" violence that many primitive cultures practiced. An early theory had been because the diets of the more violent cultures were more heavily supplemented in meat and dairy, this food and the "animal hormones" it contained made those people bigger and more aggressive.

But another theory refuted this claim, noting that it was not the diet that granted those cultures their advantages, but the actual practice of herding and butchering animals. Herders who worked together to move and control large masses of animals practiced communication, coordination, and tactical control of the land that aided them on the battlefield. Beyond this, a people who were used to the act of killing large mammals, of seeing and smelling large pools of blood, of butchering game and seeing raw meat laid open; these cultures were much more able to handle the visceral shocks to the senses that came from the horrors of close-quarters combat, something that set truly violent cultures apart from their posturing counterparts.

Boiled down to its most pragmatic terms, a warrior from a herding and butchering culture had the know-how and stomach to advance in a coordinated fashion against an enemy, rout them by forcing them into close combat, and cut them down like animals when they fled. A rival culture who had only progressed warfare to the point of hurling missiles and insults, with the occasional ritual duel thrown in for good measure, had no hope against an enemy who would come at you undaunted through a hail of slings and arrows in order to bury a sword in your guts, and not even blink when your blood hit him in the face.

It came to me then, that the last two weeks had been my electro-shock treatment, my swift immersion into that pragmatically bloody mindset. Richard knew I came from the modern equivalent of your typical segregated agrarian society; someone who looks at cute cuddly animals as pets to be loved, and whose meat is killed and prepared by someone else so I never had to see or perform the deed myself. I had to be forced into the role of the pastoral herder-slaughterer, to smell fresh blood and not be sick, to not faint at the sight of a raw wound. I needed to be able to think of the men I was going to kill in the same way a herdsman would separate out the sick animals from the pack and cull them so the rest could flourish.

Richard was doing his job remarkably well. He was worth every penny.

We got back to Richard's cabin around eight in the morning. We had only eaten some dried fruit, jerky, and nuts while breaking camp, so after Richard entered the cabin and disarmed any "surprises", we set about preparing a better breakfast. We ate powdered eggs, canned beans and tomatoes on crackers, along with a pot of tea and some reconstituted milk. Funny how a meal you'd turn your nose up at back home tastes like a feast after you've been living out in the desert for a week.

After putting some food in our bellies, Richard and I took turns cleaning up. For the last two weeks I hadn't had a decent shower, but at least while staying at the cabin I would wash up every night with a small bowl of hot water and a washcloth. Out in the desert, I had lacked that small comfort, and I realized we were both utterly filthy, and pungent to boot. We hadn't shaved for a week, either, and we could pass for a pair of vagrants. A thorough wash-up, a shave, and a new change of clean clothes, and I could tell even an old campaigner like Richard was feeling remarkably more put-together.

Next, Richard led us through a set of stretches and light calisthenics, and we went for our customary run, although Richard kept it short. I could tell I was sore and out of practice; although we had finished every day out in the desert exhausted, we hadn't done a lot of running. Getting in even a short run was remarkably refreshing, and I noted with satisfaction that I had, if anything, more energy and stamina now than last week, despite the weariness I had felt at the end of every day.

Richard and I returned to the cabin around eleven in the morning.

"Now that we're back into the routine a little, let's strip down and clean everything. Guns, gear, even the Suburban's cargo bed."

We spent another three hours going through our gear and making sure that not only was everything accounted for - including the spent brass - but that our packs were clean, the carbine and the AR-15 were stripped, cleaned and oiled, and both pistols given the same treatment. After two weeks, gun maintenance had become second nature to me.

By the time all our equipment was attended to, and the Suburban was cleaned, it was early afternoon. I prepped a quick lunch of canned beef stew with added vegetables. Sitting at the table together, eating our lunch, Richard looked at me thoughtfully over his bowl.

"Hmmm?" I asked.

"You ever play checkers?"

"The board game, checkers?"

"That's right, checkers."

"Back when I was a kid, yes. Played against my kid sister a lot. Probably haven't played a game in ten years."

Richard chewed another mouthful.

"Reckon you'd be up for a game?"

I laughed. "After the last week, anything that involves sitting in the shade and not crawling over rocks and dust sounds fantastic to me."

Richard chuckled for a moment, then got up and walked into his room. A few moments later he brought in an old, battered cardboard checkers box. Laying out the board, he deftly populated the squares with the red and black playing pieces, save one of each. Holding them behind his back, Richard asked me, "Right or left?"

"Left."

He held out his hand. A black disk.

"Smoke before fire, kid. Your move."

I had always been an indifferent checkers player, and over the course of the first game, I realized I had forgotten most of the rules. Richard coached me through the game, reminding me where necessary what moves I could and could not make. It was mostly a confusing muddle, and although I lost the game, I felt I finally had a grasp of what to do, so I asked Richard for a rematch.

Ten minutes later, the game was over. Richard had won again.

I asked for another game. Richard beat me after twelve minutes.

We played for a couple of hours, and game after game, Richard came out on top. Some of the matches I just got frustrated and made stupid mistakes that were quickly exploited, while other times I felt I was being clever and sneaky, only to have it all fall apart a few moves into my "master plan". Either way, Richard played with an infuriating calm, taking his move the moment I finished mine, without any need to think about what he was doing.

Finally, after what must have been a dozen games, Richard looked up at me from across the board.

"Why do I always win?" he asked me.

"Because apparently, you are a master of the checker board."

"No, seriously. I haven't played a game of checkers in years. I probably haven't played it since the last time you played. But why do I always win?"

"I dunno, you've probably still played more games. You've got several decades of experience over me."

"What else? What am I doing that you aren't doing?"

I stared at the board for a long moment. "You make your move as soon as I make mine. It's like you don't need any time to think about what you're going to do."

"But that's ridiculous, right? Of course I'm thinking about my moves."

"But you don't take any time," I countered.

"Says who?"

"Then you...you're thinking about your move while I'm thinking about mine. But how do you know what to do when I haven't done it yet?"

Richard smiled. "Mhmmm?"

I stared at him, annoyed. "'Mhmmm' what?"

Richard began to put pieces onto the board at

random, setting up what looked like a mid-game distribution.

"What are your options?" he asked, pointing to the board.

I looked the board over for a minute, then told Richard the half-dozen possible moves I could see. Richard nodded along with each of them, and when I finished he looked at me.

"Every time we play, every time it's your turn, I can practically hear you thinking out your moves, just like that. Your eyes, your body language, sometimes even your lips move. I know the move you're going to make before you even reach for the piece."

I just looked at him.

Richard continued. "Furthermore, because you take so long and make your move so obvious, I've got plenty of time to plan my move, so that when I make it, you now have to react to it instead of planning your own strategy. Do you see what I mean?"

"Uh..."

Richard leaned in over the board. "Let me ask you again, why do I win?"

"Because you can plan faster. Because when I'm figuring out what to do you're already figuring out how to counter my move."

"And what does that mean?"

"You've always got me on my back heel. I'm not playing to win, I'm playing to try and not lose."

Richard smiled at me. "Give the kid a cigar."

"So is that it?" I asked.

Richard barked out a laugh and threw his arms up over his head. "Is that it? Is that it? Son, you are talking about the single most fundamental point in the art of war; making the enemy react to you instead of you to him. Action-reaction. Offense and defense. The man who never manages to throw a punch never wins a fist-fight."

"But you have to be able to protect yourself against the other guy's moves," I protested.

"What moves? If every move your opponent makes is to defend against one of your own, you already know what he's going to do. You utterly dominate the battle because you control everything your enemy does. You guide his movements because he is constantly moving to defend against you. You control his attacks because he can only attack from where you left him. You offer him only what you want him to attack and force his strategy to conform to yours. In this situation, he is left so busy reacting that he never has a chance to act himself."

I shook my head. "Okay, that's great, but how do you do that?"

Richard folded his arms across his chest. "When you were playing baseball in little league or summer camp or wherever, what was the most important thing you needed to do in order to make contact swinging your bat?"

"Keep your eye on the ball," I said.

Richard nodded. "What does that mean, exactly?"

I frowned. "Uh, it means watch the ball so you know where to swing."

Richard shook his head. "It means much more

than that. It means you need to pay attention to what you want to achieve. The goal of swinging the bat isn't to swing the bat well; it's to make contact with the baseball. Do you see the difference?"

"I think so, maybe. No."

"Think about checkers. What is the goal of the game?"

"To eliminate all the opponent's pieces."

"So, it's not moving your pieces around on the board?"

I sighed. "Get to the point, please."

Richard waggled his finger at me. "This is the point. In any combat situation, the end goal is to defeat your enemy. It is not to avoid getting hurt yourself, although that factors into it. It is not to shoot the bad guy; that is just a means to an end. If the most fundamental point in the art of war is to make the enemy react to you, then the path to performing this feat is keeping your end objective foremost in your mind and always be moving towards that objective. If you are playing checkers, always ask yourself, 'will this move contribute to winning the game, or am I just moving a piece because it's my turn?'. If your answer is the latter, then you are failing to keep the end goal in sight, and you are going to lose every time."

After his lecture to me, Richard decided it was time to introduce me to a greater portfolio of weapons. We unpacked ammunition for his scoped AR-15, as well as the Remington shotgun Richard had shown me on my first day, but never took out to the firing range. We also stripped and cleaned all the weapons we scavenged from the meth lab. Richard had ammunition for everything, and in large quantities.

One by one, I took the guns out to our makeshift firing range. Richard walked me through loading and unloading each weapon, any special features they had, and any tips on how to handle each weapon. By now, I was getting to the point where I could figure most of it out on my own; a safety lever is a safety lever, a bolt is a bolt, a magazine is a magazine. For a few hours, we blasted paper targets and Richard's much-battered five-gallon buckets filled with sand.

"I've told you this before, but it's worth repeating; you want to be able to pick up a bad guy's gun and use it just as well as your own firearm. Guns jam, break down, get shot up, run out of ammo, fall down elevator shafts...anything that can go wrong, will go wrong."

That night, Richard started me on a regimen of reading a steady stream of excerpts from "books about war", for lack of a better term. Sun Tzu, Clausewitz, Miyamoto Musashi, Julius Caesar, Wang Jingze, and a plethora of more modern sources, from US military field manuals to excerpts from military biographies and after action reports. Richard had boiled the readings down to a manageable degree, but there was still a couple hours of reading every night.

During my last two weeks, we made several trips into town, mostly to purchase building materials; two-by-fours, sheets of plywood, nails and hinges and the like. Richard and I spent our evenings constructing target stands, doors and doorways, partial walls of various shapes and sizes, even windows and railings. Richard wanted me to be comfortable moving through a doorway with a gun, being able to engage targets not only while moving, but moving into a space, over a railing, leaning around a wall or through a window.

With these more sophisticated drills came equally sophisticated scenarios. I could see now why Richard had begun with checkers and moved on to The Art of War; he was conditioning me to see each confrontation as a series of moves and counter moves, and to understand that the way to survive the confrontation was to have my game plan in place before the first shot was even fired.

"The trick is to practice positive visualization," Richard told me one day. "You have to not only see yourself progressing through your plan of action, but you have to see success at the end of every scenario. Victory often goes to the side who can see themselves winning before the battle has even been joined."

"Isn't that being over-confident?" I asked. "What about 'plans never survive contact with the enemy'?"

"There's a big difference between being cocky and never believing in the no-win scenario. If you are confident that there is no situation so dire that you can't find a way out, you've taken the first step towards succeeding where others would give up and fail. You can read accounts of battles where time and again, the side who won was simply the side that refused to accept the odds stacked against them, and kept working to come out on top."

"It sounds like you've been there a few times yourself."

"You have no idea. But, I'm still here because I never quit when another dummy would have just stood up and ate some lead to get it over with. I've fought to the last bullet, and when my guns ran dry I've used my knife, and when that broke I've used my fists until my knuckles were bloody. But every time, I won through."

By the middle of my third week, we had a pretty solid routine. Up at dawn for exercises and our run, a light breakfast followed by setting up a combat scenario that I worked through in several different ways under Richard's tutelage. After lunch, while cleaning our weapons and making repairs to our target range, Richard and I would play out games of "What if".

"Have you ever tried a role-playing game?" Richard asked me one day over lunch.

"I don't know if that's any of your business, pervert."

Richard sneered. "Not sex, idiot. It's a kind of game."

"You mean like, what, Dungeons and Dragons? Wearing a cloak and pretending to cast magic spells with elves? No, I've never done that."

"I'm not talking about pretending to be an elf, dummy. Not every role-playing game is about dragons and gnomes. Some of them are about secret agents, or commandos, or anything else you can think of. A role-playing game is a natural evolution from cops and robbers or cowboys and Indians into something much more structured and codified. The principle, however, is the same. A scenario creator posits a challenge, and the participants offer up ways in which they would overcome the challenge, with the creator acting as a referee, determining success or failure."

"If I checked under your bed, I wouldn't find a wizard's hat and a magic wand, would I?"

Richard flicked a cracker crumb at me. "It is a tool for training your mind to approach situations analytically, and quickly find a solution to the problem."

"Okay, you win, Bilbo Baggins. Give me a challenge."

And so, Richard and I played out what-if scenarios. Your target is in a sedan and you are trying to engage from a distance, how do you do it? Ground level or from a rooftop? Is it better to take the shot at night or during the day? Do you shoot through the sheet metal roof or the windshield? Do you go for the kill first, or do you try and immobilize the vehicle? Is it better to keep the target pinned down in the car, or get them to exit the vehicle? What if the target has a bodyguard? What if you want to take them alive?

Richard's ability to come up with a scenario that became increasingly more complex and convoluted was remarkable. Every time I found a solution to a problem, Richard would add another element or complication that forced me to step back, re-evaluate, and come up with an alternate plan. Our discussions became so complex that after a couple of days we drove into town one afternoon and bought ourselves some plastic soldiers, toy cars, and other visual aids. We built a "sandbox" that we could set up on the dining table in order to build out the imaginary terrain, erecting buildings made from cracker boxes, toy cars, soldiers representing both targets and innocents. These sandbox scenarios grew increasingly more involved, and the lessons I learned from playing checkers against Richard served me well. I would plan my "moves" while Richard adjusted the position of the enemies and the civilians, and I focused on making Richard react to me, and not the other way around.

"When we first tried this," I said to Richard, "I felt kind of silly. But now, I see how helpful it is to visualize all the players in the scenario and their spatial relationships."

"There's nothing silly about it. There is a reason they call chess 'The Game of Kings'. For thousands of years, generals have played out similar war games, sandbox battles pitting one enemy force against another in mock table-top warfare. Even professional sports teams use similar techniques; every football coach has a chalkboard with arrows showing sweeping flank maneuvers or headlong charges. Now that we've entered the computer age, programs have been written to pit opposing forces against each other on a virtual battlefield, calculating such minutiae as how weather, terrain, hunger and thirst affect the performance of the soldiers on the field, determining trajectories and percentages of rounds delivered on target."

"I've heard the Army encourages their soldiers to play computer games in order to develop their reflexes and understand the benefits of certain tactics."

Richard nodded. "There will come a day when much of a soldier's training will happen in virtual reality, although nothing will ever be able to fully replace the experience of live field exercises."

My last week in Texas was an unrelenting grind of training and study. Although Richard had said in the beginning we would focus on "guns, not Judo", he felt I had progressed far enough in my marksmanship that some basic unarmed fighting techniques made their way into our training schedule. First I was taught what Richard claimed was the most important skill: how to fall.

"If you're going to get into a fight, you're going to wind up on the ground at some point. The most important thing to know how to do is take that fall well, and recover from the impact."

Along with falls, Richard and I practiced throws. Against your average person with little unarmed combat training, the key was to lower your own center of gravity and widen your stance in order to keep yourself stable, while raising your opponent's center relative to your own and destabilizing them to provoke a fall. The ease with which Richard threw me around was astonishing; it seemed to take no effort on his part at all, he would just shift his body in relation to mine, and I'd find myself tumbling to the ground. Although Richard allowed me to throw him to see how the techniques worked, it was clear that in a real fight against the old man, I'd never have a chance.

Beyond throws and falls, Richard and I discussed and practiced simulated blows to the body's weak points. Strikes to the groin, the instep, the knee and the base of the skull were all good because there was little muscle mass to pad the impact. The fragility of the knee and elbow joints, the usefulness of dislodging and breaking an enemy's pinky or ring finger, and the ultra-sensitive bundle of nerves right under a person's nose were discussed in detail. Techniques such as kicks or punches to the juncture of the inner thigh to strike at the femoral artery, clapping blows to the ears to rupture an eardrum, or the best way to shove one's thumb into an opponent's eye socket were topics for our dinner conversations.

"What about knives?" I asked Richard one evening.

"Stay away from knives," he replied.

"What do you mean, stay away from them? Wouldn't it be easier to stab a guy then have to go through the trouble of ramming my thumb into his eyeball?"

"I don't have time to teach you anything about knives. They are messy, they can slip and twist in your hand and cut you as badly as they'd cut your enemy, and they can be taken away by a lucky or trained opponent and used against you. They can even break, snap, or get stuck in the other guy and become useless. Better to not rely on a knife at all than be inexperienced and try anyhow."

"What if the other guy's got a knife?" I asked.

"Run away. The guy who pulls a knife on you is either real dumb, or real good, and you don't want to take that gamble."

Nevertheless, Richard showed me a few last-ditch techniques for catching a knife hand and gaining control of the weapon, but he stressed this was a do-or-die technique for me, and performing it incorrectly could get me into deep shit real fast.

"Go for that knife hand at the wrong angle, you're going to wind up with a blade sticking out of your palm or lodged in your wrist, and then your goose is cooked for sure."

Chapter 13

My last day in Texas arrived with unexpected quickness. I simply woke up one morning, and it struck me that this was my last day of training. In twenty-four hours, I would be flying back to Boston and starting to take my revenge in earnest. Richard and I went through our morning workout and run, and over breakfast we discussed tomorrow's schedule.

"We'll skip the run and get some grub in you, then I'm going to drive you out to the airfield where I picked you up. Chuck is supposed to be there at seven tomorrow morning. From there you have an 11 AM flight out of San Antonio, so take a cab from one airport to the other, then slow down a little, get a meal in your belly, and get some sleep on the flight up north."

"What do I do when I get to Boston?" I asked.

"Your gardener will meet you at the airport and get you settled into your new apartment. He'll also provide you with any last-minute details."

"What does this guy look like, or is he just going to find me?"

"He'll find you, but just in case, he looks like you, more or less. Same height, same build, same hair color and eye color, same haircut."

"That's kind of creepy, actually."

"The gardeners bear a superficial resemblance to the operatives they cover for because it helps make the illusion more realistic for the neighbors. If your cover is ever investigated and the enemy learns from the neighbors that "you" appeared to be a five-foot tall Asian man, the cover wouldn't last too long."

"Makes sense."

"Trust me, if it didn't make sense, we wouldn't do it, because people would get killed."

The rest of the morning, Richard and I went through all the weapons I had trained with over the last few weeks to see if there was any change to Richard's original recommendations. I still liked the Uzi, the Glock, Beretta .32 auto, the Smith & Wesson .38 snub-nose, the DeLisle carbine, and the cut-down Remington 1100 shotgun.

Richard and I had focused the least amount of time on the Remington, not because a shotgun was easy to use; in fact, it was the most difficult and the most specialized of all the weapons I would have at my disposal. With limited ammunition, and a slow reload time, coupled with its tremendous recoil, blast, and the weapon's bulk, we both agreed that it was best suited for situations where I would be immediately emptying it into a room or a vehicle, then switching to another weapon for the rest of the engagement.

After spending a final few hours working my way through using these firearms under Richard's mentorship for the last time, he agreed that I was as ready as I was going to be, given the time frame.

"I could say you needed to stay out here for another month, or six months, or heck, even a year. But the work I can do with you here can only take you so far. Right now, the biggest challenge for you is going to be finding the right time and place to strike, and I've got assets working on that as we speak."

"You do?"

"Along with your gardener, there's an intelligence operative in place right now, whose job is to keep an eye on the Paggianos and begin tracking patterns and familiar faces, strengths and weaknesses, hard points and vulnerabilities. Once you get into Boston, your operative will make contact with you."

"How will I know who it is?" I asked.

"Son, how many people in Boston are going to walk up to you and hand you an intelligence dossier?"

"Good point."

Richard offered to treat me to dinner on my last night in Texas. We drove into town and went to the same restaurant we visited three weeks ago. I got myself a ribeye steak and a beer, while Richard had pork chops and iced tea. Biscuits, greens, potatoes, and gravy were never in short supply.

"May I ask why you don't drink alcohol?"

"Alcohol makes it too easy to disguise something slipped into your drink."

"Do you think that's going to happen here?"

Richard gave me a look and a shrug. "It's an old habit, and if I have to ask myself every time if I think it's safe enough, I'll make a mistake when it counts. I have been in this business forever, and the list of people who'd like to see me dead is longer than you can imagine."

I considered my next words carefully.

"When I first heard about you from my uncle, he said he didn't know how you got into this line of work, only that you were already well-regarded when he met you after the war, and that he was certain you were never a military man."

"Well, he's right on both counts."

"So if it wasn't the military...?" I let the question hang in the air.

Richard shook his head. "You never paid to hear my life story. Let's just say that I was in deep with some bad hombres, and after cutting myself loose I settled back into doing the only thing I was ever good at, only I sold my skills to those I thought to be the good guys."

"I guess by that you mean, the U.S. Government."

Richard shrugged again. "Most of the time. During the height of the Cold War, who was a good guy and a bad guy changed with surprising frequency. Sometimes I worked for Uncle Sam, sometimes I worked for one of his friends, and sometimes I worked in the private sector for people who had government ties, people who could ask around and find out how to be put in touch with someone with my skills."

I paused for a long moment. "Do you know why my uncle quit doing...what it is you do? I guess that's how you two met."

Richard gave me a wistful smile. "When it comes to this kind of life, you sometimes feel like you've plummeted down a rabbit hole and can't see the light up above you. Tell me, did you see that movie, The Matrix?"

"Uh, yeah."

"Although your uncle was coming out of a long, dirty war, and had spent a while serving at the sharp end of a very shadowy organization, he wasn't really privy to the world that lay beneath it all, the shadow world that I had operated in for years by the time I met Jamie. In a way, you could say that our relationship was much the same in those early years as that of Morpheus and Neo. Your uncle was a very skilled protégé who had a sense that there was something going on under the surface of the world, while I was the one who showed him just how deep the rabbit hole could go."

"So what happened?"

"Your uncle got out of the game before it consumed him. He became like Obi-Wan Kenobi, living out his days far removed from his past, content to let the world and current events pass him by. But you, young Skywalker, you came along and reminded him of what he once was, reminded him of the days when he fought the good fight."

I smiled. "I think we're mixing our movie metaphors a little?"

Richard waved his steak knife in the air and made wooooommm woooommm noises. "An elegant weapon, for a more civilized age."

I chuckled. "Oh my god, you're a closet nerd."

Richard smiled. "Your uncle and I saw Star Wars in the theater together the week it opened. We were in Los Angeles at the time, not working, just some R&R. You might laugh, but in those days, we could relate to those cinematic adventures and escapades, living in the shadow world of the private contractor, fighting all over the map against the communists, the Islamic extremists, terror cells, organized crime, civil wars in Africa. We worked with guys like Han Solo or Boba Fett on an almost weekly basis."

I just shook my head. "I can't imagine what that must be like."

Richard barked out a laugh. "You can't? Well hell, son. What do you think you're doing right now?"

It was a sobering thought, one that continued to haunt me as I tried to get a few hours of troubled sleep that night.

In the morning, there was little that needed to be said. I was up by five, a quick but thorough ablution and a change into presentable clothes. Richard and I had a light breakfast of tea and dried fruit, saying nothing of consequence. My bags went into the back of the Suburban, and we drove away from the cabin. I resisted the sentimental urge to look back at the place that had changed me in such a profound way.

We drove to the tiny airfield in silence. I had

learned from experience that when he had nothing important to say, Richard could go hours without the need for small talk, and so I didn't think much of his quiet now. We reached the airfield ten minutes before Chuck was scheduled to arrive, and as before, we rolled down the windows in order to listen for the drone of his aircraft's engine.

"I had always thought I didn't possess the patience or temperament for instruction," Richard said to me suddenly, "but I hope I served you well, even when I wasn't very easy on you."

I turned and looked at him, illuminated in the early morning sunlight. Richard wore his straw cowboy hat, long-sleeved shirt and a pair of faded jeans, much like the day I arrived in Texas. His Delta Elite sat on his hip, hammer cocked, safety engaged. I knew in his left front pocket, Richard had two extra magazines. There was at least one other firearm in the Suburban's cab, possibly another in the back seat. I wondered what drove a man to live his life in such a way.

And then it struck me. I already knew.

"When I came here," I said, "I had a purpose, but I didn't have a plan, I didn't have the means, and I didn't have the faith in myself to see the job through. You've given me all those things, and much more."

Richard nodded. "People like myself, we live in another world, the shadow world, and stepping into that world can be quite a shock. You handled yourself all right though, better than many I've seen. Your uncle, he was able to handle it too, at least for a time, but that's because he didn't have a choice. Vietnam made him what he was, what he became. You made the decision to step through the door on your own. I think you'll handle it even better than he did."

We both heard the drone of Chuck's engine at the same time, and paused to see him come in for a landing. Without any urging, I felt under the seat and drew the Glock I knew was there, just in case. We waited until Chuck had taxied to a stop and stepped out of the plane, at which point I tucked the gun away and exited the Suburban. As I unloaded my two bags, Richard climbed out as well, and he offered me his hand before I started out for the waiting plane.

"Give 'em hell," Richard said as he shook my hand.

"Happy trails, Richard. Enjoy that money a little - you can't take it with you."

I shook Chuck's hand again as I stepped up to the plane, and he took my bags to throw in the rear as I moved to climb into the cockpit. Just before I shut the cockpit door, I heard Richard holler out to me over the rumble of the engine.

"Hey, William!"

I looked over to him, standing with one thumb hooked into his belt, the other raised in farewell.

"Yeah?"

Richard gave me his most mirthless smile.

"Welcome to the brotherhood."

Chapter 14

After my extended boot camp in the Texas desert, the first-class flight from San Antonio to Boston felt like I was enjoying the comforts of a five-star hotel. Comfy seats, a not-half-bad airline meal, and (after showing my ID) a couple scotch and sodas. In-flight movie, blanket and pillow, cool air conditioning, and thankfully, no screaming children or hacking coughs anywhere within proximity to my seat.

I knew my "gardener" would find me somewhere around baggage claim, and when I went downstairs to the carousel area to wait for my suitcase, I gave the area a sweep, but spotted no one who matched, well, the description I would give if I were looking for someone just like me. After a few moments the carousel started up, and eventually I spotted my suitcase. Taking it from the carousel, I turned around, and almost walked straight into myself.

At least, that's how he appeared. The "gardener" was my height, just about my build and weight, his hair the same glossy black and of similar length and style, the same blue eyes, the same fair, slightly freckled complexion. It was absolutely uncanny. I judged him a few years older, but beyond that, he could have been my older brother, it was such a similarity.

"You all set?" he asked.

I nodded. "You got a car?"

"It's your car, dude, and yeah, parked in the short term lot across the way. Let's go."

The car was a silver Volkswagen Jetta, just hip enough for Boston but simple enough to not stand out. We threw my suitcase in the back and climbed in.

On the drive into the city, the gardener laid it out for me.

"I've got you a one-bedroom apartment along Park Drive, over in the Fenway area. It's good sized, parking in the back behind the brownstone, and you're on the first floor, so there's less of a chance anyone will notice you coming and going at odd hours. Ever live in the Fenway?"

"Never had an apartment of my own," I replied.

"It's alright. Not a bad area, but not great. Now, this is important. You might hear shit or see shit with your neighbors: asshole boyfriend, couple always getting into fights, some dude who listens to his stereo too loud, whatever. The point is, you see nothing, you hear nothing, you say nothing, you do nothing, all right? No heroics, no calls to 911, no anonymous tips, no having a quiet word or playing Leon the Professional, you got me? You keep your head down, you maintain your cover."

"I got you, don't worry."

He looked at me out of the corner of his eye. "Yeah, you say that now, but I know it can happen. Someone is a dick to his girlfriend, you think she's cute, you catch her in the hall and ask if everything's okay, she thinks you're nice, and the next thing you know, she's banging on your door at three in the morning asking to come in because he's a mean drunk. That is the shit you do not want. Next day you have police knocking on your door, asking you questions, like why you didn't call 911, shit like that. Attention you do. Not. Want."

"I got it, okay? I got it. Believe me, I have no interest in getting scooped up because of some domestic trouble that's not even my deal."

He was still skeptical, but moved on. "I've already taken care of the rent. A check under your white identity will land in the rental company's mailbox a couple of days before it's due every month. I'm guessing this op isn't going to take very long, month or two at the most, but it'll keep being paid until I hear otherwise from your handler. Utilities are all set up to be paid electronically, so you won't even have to touch those. You have cable, full package, plus a phone line and a DSL connection for the computer."

"Computer already set up?"

"Yeah, got you a good laptop, and a color printer as well."

"Works for me."

We eventually reached the Fenway area, coming

off of Storrow Drive and hopping onto Park Drive via Charlesgate. Within a few minutes, we cut down one of the side streets and parked behind the four-story brownstone. Taking my suitcase and my carry-on from the Jetta, the gardener handed me the keys and I used the remote fob to lock the doors.

"There's a full tank of gas and I had the car serviced a week ago. Shouldn't have any problems."

We came in through the parking lot entrance and took a single flight of stairs to the first floor. The gardener pointed out the right key, and I let myself in through the door just to the left of the stairwell. The apartment was simple and functional. The front door opened into the living room, while straight ahead was a small kitchen space. To the far left was the bathroom, and to the right, over near the far corner of the living room, was the bedroom. A couch and a reading chair dominated the living room, with an end table and lamp in the corner between the two, and a bookshelf in the middle of the left-hand wall near the bathroom door. To my immediate left, there was a small coat closet. The television and VHS/DVD deck was straight ahead, facing the front door and the couch. The floors were hardwood, with a simple Berber rug in the living room.

Decorating the living room, there was a poster of Bruce Lee in Enter the Dragon hanging over the television, while a poster for The Matrix hung on the wall behind the couch, and a third poster for Eastwood's The Outlaw Josey Wales occupied the wall behind the reading chair. The bookshelf was about half-filled with old economics textbooks, a few hardcover and paperback thrillers, some violent comic books, about two dozen DVDs, and a stack of various military-themed reference books, seemingly not out of place in a living room that was obviously used by a guy who liked violent films.

I nodded my approval. "Wow, this really looks good. You set this up over the last month?"

"Yup. This is what a degree in theater gets you."

"You were a theater major?" I asked.

"Undergraduate and grad school. A couple hundred thousand dollars down the tubes. Well, until I stumbled across this line of work. It's all about the little details, you see? We can lump in military manuals about urban combat tactics if it's sitting next to some Punisher comics and a couple of action movies. Might raise an eyebrow, but no one is going to take it seriously. Just another young guy who digs action flicks and graphic novels."

Stepping into the kitchen briefly, I opened the refrigerator; filled with sodas, sandwich makings, milk, eggs, sliced ham and turkey, OJ, and a few bags of veggies. The freezer had some frozen goods, the shelves contained canned foods and boxes of pasta and cereal. There was a microwave, a toaster, a coffee maker, and a tea kettle on the stove. Simple but attractive flatware and silverware filled the remaining shelves and drawers, along with pots, pans, kitchen cutlery, and other necessary utensils.

"Hey, thanks for doing the shopping. Much appreciated."

"You're going to be busy, so I figured I'd stock up.

Besides, the fridge is often a give-away that some-one isn't really living there when you find it empty or filled with spoiled food."

The bathroom was also well-equipped, with all the necessary soaps, shampoo, toothpaste, and other toiletries, as well as a stack of good quality towels and washcloths. The bedroom contained a full-sized bed, a bureau, a night-stand, and a small desk in the corner, where a laptop and color printer were set up. The laptop was open and running, and just then, I noticed a few odd devices plugged into the wall outlets in between the outlet and the plugs themselves.

"The laptop runs a program that controls the timers throughout the apartment. The TV is turned on, lamps turned off and on, radio, that sort of thing. The times are adjusted randomly so it's not obvious that the TV comes on at, say, six o'clock exactly every weekday. Now that you're here, you'll want to disable the program, but if you're going to be absent a while, could come in handy again."

"Very cool," I replied.

I noticed that on one side of the laptop, there was a small red sticker.

"What's that?"

The gardener leaned down and pointed to a small appliance plugged into the wall, resting on the floor near the desk.

"This is a hand-held degausser. If you ever feel this place has been compromised, or that you need to ditch the laptop, turn it on and scrub this back and forth over that sticker for thirty seconds. It's sitting right over the laptop's hard drive. You'll completely paste the magnetic drive platters and anything on the laptop will be unrecoverable."

I nodded. "Good to know."

Opening the bureau's drawers, I found a selection of casual late spring and early summer wear; polos, t-shirts, shorts, jeans, underwear, socks. In the bedroom closet hung a handful of shirts, both short and long-sleeved, as well as two full suits; one black, the other a very light tan. Matching two pairs of dress shoes sat on a shoe rack below the suits in the closet, along with a pair of flip-flops, a pair of light trail shoes, and a pair of running sneakers.

"You really think of everything, don't you?"

The gardener smiled. "That's my job."

We moved back into the living room, and the gardener reached into his jacket and handed me a thick white envelope. Looking inside, it was filled with several sheets of computer paper, a fat wad of used bills, and at least two dozen pre-paid calling cards.

"The first page details contact info for getting in touch with your handler. There is a list of numbers. Never call the same number more than once. Never use a pay phone within five blocks of this apartment, and never use the same pay phone more than once. Those cards should give you an hour's worth of call time apiece; never use a card more than once. The cash is five grand in mixed, used bills. Try not to use the credit or bank cards for your alternate identities unless you have to. If you need more money, contact your handler and we can get you some cash within four hours."

"All right, what about these?" There was a print-out of several dozen email accounts and passwords, all free web accounts from Hotmail and Yahoo.

"Those are one-time email accounts we've set up for you. If you contact your handler and need to get information quickly, he will email you at the specified address. Log in, get the info you need, then delete the account."

"I'm guessing he'll be using one-time accounts as well?"

"Yup. We want to keep all these channels as disposable as possible."

"I was told I've got an asset in the city gathering intelligence for me. How do I get in contact?"

The gardener shook his head. "No idea. Your handler will probably arrange for the asset to contact you somehow. I know nothing about that, and it's the way I like it. Keeps it compartmentalized."

"What about my gear; the guns, ammo, that stuff?"

"Being shipped to you by courier. Should be here a couple of days. Plenty of time to get settled, get the vibe of the city back in your head."

I nodded again. "I guess that's it?"

"Yeah, I think my work here is done. Like I said, just keep your head down, focus on your mission, and follow the operational security procedures we've given you."

I offered the gardener my hand, and after a moment's hesitation he shook it.

"Thanks for getting me set up. I don't even know your name."

He nodded. "That's because you don't need to know it. Good luck."

Without another word, he left the apartment.

For the first time in six weeks, the next move was entirely my own.

I looked at the time on the VCR display; it was almost five o'clock. I went into the kitchen, made myself a sandwich, grabbed a soda, and clicked on the TV to catch some news. I hadn't watched television in close to two months, and it felt surreal to just sit back on a comfy couch, drink a soda, eat a sandwich, and watch some TV like a normal human being who wasn't planning a vigilante crime spree.

The news was the usual nonsense. More work on the Big Dig. More talk about how President Bush takes a lot of vacation time. Later I watched some X-Files and The Lone Gunmen. After a while, I shut the television off and stared at the ceiling. A sense of fitful depression overcame me. What am I doing here? Do I have the will to go through with this? Even after all that time in the desert, am I fooling myself to think I have what it takes to earn my revenge?

I needed to do something. I took a shower, changed into some running clothes, grabbed my sneakers, and went out. I didn't have a plan, I just started running, Forrest Gump style. I was not particularly familiar with the area, aside from being at a couple of Red Sox games over the years, so it was good to get a sense of the neighborhood. I just took off down Park Drive, heading towards the MFA, cutting through the park, then past the Isabella Stuart Gardner Museum and Simmons College. Eventually I made my way into Brookline, jogging down one quiet street after another, and an hour after I left my apartment, I finally jogged back along Beacon Street and then Park Drive.

The exercise definitely cleared my head. I took a second quick shower, unpacked my suitcase and carry-on, and called it a night. Looking at the clock radio next to the bed, it was only eleven o'clock, but it might as well have been near dawn, I was so exhausted. Closing my eyes and willing myself to relax, I fell asleep in a real bed for the first time in a month, and dreamed of revenge.

Chapter 15

I wasn't immediately aware of what woke me that morning; one moment I was sound asleep, the next I was completely awake, the skin along my arms and the back of my neck prickling, a jolt of adrenaline running through me. At first I thought it was because of the strange bed I found myself in, but after a few seconds' reflection I realized there had been a sound, not a sensation, that had woken me up. Something intrusive beyond the usual noises of an urban morning.

I slid softly out of bed and padded into the living room. I saw the culprit immediately; a piece of folded white paper had been shoved underneath my door and slid across the hardwood. I studied it bleary-eyed for a moment or two, and then decided - fuck it - to pick it up. Unfolding the paper, I saw only a handful of scribbled words:

INTEL BRIEF
SEVEN PM HERE
SEVEN KNOCKS
HAVE PIZZA AND BEER

The handwriting was, if I had to hazard a guess, feminine. Richard had never mentioned that his "asset" was a woman, but then again, he hadn't stated anything to the contrary, either.

Hmmm, a woman? I had a sudden jolt of anxiety. I hadn't spoken to a woman for any reason other than to order a meal or ask for an airline pillow in over a month. Now I was going to be working with a woman, have her here in my new home, and I was feeling foolishly uncomfortable about the idea. At least I hadn't been here long enough to accumulate piles of dirty socks and porn, and the sink was remarkably free of dirty dishes, but I still had the anxiety any young man has when a member of the opposite sex visits his home for the first time. It was a surprisingly normal thought and it brought on a wave of bitter nostalgia, because the last time I had felt that way, I was showing Beth my bedroom while she visited my home in Providence.

The thought that my old room, along with everything else, was now just a pile of cinders put me in a dark mood for the rest of the morning. I went through the now-ingrained routine of stretches, calisthenics, and a hard run around the neighborhood. After a post-run shower I made myself a big breakfast; coffee and OJ, scrambled eggs, toast, and ham. Thanks to my extremely lean diet over the last month, I had ramped my metabolism to absurd heights, and I knew I'd be hungry again by noon.

After fueling up, I decided to head downtown. I wanted to get the feel of a city back under my skin, the noise and the smell and the constant energy and motion. It took me about an hour, but I walked from my apartment to Government Center, where Boston's city hall stood gray and monolithic over the plaza. I had no particular agenda, I just wandered through crowds, maneuvering through Faneuil Hall and around the milling tourists, past the performers and buskers. Although it was only the beginning of May it was already warm and sunny for Boston, but compared to Texas it was almost cool. Still, everyone was taking the opportunity to wear their summer apparel, and the college girls who walked by me were definitely making the most of the few weeks they had left in the city.

As I moved through the masses and soaked it all in, I couldn't help but feel a shocking degree of antipathy, even disgust, towards everyone I passed. Families walked around me, smiling and laughing without a care in the world, while my own family was buried in the dirt, their bodies broken and burned beyond recognition. The unfairness of it all, the loss of anything approaching a normal life for me, suddenly became overpowering. I wanted to punch every smiling couple in the face, smash an elbow into the gut of every proud father, hammer a heel-kick into the knee of every loving mom. There's nothing like rage and jealousy to drive fantasies of indiscriminate violence on a gorgeous spring day.

I needed to get away from all the crowds, so I took a couple of hours and slowly worked my way along the wharves and docks, past the private yachts and the condos and high-priced apartment buildings that lined the waterfront. Eventually I made my way into South Boston, past the tea party ship, out along the piers, walking by Fish pier and right out as far as I could get before hitting a chain link fence and staring out into the Atlantic. There wasn't anyone around, and although I'd see a person here and there at a distance, this part of Boston was practically a ghost town. Briefly I wondered if I might encounter someone looking for a lost tourist to mug. The thought gave me a thrill, and I realized I had wandered this far subconsciously looking for a fight.

Enough was enough. I headed west, only vaguely aware of where I was going, but eventually I found the Broadway T station and headed home. I remembered the note from this morning, and checked my watch; it was five in the afternoon. I walked back to my apartment, showered and changed, tidied up the living room and the kitchen some, then went out looking for pizza and beer.

My gardener had been kind enough to leave several take-out flyers stuck to the refrigerator, and I was able to find a place right around the corner, a little hole-in-the-wall pie shop just down from a tiny, dingy hole-in-the-wall liquor store. I put in an order for a large pizza with loaded toppings, then went next door and picked up a six-pack of Bass ale. By the time I returned to the apartment it was six-thirty, and with little to do but wait I set the pizza on the kitchen counter, popped the beer in the fridge, brushed my teeth, checked my hair, and changed my shirt twice.

There was no warning before the knocks, no buzzer for the front door, no sound of footsteps on the hard tile in the corridor. One moment I stood in the living room listening to nothing, the next moment a hard-knuckled series of seven fast raps struck the door. Taking a deep breath, I stepped softly to the door and looked out into the hallway. I didn't see anyone. Whoever it was, they stood to the side of the door, cautious about being seen. It struck me that I was unarmed. In order to keep the cover of the apartment secure from the landlord, there were no weapons left here, and my hardware was still on its way from Texas. A stupid thing to worry about, seeing as I had no reason to suspect my plan was known and someone was acting against me, but I realized now that Richard's paranoia had worn off on me.

"Hey, asshole. Let me in. This is getting awkward."

She whispered it into the crack of the door, just loud enough for me to hear.

"Then stop hiding away from the peephole," I replied.

"Fine..."

She stepped into view from the right side of the door. She was short, dark-complexioned, with long hair and wearing casual street clothes. She had a big book-bag over her shoulder, but her hands were empty.

"Gimme a sec." I unlocked the deadbolt and slipped the chain, then stepped clear and opened the door for her to come inside.

"Thanks." She stepped into the room, and although it wasn't obvious, I saw her eyes move around all the entrances, scanning and cataloging the room. I could tell she was looking for blind spots, available cover, windows and doors to observe. She had either received training, or she was naturally very observant and paranoid.

She looked to be Hispanic, somewhere in her mid-20's, a few years older than me. Attractive, cute even, but not a girl you'd immediately think of as hot or sexy. She was slim and athletic, with strong looking arms and shoulders, a small, high bust and lean legs. Her hair was black and straight, worn long and loose, about mid-way down her back. She stood with an air of assured strength; not afraid, just cautious and ready to act if need be.

"I smell pizza," she said.

"A loaded pie from down the street. I've never ordered from there, so I hope it's good."

"And beer?"

"Picked up a six pack of Bass from next door, hope that's good enough?"

"A little heavier than I like, but not bad."

"You hungry now?"

"Yeah, starved."

"Drop your bag on the couch, let's eat."

I fetched plates from the cabinet and napkins from the counter. While she grabbed a slice for herself, I grabbed beers from the fridge for both of us before fetching my own slice and joining her in the living room.

We sat in silence for a few minutes, devouring pizza and washing it down with beer. I glanced at her now and then out of the corner of my eye. She seemed extraordinarily at ease for someone sitting alone in an apartment with a man who was on a mission to kill a number of other human beings in cold blood. I was guessing this wasn't her first rodeo.

Once we plowed through the first slice and the first bottle, we both paused for a minute.

"Want seconds?" I asked.

"Sure. I'll get out your materials while you do that."

By the time I had loaded the plates and uncapped the bottles, she had pulled several folders from her book-bag and arranged them on the table. Opening them up, I could see she had photos, diagrams, charts, notes...she knew what she was doing.

I sat down next to her again, and she began taking me through it all, one folder at a time.

"Okay, here's the deal. The Paggiano family is one of the last Italian crime families of any real weight in the Boston area. They still cling to the old ways of doing business; muscle, hustle, fear, intimidation. The Irish, the Russians, the Chinese, various black and Latino gangs, that's where organized crime is at in Boston right now. But the Paggianos survive, mostly because they are a bunch of ruthless motherfuckers, and they have a lot of old, long established connections with families in Rhode Island, New York and New Jersey. They are the mom and pop store of organized crime, still doing business in a world of Wal-Marts because they have a rent-controlled storefront and a loyal customer base that keeps coming back for more."

"So what are we looking at?" I asked. "How many trigger-men? I need to know numbers, quality, resources, hard points."

"Calm down, Sergeant Rock. We'll get to all of that."

I gestured to all the folders. "Where to start?"

She handed me the first folder and I began to sort through photos and hand-drawn diagrams while she spoke.

"The Paggiano family has its heart in this estate, up in Swampscott. About twenty acres right on the ocean. There's a wrought-iron gate that goes around half the property, with the other half bordered by the cliffs. Those are pretty sheer, but there are a couple of places where you could hopscotch down to the waterline if you wanted, but there's no sand down there, just rocks and water.

"Aside from the main house, which is three stories and a basement, there is a large four-car garage and a grounds-keeper's cottage right by the front gate. The gate is motorized and controlled by a remote in the cottage. The cottage is a house in itself; two floors, a basement. Two guys stay there at all times, taking turns to keep an eye on the security cameras, watch the gate, handle any deliveries or parcels that come to the place. They take turns sleeping at night, so there's always someone awake. It's not always the same two men, but there are always two of them."

"You said security cameras?" I asked.

"Yeah, here, see the diagram? That's where they are. Two on the cottage, one covering the gate, the other looking back up the drive towards the main house. Then up at the main house, there's one on each corner, covering the property itself. I know there are monitors in the cottage for all the cameras, but I'm guessing there's another control room somewhere in the main building as well."

"What other security measures are in place?"

"They have dogs, at least two. Dobermans, running free on the grounds at night. During the day there's a fenced-in kennel, right here next to the garage, where the dogs are kept so they don't get out or go after anyone who brings in deliveries."

"The guys in the cottage, do they have guns?"

"I've never seen any, but I'm sure they do. No idea what kind, though."

"And the house?"

"As far as I can tell, there are eight bodyguards who live on the estate itself. Two of them are always in the cottage, six of them up at the house. I'm guessing three stay up at night, three go to sleep. Beyond that there's a cook, a maid, and a butler. Of the Paggianos, right now Pauly, his older brother John, John's wife Mary, and their son Adam stay on the estate. Then there's the head of the family, old man Dominic Paggiano, and his wife, Maria."

"That's a pretty big house. What...fifteen people up there at any one time?"

"Yeah, about that. It's immense though. One of those labyrinthine old mansions with dozens of rooms and no order or symmetry whatsoever."

I gestured to the other documents. "What else do you have?"

She shuffled through several folders. "Brief dossiers on all of the Paggianos and their worker bees. The estate crew does some enforcement work; they aren't just babysitters. Outside of that bunch, there are only a couple hard-hitters worth looking into. I've got photos, homes, schedules, routines, weaknesses, anything you want."

I nodded and finished off my second beer. "Looks like you're pretty good at this."

"I should be. Undergrad at Northwestern, Master's at Cornell, focusing in investigative journalism. Been doing lightweight freelance investigation work for a couple of private dicks here and there, but I spend the bulk of my time working for Richard."

"So you know him too?" I asked.

She was quiet a moment. Getting up, she finished her beer, then went into the kitchen and returned a moment later with the last two bottles opened. Handing one to me, she sat down on the couch again and took a long pull on her bottle before speaking.

"I was born in El Salvador, 1975. It wasn't a very friendly place back then. By the time I was ten, every relative I had was dead, or missing and presumed dead. Although I don't really remember it well, I know Richard was working with the CIA as some kind of freelancer, and he helped get me and some other orphaned children into the States. He found us good homes and made sure we got into good schools. I went to college on his dime. Now I work for him."

"Wow. To tell you the truth, I'm kinda surprised. I wouldn't have thought a tough nut like Richard would have mustered up that sort of kindness."

She tipped her beer bottle back and drained what was left in several fast gulps.

"What fucking kindness? He acquired, educated, and established a network of intelligence assets. We're indentured servants, not charity cases. I don't know what he'd do if I tried to leave, but I know I can't just up and walk away from him. If he hadn't gotten me out of there, I'd have been dead before my next birthday."

I didn't know what to say. A minute passed, and finally I asked, "Do you think this is a bad idea?"

She shrugged. "It's not my place to say."

"But if it was? If I told you I'd walk away if you said it was a bad idea?"

"Would you?"

"What?"

"Would you walk away if I said it was a bad idea? Would you let the people who killed your family and burned your house to the ground go on living?"

I hesitated. She smiled.

"He's gotten into your head, too. Richard. You're a part of his insanity now."

I shook my head. "The plan was my idea. My uncle wouldn't go along with it, so he put me in touch with Richard. Richard said he didn't have an opinion on way or the other, he just said he didn't see a problem with a man taking his own vengeance."

Now it was her turn to shake her head. "Two men who've both seen terrible things in their lives, and they let a young man, with his whole future ahead of him, throw away any chance at a normal life, and you don't think you're being manipulated?"

I was taken aback by this. "I can't imagine my uncle would let me get manipulated by someone like Richard. It doesn't make sense."

She leaned in to me now, only inches away. Her stare was shocking, piercing in its intensity. "Richard has made a pact with Death. He sold his soul, and to keep the Grim Reaper from collecting on the deal, Richard keeps feeding people into the mouth of Hell. It doesn't matter if he pulls the trigger, if you do it for him, or even if it's you who dies. Everyone who comes into contact with him gets sucked into oblivion. You, your uncle, everyone."

There was the beginning of a laugh in me, but it died when I realized she wasn't kidding.

"Sold his soul?" I said. "You can't really mean that. No one makes a pact with Death. That doesn't even make sense."

She sat back. "There are certain men, certain violent men, who live through the blood and the death all around them, surviving when they should've died a hundred times. These men have made a deal, a pact, with Death. In exchange for their lives, they must offer up lives in return. It is an old magic. A dark magic, a warrior's magic. That is the magic of blood and murder, and Richard has practiced it all his life. He's a sorcerer. A vampire. He may never die, he has seen and caused so much death."

She was breathing hard now, her eyes wild. For no reason I could fathom, the skin at the back of my neck and along my arms prickled, the hairs standing on end.

An idea came to me.

"The brotherhood," I said.

She nodded.

I looked at her. "And you?"

She shook her head. "I'm just carried along, helpless on the wave. One day it'll crash and I'll be swept away like all the rest. Dragged down into Hell, useful while I lasted, but not anymore."

"But he's known you since you were ten years old."

"By the time Richard met me, he'd killed a thousand men, and he's probably killed thousands more since. I wouldn't be worth a thought to him."

"Do you really believe that?"

She paused, looked away, glanced at the empty bottles in front of us, then back to me. There was an unspoken question in her eyes. We just stared at each other, and the silence dragged out into an awkward tension before she finally turned away and looked at my bedroom door.

"I want to get fucked," she said.

The sex was rough, almost desperate. At one point she hauled off and slapped me across the face, hard enough to make me see stars.

"What the hell?" I said, stopping in mid-thrust.

She slapped me again, tears in her eyes. "Don't stop, you bastard! Don't you fucking stop!"

I tried my best to drive her through the mattress.

Later that night we lay awake, sprawled across the bed sheets, neither of us moving. I was almost afraid to say anything. She was clearly damaged goods, damaged in the worst way, although I had no idea how or why. Finally I turned to her, silhouetted next to me in the dark, staring at the ceiling.

"You don't have to tell me your name, but I'd like to know what to call you."

"Call me Sophia," she said.

"All right, Sophia. Do you really believe what you said earlier? About Richard having a pact with Death."

She turned to me. I could see the whites of her eyes in the dark.

"Even though I was very young, I still remember some of the men who would come into my village, the soldiers, the death squads. Most were nothing but jackals, men who killed and raped and looted for fun, because it was the easy thing to do. But some of the killers, they had a fear about them, like an aura of death. They would look at you and your blood would turn to ice and your heart would feel like it had stopped beating in your chest. Those were the men who killed and killed and would never die themselves, time after time. Whether they knew it or not, they had made a pact with the Reaper, a pact to stay alive as long as they kept sending souls in their place."

"And you think Richard is like these men?"

"Don't you? Killing is like breathing to him. He has bathed in the blood of countless murders. I have seen him kill three times, and on each occasion, he should have died time and again, but the other men were a heartbeat too slow, or the bullets a few inches to the left or right. No man is so lucky for so long without something making that luck for him."

"Do you think he is evil?"

"Killing and evil are not always the same things. I do not think he is a good man, but I don't think he is an evil man, either. I think he is like an earthquake, or a bolt of lightning. If you are in his sights, you die. The only question is, what put you there."

"Do you feel the same aura around Richard that you felt around those men in El Salvador?"

"You are comparing a candle to the sun. Those other men, they were apprentices in the ways of Death. Richard is a master."

"And what about me?" I asked.

"I feel it in you too, a spark. I imagine you are as Richard was forty years ago."

"Then why did you sleep with me?"

Sophia rolled onto me, climbing up and straddling my hips, moving to slip me inside her again.

"Because until I die for Richard, I want to live for myself."

Chapter 16

A week after meeting with Sophia, I sat on the roof of a four-story brownstone in Brighton and looked down on the evening's killing ground, half a block to the south. Donnie DiMarco, aka Donnie the Dick-Kicker, first-class knuckle-dragging muscle for the Paggiano family, liked to get his knob polished on a regular basis. Donnie kept a dirty little thing by the name of Tina Greene in a one-bedroom on the third floor of the apartment building fifty meters down the street.

At least three times a week, after a long day of kicking the living shit out of anyone Dominic Paggiano didn't like, Donnie dropped by Tina's place and got his ashes hauled. Apparently Donnie was a little possessive of Tina, because one of his toadies tried to swing by Tina's pad a couple of years ago and convince her that Donnie had "rewarded" him with a visit. Apparently Tina was to fellatio as Kristi Yamaguchi was to figure skating, and her performances were legendary and highly coveted.

Upon discovering this little ruse, Donnie beat his flunky into unconsciousness, and then, for good measure, crushed his skull by repeatedly stomping on his face.

Donnie was also, as best as Sophia's investigations could determine, the man who beat my mother and sister to death. It would be difficult to tell for certain, what with the house fire that incinerated their bodies and all, but the coroner was sure that all the breaks and fractures their bodies sustained were the result of a beating severe enough to kill, not just damage due to the fire.

Not surprisingly, I made Donnie DiMarco the first target on my list.

Donnie was a man of inviolate habits. Thanks to Richard's incredibly capable intelligence asset, I knew that Donnie almost always visited Tina after drinking with the boys for several hours, so he never arrived until at least ten o'clock, sometimes later. Doing my due diligence, I'd been up on this roof since eight-thirty, before the daylight had completely disappeared from the horizon. I was hunkered down low, peering over the ledge at the top of the building every few moments to make sure I hadn't missed him due to some quirk of circumstance.

But no, Donnie pulled up in his black Mercedes S-Class at 10:23, coming from my direction and parking in front of Tina's brownstone so that his car was facing away from me. There was plenty of room out in front of the apartment building. I was sure no one, but no one, takes the last spot and forces Donnie the Dick-Kicker to go find a parking space.

Sitting next to me on the rooftop gravel was the DeLisle carbine. I had unfolded the small bipod underneath the barrel, and at a suggestion from Richard, the DeLisle wore a black wire mesh "brass catcher" fitted over the ejection port. When I worked the bolt and ejected the spent brass, it was caught like a hockey puck in the goal net, not kicked out into space where I'd never find it. This kept the casings from being found by some eager police forensics technician, reducing my "forensic footprint".

The moment I saw the car nosing into the parking space, the moment I knew it was Donnie's black Mercedes and not that of some poor unfortunate who'd later get a beating, I had the DeLisle's bipod propped on the roof ledge. There were other, better vantage points on other buildings along the street, but this was the only building with a ledge of any appreciable height facing the street. I crouched low, decked out in blue jeans, black sneakers, and a dark green windbreaker. I wore a sandy blond wig and a navy blue baseball cap pulled low over my eyes. Good dark colors to blend in with the night, but not some wannabe ninja outfit that'd make me look a little too obvious coming to or from the scene of the crime.

Back to Donnie. I watched him shut off the engine and open the car door, and I couldn't help but notice how utterly massive a creature he was. I knew Donnie was six foot four, well into the mid two-hundreds, with hands like slabs of concrete and a closely shaved, bullet-like skull. A man of Donnie's size can kill a person with a single punch, crushing ribs and causing internal bleeding with a body blow, or delivering a depressed skull fracture with a fist to the head. That is, of course, if the punch doesn't just break the victim's neck. I had to force myself to breathe deep and pull in the air I'd need when I settled in for the shot. I tried to ignore the mental movie playing in my brain, showing Donnie knocking my sister and mother around my mother's bedroom, like a child might slap and punch a couple of insolent dolls during playtime. My teeth clenched so hard, I could hear them creaking though my skull.

Donnie finally extracted himself from the confines of the Mercedes and stood to his full height, turning away from me as he closed the door of his car. I tried to time the shot so it would coincide with the metallic thump of a heavy car door being slammed shut. As the door closed, I saw the puff of fabric in the middle of Donnie's broad back, as the bullet tore a hole in his tent-sized polo shirt.

Donnie's body didn't even rock from the impact of the subsonic .45 caliber hollowpoint. For a second or two I wondered if Donnie wore some kind of concealable body armor under his shirt, something that had absorbed the impact of the bullet and kept Donnie upright. But by the glow of the streetlamp a few meters from my target, I could see the dark stain spreading between Donnie's shoulder blades, and I knew I'd got him. But still, Donnie stood.

I fired another shot. My hands had cycled the bolt automatically the moment I fired my first round. The second bullet struck Donnie square in the right shoulder blade, landing a little off-target as he turned slightly, his body coming around to look behind him, his movements as sluggish as an oil tanker at sea. That shot caused him to rock back against the side of his Mercedes, but Donnie remained on his feet, one massive paw extended out to steady himself on the car. Donnie didn't shout or cry out or move to cover. At that point I realized he was probably drunk as a skunk, having been out with his wrecking crew for the last couple of hours.

Fuck this, I decided. Working with assembly-line speed and economy of motion, I fired off four more .45 caliber slugs. In the indistinct light of the streetlamp, Donnie's pale yellow polo shirt began to look like blooming sunflowers, as one by one, dark blotches flowered across his chest.

And yet, Donne didn't die. With six bullets in him, Donnie remained upright, though brought to his knees, clinging to the side of his car. Donnie kept himself from collapsing into death by sheer drunken stubbornness and his immense physique. The gleaming bullet head was raised, looking for the source of the gunfire but staring into the shadows of doorways and down the street, not up at the rooftop where I sat, invisible and silent, raining down death.

I realized now why Richard had suggested, when we talked over the phone two nights ago, that I kill Donnie from a distance with the suppressed carbine. If I had attempted to kill him up close and personal, using the Glock or even the shotgun, I might have panicked when confronted with Donnie's sheer intimidating physicality. If I had shot him, and he didn't drop, I might have paused just long enough for Donnie to cave in the side of my skull with one of his wrecking-ball sized fists. Sniping at him from the rooftop, his intimidation factor went away, and I could kill him without experiencing the fear that close proximity would have created.

Richard, you are one crafty motherfucker.

No man, not even Donnie, was going to live through the punishment I'd delivered. On the other hand, I had no idea how long it would take for his body to finally accept the fact that it was going to stop functioning. Already I could hear shouts, and I saw someone down the street hurrying over to Donnie, mistakenly assuming he was having a heart attack or some other ailment. With my mental countdown ticking away, I centered the crosshairs on Donnie's forehead and sent him my last bullet, just before a concerned citizen reached him to see if he needed help. The bullet caught Donnie just above his right eye, dropping him face-down on the pavement like a felled ox. The hole in the back of his head was big enough to hide a billiards ball. The concerned citizen, a paunchy fellow in his late 40's, promptly turned and puked, then scrambled away from Donnie as if his body was about to explode.

That was the end of Donnie the Dick-Kicker.

I needed to get moving. I folded up the bipod and the stock of the DeLisle carbine, and then slipped the weapon into my backpack. Walking in a crouch to the rear of the building, I double-checked the line I'd looped around a rooftop ventilation pipe. The old iron was still strong, without any wiggle or sag that might suggest it had rusted out of its fittings over the years. I'd looped a rappelling rope around the base of the pipe, locked to itself with a carabiner. I snapped the line into my own rappelling ring, having put my clothes on over the harness. Hiding the repelling rig this way wasn't comfortable, but it did prevent stares and questions.

Holding onto the line, I stepped to the edge of the rooftop and dropped into space, letting the line slip through my gloved fingers as fast as I dared, feet skipping and skimming along the side of the building so I didn't bounce or flail about in space. In three seconds, I was on the ground in the alleyway behind the brownstone, unsnapping the line from my harness.

To retrieve the rope, I used a little trick Richard had taught me involving a fly-fishing reel and some line. I reeled down the carabiner securing the line around the pipe on the rooftop. Once in hand, I unclipped the line from itself, then pulled the line up and over the pipe, letting it go slack and drop from the roof. All in all, the process took about thirty seconds. Once I stuffed the line in my pack, I walked out of the alley and assumed a leisurely gait, hearing the first wailing sirens as police cars responded to reports of Donnie's shooting.

Scratch one off the list, I thought to myself.

A short walk to the B-line and one T ride later, I was back at my apartment. Without really thinking about it, I broke down the DeLisle, cleaned it, oiled it, and stowed it away before I did anything else. Next was a scalding hot shower, where I vigorously scrubbed my arms, hands, and face. I knew that gunshot residue tests could still find evidence even after a shower, but I wanted to be sure as little evidence as possible remained. Once I was out of the shower, I threw the clothes I had worn into my kitchen garbage, dumped in a few broken eggs and some lunch meat, and took the trash out to the dumpster, making sure the bag was buried as deeply as possible.

Back in the apartment, I went to the fridge, grabbed a beer, flopped on the couch, and drank the entire bottle in about thirty seconds while just staring off into space. The killing of Donnie couldn't have gone better, and although I had discussed a few of the details with Richard, ultimately the job had been mine, start to finish. No Richard, no Jamie, just me. I had taken the first step on the road to revenge, and it felt great.

I got up off the couch and went into the bedroom. Opening my closet, I dressed in my black suit and slick shoes, foregoing a tie. I dug out my spending money and pocketed two thousand dollars in a silver money clip. I grabbed my keys and my "white" identity wallet, and I went out the door.

One cab ride later, I was downtown. I spent a few minutes wandering the mostly deserted streets until I found a nightclub that seemed to have some action going on. There was a bouncer all in black, wearing a suit and an ear piece. There was a velvet rope across the entrance, and a half dozen men and women looking to get inside, all of them well-dressed and looking to party. I played it cool and soon enough, I found myself past the velvet rope, making a beeline for the bar. The music was shockingly loud, a deep techno dance beat that I could feel in my diaphragm. I elbowed my way through the milling crowd, and although I received a couple of dirty looks from the posturing males I bumped along the way, none of them took it any further after I returned their looks with a flat, don't-fuck-with-me stare. That night, there was an aura about me, an almost sexual afterglow that marked me as an alpha predator.

I made it to the bar and scanned the top shelf liquor. I had a tumbler of eighteen year-old Scotch in my hand a few moments later, and I surveyed the crowd, not sure of what I was looking for, only that I'd know it when I found it.

She was blonde, built tight, and already half in the bag by the time we made eye contact. A wispy black dress that barely covered her ass, no hint of a bra or panties anywhere to be found. Black fuck-me pumps and gold hoop earrings, bubblegum-pink lipstick and long, come-hither eyelashes. I bought her a drink, there was about three minutes of small talk, and we were all over each other before we made it into the cab.

At this point I was operating purely on adrenaline-fueled hormones, so I directed the cabbie to make for the nearest, nicest hotel he knew. The concierge gave us the stink-eye the moment we walked into the lobby, but I handed him my credit card and tipped him the cost of the room in cash. Suddenly, but not surprisingly, we were the best of friends and the most valued of guests. Funny how that works.

My hands were under her dress and hers were down my pants before we even got off the elevator, and I dropped the key card twice on the way to the room. Inside, I practically threw the girl - her name was Staci - onto the king-sized bed, and thirty seconds later, no one was wearing any clothes and her fingers were raking my back. While the sex I'd had with Sophia was violent, scary, and sometimes downright disturbing, Staci and I just fucked like champs. I had never considered myself a loser in the sack, but that night, I was a sexual dynamo. At one point, I found myself looking into the mirror over the bureau, and I posed for myself while maintaining my rhythm just like Christian Bale in American Psycho.

Some interminable time later, we were both collapsed in the tangle of bed sheets, and I stared out the window, looking over the nighttime Boston skyline with an exhausted smile on my face. Tonight

I'd killed a man in cold blood, and without skipping a beat, I'd gone out afterward and scooped a ten off the dance floor, thrown several hundred dollars at a hotel clerk just for the hell of it, and fucked until I was fairly certain any more sexual activity would result in permanent damage to my nether regions. I felt no fear, no regret, no remorse for what I'd done, and zero trepidation about doing it again.

Truth be told, I could get used to this.

Chapter 17

Three weeks after Donnie met his end face-down in a Brighton street, my sights were set on the reason for all my miseries, the rapist and murderer Pauly Paggiano. The first night we met, Sophia had provided me with Pauly's schedule, and I was able to find a small but practical window of opportunity, during which he would be vulnerable. I made sure to confirm my hunch for two weeks straight before deciding it was the right move to make. After a lot of leg work and a lot of unobtrusive observations from here and there, I confirmed that on Thursdays, Pauly would treat himself to the lunch special at Gianouli's, an Italian seafood restaurant tucked back into Boston's North End that was "protected" by his family, and of course, that meant Pauly ate for free. Thursday was the day Gianouli's offered their seafood pasta lunch special, and whatever was in it, it kept Pauly coming back for more. He apparently liked to get there right as they opened for lunch at 11:30, and he'd stay there until roughly 1:00, after which his mother hens would bustle him into his Cadillac and they'd depart for the day's business.

I was sitting at a little coffee shop four doors down across the street from Gianouli's, sipping a decaf latte and keeping an eye out the window. Whenever Pauly was done with lunch, his driver would go and fetch the Cadillac and bring it around, so Pauly didn't have to walk to his ride. I'd seen this little routine twice now, and it didn't vary. The driver always parked the Caddy in a "reserved" parking space a block further down the street, and from the time he left to fetch the car to the time he pulled up, it always took between four and a half and five minutes.

Once the car was out front, one of Pauly's two bodyguards would step outside, give the sidewalk a brief look-over, and then open the rear door, at which point Pauly and his remaining bodyguard would exit Gianouli's. Pauly would get in the back and sit behind the front passenger seat, while the second bodyguard would walk around and get in behind the driver. Once everyone was in the Cadillac, the first bodyguard would get into the front passenger seat, and the car would pull away. It was a good arrangement; the principal was out in the open for perhaps four seconds, flanked the whole time by his two bodyguards, and once in the vehicle there was a guard in the front and in the back, one to the right watching the sidewalk both ahead and behind through the side-view mirror, one to the left on the street side keeping an eye out for anyone attempting to cross the street or make a drive-by.

And this is why my timing had to be spot-on. I wanted them all trapped in the vehicle, where bringing their guns into play would be that much more difficult and I had a small, target-rich environment to fire on. But once they were all in the vehicle, I only had a second or two before the Cadillac pulled away and I was out of luck. It was a very small amount of time in which to do the maximum amount of hurt, and I needed to get to that window without alarming Pauly's bodyguards and giving away the game.

At 12:53, the driver emerged from Gianouli's and began walking up the street towards the parking spot. Clock ticking, I finished my latte, collected my red-and-white striped gym bag from the floor next to my chair, slipped the cup into a side pocket of my bag, and stepped out of the coffee shop. I turned left and walked away from my target, towards Commercial Street and downtown. I walked up to the end of the block, waited patiently for the light to change, crossed at a leisurely pace, and turned right, now facing the restaurant and walking back into the North End. I'd walked this little roundabout path a dozen times over the last two weeks, timing myself at various speeds and trying to mentally judge where the car would be at any one time. Because of this, I put myself on a path towards Gianouli's just as I saw the Cadillac approaching the restaurant.

Now my pacing wouldn't just be the most important thing, it would be the only thing. Too fast and I'd be noticed, and even if I wasn't considered a threat, the bodyguards would be watching me and I'd lose the element of surprise. Too slow and I wouldn't get there in time, which meant the Cadillac would be driving away by the time I got into position.

Luck, however, was on my side. I had timed it right, and as I closed in towards the front of the restaurant, I could tell I would reach the car just as the first bodyguard slipped into the front seat next to the driver. Thirty feet away, I recalled Richard's advice about moments like this.

"The most important thing for you to do," he'd said, "is to make your aura as benign as possible."

"My aura? You mean, what, like my chi or something? Give off warm vibes before I blow them all away?"

"You laugh, but it's true. The best close-in killers are able to mask that predatory vibration they send out, the thing that tickles your animal hindbrain when you're on the receiving end and causes all the hairs on your neck to stand up, the old ancestral genetic early-warning radar that told you something had you zeroed in and was moving to make the kill."

"Are you saying they'll be able to sense I'm going to kill them?" I had asked.

"If they are good at their jobs, yes. A good bodyguard, really anyone with true combat instincts, can tune in on that aggressive mental energy when it's pointed their way. For most people, it only works at a subconscious level - like instinctively moving out of the way of someone because they make you uneasy and you can't quite put your finger on why, or turning around for no reason and seeing that someone across the room is glaring at you. We all do it from time to time, but it's not conscious. But the real survivors, the operators who dodge those shots that should have taken them down, but they somehow avoid at the last millisecond, those people can use their inner threat radar actively, and can pick up on the predatory vibe coming their way."

"So you're saying I need to act casual, and not give them the stink-eye to keep from tipping them off."

"It's more than that. You need to learn how to control that aggressive aura, make it work for you. A good killer can put themselves into stealth mode right up to when they pull the trigger, and then when all the innocent bystanders are getting in the way and slowing you down, milling about in a panic, you dial it up all the way and blast it out like the bow-wave on a ship running at flank speed. You can clear a path through the crowd; they'll get out of your way without even knowing why. I've made it work for me, and I've seen others do it as well. It's just another weapon in your arsenal."

And so, I did my best to control my aura now. Richard told me the easiest way to accomplish this is to focus your mind on something completely trivial - the weather, a pretty girl walking by - anything to put your mission into the background of your mind right up to the moment when it's show time. I looked at my watch and looked across the street and thought about the bagel and cream cheese and banana I had for breakfast, and how the latte I had just finished was a little weak for my liking.

Out of the corner of my eye, because I didn't look at the man directly, I could see the bodyguard - a big, blocky figure of a man in a well-cut charcoal suit - step out from the restaurant and look at me. I could almost sense his own predatory bow wave as it hit, a pulse of threatening aggression. Don't fuck with me, it said. Don't even think about it, just walk by, shithead, and don't even look at the chubby guy in the nice expensive suit walking out from the restaurant and getting into the Cadillac.

But I knew what he saw. I could almost feel his own early-warning radar scanning me and finding nothing. I was wearing a baggy red t-shirt, white basketball shorts, and a pair of high-top sneakers. I had my gym bag slung with the strap crosswise over my chest, just another college-age kid coming from or going to a pickup game of b-ball and minding his own business. I had on a blond wig, a pair of sporty Ray-Bans, and a Celtics cap turned backwards on my head. As I felt the bodyguard's eyes sweep over me, I glanced down at my cheap athletic sports watch and I filled my mind with the thought of how I would be on time for that game, and all was cool with the world.

Fifteen feet away, I forced myself to just barely notice the bodyguard on the sidewalk climbing back into the front passenger seat of the Cadillac. At ten feet I distantly registered the car door shutting. At eight feet, almost of its own accord, my hand dropped into the open top of my gym bag. At six, almost surprised at what I found inside, I pulled the cut-down Remington 1100 semi-auto from the gym bag, the folding stock replaced with just a simple pistol grip. At four feet, I saw the bodyguard in the front seat staring at me, eyes wide, bellowing something I couldn't hear within the vehicle's luxuriously soundproofed interior.

At two feet from the bumper of the Cadillac, the muzzle of the Remington pointed itself at the driver, and the shotgun roared twice in the span of a second. The driver's side of the windshield turned into stars from two distinct impacts. Not a killing spread of buckshot, but two rifled shotgun slugs, each an ounce of hard-nosed lead alloy, that punched through the tough curved windshield glass. The first slug tore through the top of the dashboard, passed through the opening in the steering wheel, and bored into the driver. The slug shredded his heart and spine with enough energy to pass completely through the back of the seat and shatter the knee of the bodyguard sitting behind him. The second shot, coming in high as I rode the recoil up, caught the driver right at the hairline, turning his skull into a valley of bone and brains. The slug painted the injured bodyguard with gore as it passed by his head and blew through the window of the left rear door, eventually lodging itself in a Toyota parked across the street.

It was only then, after I had fired the first killing shots of my ambush, that I channeled the full force of my aggression at the occupants of the car, specifically the bodyguard sitting up front, who I saw scrambling at his coat, all thumbs, in an attempt to draw his gun from its shoulder holster. I took two quick steps forward, placing myself so that the two bodyguards, front and back, were in a direct line with my shotgun's muzzle. I could see the closest bodyguard's eyes, see the naked fear as he stared, not at me, but into the smoking muzzle of the Remington. I knew he saw death in that dark circle of steel, because he knew what was coming in the next heartbeat and he was too slow to stop it.

I pulled the trigger three times, slightly slower now, one measured pull a second so I had time to aim after every load of buckshot did its gruesome work. The front bodyguard's head came apart with the first load of double-ought, disappeared entirely after the second, and even the headrest behind him was a tattered ruin after the third. I noticed, out of the periphery of my vision, the right rear door flinging open and Pauly Paggiano clawing himself out of the back seat, flinging himself out of the car, and stumble-stagger-running from me down the sidewalk, arms flailing, an inhuman shriek of pure horror tearing from his throat.

I slipped the emptied Remington into the gym bag, and pulled from a side pocket the sleek little Beretta automatic. I sighted down the pistol at Pauly's back and aimed low, firing three shots that struck him high in the buttocks and the lower spine. Pauly dropped face-first to the pavement with a hard thwack, like a man who'd been tripped while sprinting, earning him broken teeth and a bloody nose. I stepped around the open rear door and glanced inside at the bodyguard in the back seat. The man was a ruin, pieces of his skull torn away, scalp shredded, sheeted in blood from his head to his lap. His right shoulder was torn to dangling fragments of muscle and bone, while his left hand was clutched around his throat, bright arterial blood pulsing between his fingers.

I crouched low, leaned into the Cadillac, and fired two shots through his skull. The clutching hand flopped into his lap.

I stood back up and walked over to where Pauly Paggiano lay blubbering and wailing on the side-walk. He had scrambled and dragged himself a few feet from where he had fallen, and there was a smear of blood by his dead, dragging legs where his face had bled all over the concrete. I thought of making some pithy little speech about revenge being a dish best served with a smoking pistol or some other cold fucking action movie one-liner.

But looking around, I could see people staring at me, screaming and sobbing in terror up and down the block. Off to the right, across the street, some-one who'd kept his head was crouched behind the back end of a blue sedan, a cell phone held up to his face, frantic words pouring out. I stood over Pauly Paggiano, the worthless, piece of shit, the scumbag rapist who'd set all this in motion, and I fired three hollowpoint bullets into his back, and two more through the base of his skull.

After the echoes died away, I shouted at Pauly's corpse at the top of my lungs. "Idi na hui, zas-ranetz!" which, roughly translated from Russian, meant "Go fuck yourself, shithead!"

Having a Russian roommate my sophomore year bore surprisingly helpful fruit.

Now it was time to run, as Richard once said, as if the Devil himself were dogging at my heels. Half of the police cars in Boston were probably descending on my location at the moment. I dropped the pistol into my gym bag, zipped it shut, and pushed it around so it was slung across my back, cinching the shoulder strap tight. This done, I took off at a dead sprint, running as fast as I possibly could. As I ran, I shouted "Ubiraisia c moyevo puti!" as loudly and clearly as I could at the gawking bystanders, another purloined Russian phrase that meant "Get out of my way!"

That one I had to find on the Internet.

I ran down the sidewalk until I reached the corner, turned left, sprinted diagonally across the street, ran up half a block, turned right down a narrow side alley, ran the length of the alley, turned left again as it opened onto the next street, ran down another full block, crossed right at the next intersection, and finally came to another alleyway. I could hear sirens passing to my left, closing in on the scene of the shootout, and I knew it was a matter of moments before the first witnesses turned to the police and screamed "He went that way!" while pointing in the direction I'd fled.

Halfway down the alley, I ducked between a pair of dumpsters and into a little hidden nook I'd prepared two hours ago. I kicked aside a stained and crumpled cardboard box and revealed a bright pink gym bag, and into this open bag I stuffed my red and white gym bag. Then with a single, practiced motion, I stripped t-shirt, wig, cap, and glasses off my body and crammed them into the bag. I followed this a moment later with my baggy white basketball shorts.

Underneath those garments, I wore a hot pink athletic tank top and a matching pair of scandalously brief running shorts. A pink sweatband went around my head, and I produced from my bag of tricks a pink water bottle with a pull-top spout. In fifteen seconds, I had transformed myself from a casually-dressed basketball player into a proudly gay college student returning from the gym. I took the water bottle, popped the nipple, and jetted a stream of water over my head and down the front and back of my neck, giving the appearance of someone who'd worked up a sweat.

Thus costumed, I took several deep breaths and emerged from the other end of the alleyway, pink gym bag carried loosely in one hand, water bottle carried in the other, the faintest hint of a sway in my step. I turned left as I exited the alleyway, eyes peeled to ensure no one noticed me emerge, and I began to walk at a natural pace towards Commercial Street and downtown, where I would avoid public transportation and any potential bag searches in favor of walking back to the Fens. I passed people along the way, someone occasionally looking at me with a second glance, but all anyone would see was my fabulous pink outfit and a big smile, and once or twice, when I thought I could get away with it, a wink to any good-looking guy who paid too much attention.

Two blocks and six minutes after I emerged from the alleyway, I saw a police cruiser turn and come down my street, the blare and glare of sirens and lights conspicuously absent. This wasn't an officer dashing hell-bent to the scene of the crime, this was a hunting hound sniffing for the scent of the prey. As soon as it took the turn, I lifted my water bottle to my lips, tilted my head back, and mimicked taking a long, deep drink, using the bottle and my upraised hand and arm to conceal my features from the passing police cruiser. The vehicle was rolling at a measured pace, not much faster than a brisk walk, and the two officers inside were no doubt comparing everyone they saw to my description.

This was the critical moment. If I could slip free of this strand of the dragnet, I would likely on the safe side of the manhunt. But what if my costume change wasn't complete enough to fool the officers in the cruiser? Rather than the pink outfit and assumed harmlessly gay personae, what if the cops notice the white high-top sneakers, the gym bag, an athletic physique, and a height comparable to the suspect? Then a street stop and a search of my bag would follow, and I was done for. All I could lay my hopes on would be a flat out dash as soon as the officers approached, and I knew there would be no hope to perform a second costume change; I would have to rely on pure speed and luck to break free. I didn't favor those odds.

And the odds became foremost in my mind when, a few seconds after the cruiser passed me by, I glanced into the reflection of a van's rear window as I walked past and saw behind me the cruiser stopping with brake lights on, then with growing dread the second set of tail-lights glowing as the cruiser began to slowly back up the street towards me. They were coming in for a second look.

I had prepared, thankfully, a last-ditch gamble for this very situation, and it was time to put it into motion. I immediately altered my course and turned up the steps of the first apartment I came to, stepping confidently into the building's vestibule and up to the row of mailboxes lining one of the walls. I dropped the gym bag, bent down and unzipped the front pocket, then pulled free a thick wad of mail; letters, flyers, and a couple of magazines.

Standing quickly in front of the mailboxes, I assumed my act just as the police car backed into view out the front door of the vestibule. Out of the corner of my eye I saw the cruiser slow for a moment as the patrolman saw me sorting through the mail, but then I heard the clunk of the transmission as the cruiser was shifted out of reverse, and the vehicle accelerated back the way it came.

Now for the final phase of my escape plan. Moving as fast as I dared, I tucked myself into the corner next to the front door, where I could put solid wall between me and the outside world. I pulled from my gym bag my last disguise: a black t-shirt, bearing some morbid skull-themed metal band logo, and a pair of cut-off dark grey sweat pants. Shedding my headband and pulling on this new costume, I went from gay jogger to metal-head slacker, slipping the pink gym bag, water bottle, and mail pile into a heavy-duty black plastic trash bag. A ragged black baseball cap completed the quick-change.

I left the vestibule and turned to walk out of the North End, just another city kid taking out the trash.

Chapter 18

"We have a problem."

I was standing at a pay phone on the street in Central Square, Cambridge. Richard had told me to never use a pay phone in the same geographic location twice when I make contact, so today it was Central Square.

"Right now, my life is nothing but a series of problems. You need to be a little clearer," I said.

"Okay, smart guy. They've brought in talent. Real talent. Cat has become mouse, hunter has become prey."

"This is what you feared, right? They'd smarten up a little, start trying to find me before I found them?"

"I told you these people were cocky savages, but they aren't stupid. Your first act was handled well, but your encore was a little too artistic. That set off some alarm bells. They think there's a real pro whittling them down piece by piece, knocking away the struts until everything collapses."

"Well, that's what you told me to do," I said, "go all Book of Five Rings on them. Cut at the hands and feet and shoulders until I could get at the heart. I've been following your advice here."

"And the advent of a pro being brought in was a calculated risk we had to take and make contingency plans to deal with. Well, now's the time to deal with it."

"Okay, so how's this going to play out?" I asked. "It's a big city. He can't just go looking for me."

"When you hunt a man-eating lion in Africa," Richard said, "you don't go wandering in the bush hoping to get the drop on it; that's its home territory. You stake out a goat and wait for it to come sniffing around for the kill so you can take your shot."

"So he's going to find some bait to draw me in?"

"He doesn't have to, kid. The bait is already in play, they're your targets. He's going to attempt counter-surveillance, pick you out of the crowd and take you out before you have a chance to strike."

"That's what those bodyguards were supposed to do, but we saw how that played out."

"Don't mistake those torpedoes in suits for real talent, son. Those guys are shaved apes, real meathead bullyboy types. They might be mean and cautious, but they're looking to pick up on their own brand of predator. This guy is going to be a jungle cat, a real hunter-killer. You might be circling the goat, but he's going to be drawing a circle of his own around the whole field, pinning you in and waiting to sniff you out."

I scratched my head and shuffled my feet in frustration. "So what's the plan, then? How do I deal with this guy?"

"You can't hope to beat the guy while you're circling the goat, kid. That'll split your focus, make you half as capable of performing either task. We need to find his den and flush him out. Maybe if you can catch him before he knows you're playing a new game, you can drop him."

"This is the real shit, then. I'm not just going for a leg breaker, I'm going to be looking for a pro, a hitman."

Richard chuckled that graveyard laugh of his. "I never told you this was going to be easy, or that you'd get out of it alive. Still want to keep walking down that long, dark tunnel?"

I let out a long sigh. "Fuck it, what's the worst that can happen?"

I could almost hear Richard's grim smile over the phone. "No one gets out of life alive, kid. I'll be in touch."

A week had passed since I'd killed Pauly Paggiano and his three bodyguards in the North End. By the time I'd made it back to my apartment and switched on the television, the shooting was all over the news, from local affiliates right up to CNN. There were artist's renditions of my face plastered all over the news, but the shaggy blond wig and sunglasses were enough to hide my appearance, and in the days after the killing, I didn't bother to shave, growing a thick stubble that further changed my look. Because of my Russian ruse, the prevailing theory was a Russian mob power-grab looking to prune the family down until they were powerless and incapable of stopping the Russian mafia from moving into Paggiano territory. There was some coverage of Pauly's rape and murder trial, and my family's name came up several times. Thankfully, it had been a couple of months since my family was killed, and when a correlation was made, the angle was always showing the Paggiano family as weak and desperate. Now, the alleged killing of my family was considered the work of a criminal organization using primitive, barbaric methods that showed how out of touch they were with the realities of organized crime in the 21st century.

The most disconcerting part of this publicity was seeing the reporting on my family's tragedy. I'd never gone back to Providence to see where the house had stood, and I'd never visited my family's graves. Photos of my parents, my sister, and myself would flash on screen and stab me in the heart, and I began to worry that someone might see me on the street and make the connection. But a close look at the photos of myself, most taken more than a year ago, showed a much different face than the one I saw in the mirror now. I was leaner, harder looking. There was no trace of softness in my features, and I'd become more tanned and mature-looking, no longer the pale, baby-faced Irish boy. It occurred to me that I looked like the photos I'd seen of my uncle in Vietnam. Someone would have to really make a reach to associate my new face with my old face.

After the phone call with Richard, I took myself out of the game for a week. I spent the time focusing myself solely on the mission at hand. I went for a run twice a day, at least five miles every time. A hundred pushups three times a day, crunches until I couldn't lift myself up off the floor. I purged the caffeine from my system, no alcohol, no jerking off, no nothing. I was going positively monastic with my regimen.

The news of another predator in the mix put me on edge, made me nervous, made me actually scared for the first time since I'd flown in to Boston. The fear wasn't of death; I think I'd moved past that notion out in the desert. No, it was the fear of not being in control of the situation, of the destabilization of the plan that I had put into motion. I had confidence in what I had started because I was calling the numbers as I put the plan into action. I was always the initiator, the instigator, never the one reacting to the situation but instead the catalyst. Being in control was the edge that allowed me to operate, to do what I needed to do. Now that edge was being dulled, ground down by the notion that someone out there was just waiting for me to wander in. I was just some fucking kid who watched too many movies; he was a guy who really, actually killed people for money and was good enough to keep doing it and become a "professional".

So I worked hard, tried to find my center. I broke down my guns, cleaned everything the way Richard had taught me. Oiled and wiped down every part, made sure to keep them as clean as possible, made sure there were no prints, dust, or fibers inside the parts, made sure each round of ammunition was also oiled, wiped down, and reloaded. I inspected the casings, the primers, made sure each cartridge was as perfect as it could be. I went through the disguise kit Richard had provided for me, and went out to acquire a few things that I thought I might need. I bought new clothes, new accessories; I even practiced dressing up in a few different "personalities" and going out to try them on for size.

Richard always told me one of the keys to his success was being comfortable in any skin he needed to wear, and if he was comfortable, he would make others around him comfortable too. You had to be more than an actor pretending to play a part: the punk, the stoner, the preppie business-school student, the starving artist. You had to convince yourself that you were who you were pretending to be, that the skin you were wearing was your own. I knew I didn't have his skill or talent in being able to do that, but I did pick up a few tricks during our time together, and I knew I was going to need them all when the time came.

That time was the afternoon of the seventh day. I came back from a run before lunch, and the mail had arrived. There was a manila envelope from Sophia crammed underneath my door. I never figured out how she got into the building, and she never saw me face to face after our one and only night together. Ultimately, I figured it was for the best.

After a shower I sat down to some interesting lunchtime reading. Apparently the professional hired on by the Paggianos was a man named Julian; no last name, no doubt an alias. He was rumored to be a cop from somewhere down south (cosmetic surgery had rendered his former identity inconclusive), who went rogue and turned his talents for hunting criminals into a more "for-profit" venture. Now, he was hunting criminals, for criminals, who apparently pay better than the police; his usual fee was $100,000. Julian's method of elimination was shooting his quarry dead, typically twice center mass to put them down, then a shot to the head to finish the job.

He was apparently a very good marksman, favored small, suppressed automatics, and tended to dress well, live well, and maintain a very slick, professional appearance. He was no coked-up 'banger, nor a needle-using addict; not a gambler or a boozer - although he favored the occasional bourbon - and tended towards expensive, very clean, very stable prostitutes who, as best as can be determined, have never voiced any complaints about his company.

Most importantly - at least from my current point of view - he had an estimated nineteen contract kills, two collateral kills (a panicking waitress and a driver, from two different jobs), and was suspected in at least three other killings, all in a four year period. It was unknown if he had killed anyone while a police officer, but it could be safely assumed.

I sat back and stared at the wall for a moment. Over a score of bodies behind this guy, and probably many more, over the course of more than four years. In the last three months I'd killed eleven men in three separate engagements. None of them was expecting me, and most of them never even shot at me. I wondered about this Julian, wondered how most of his kills went down. Was it that a guy gets in the elevator with him, doors close, doors open again, the guy's dead and Julian walks out? Did most of them even realize they were about to die until the moment they stared down the muzzle of his gun? Or did he stalk them through dark alleyways and down fog-shrouded streets, a shadowy figure relentlessly pursuing until the victim tired out and turned and uttered one final breathless curse as the first bullet struck? If this guy found me, would I even see him coming?

The last page of my "care package" from Sophia contained the address of his current apartment building downtown, as well as two photos of Julian, taken at great distance with a telephoto lens. He looked tall, slim, well-dressed, and clean shaven. A strong jawline, good cheekbones, close-cropped dark hair, and a good tan. A handsome guy but not particularly striking, he was someone who wouldn't ping anyone's threat radar. In one photo Julian was driving a black Audi TT coupe out of the apartment building's underground parking garage. A nice car, but not at all remarkable in a city like Boston.

So there it was: name, address, photo, bio, butcher's bill. If I was going to continue with my bloody business, this obstacle before me had to be removed, a chess piece to be taken off the board before we could achieve the checkmate. But Julian wasn't a pawn, he was a knight, poised to strike at me from an unexpected angle. Unless I walked away for good, and I wasn't about to do that, I needed to man up and face him.

The next day, I began by building my costume persona. Faded brown corduroys, slightly grubby white t-shirt, frayed long-sleeved check shirt. Battered green Converse all-stars, white tube socks, brown leather belt. Cheap watch, even cheaper sunglasses, wig of shaggy black curls, coupled with the careful application of matching sideburns and a little soul patch under the lip. A necklace of wooden beads, a bracelet of woven hemp. I quickly transformed myself into just another anonymous, benign, artsy-slacker douchebag wandering Boston to and from Newbury Comics, Starbucks, maybe even an art supply store. About as far from the appearance of an assassin as I could get, but the loose-hanging check shirt hid the Beretta's shoulder holster quite well, and the cords were baggy enough that I could slip the snub-nosed .38 into my hip pocket as backup. Two spare magazines for the Beretta hung under the opposite arm, doing a little to balance the weight of the pistol and its attached suppressor. I didn't know what else to bring with me, so I clipped a small Gerber lockback knife into the front pocket of my cords, slipped a pair of latex gloves into another pocket, and stuffed an unreasonable amount of cash in my wallet in case I needed to throw money around in a hurry.

Half an hour later, I was downtown. I stopped

at a nearby Starbucks, bought a venti decaf iced coffee, and found myself a good stoop about thirty feet from the entrance to the apartment building, with a good line of sight to both the front entrance and the parking garage.

I wasn't really sure why I was waiting here. I doubted Julian would just walk past me, stop to tie his shoe, and give me the opportunity to pop him in the ear. On the other hand, If I didn't stake out his apartment now, he'd be staking out one of the Paggianos while I moved in for the kill. I might be in for quite a wait, but it was better than doing nothing.

Hours passed as I sat on concrete steps across the street from Julian's apartment. I saw a number of people coming and going from the front door, and cars coming and going from the garage, but none of them were my guy, and I didn't see any black Audis. There was nothing in the information I had been provided to indicate that he used disguises. Considering his long career as a contract killer, that attested to a great deal of skill on his part, or a great deal of incompetency on the part of law enforcement.

Finally, after four hours of mind-numbing observation, I saw my man driving up to the garage entrance. He was in the Audi and wearing shades, but his identity was unmistakable. He drove up, hit the door with his remote, and drove inside. Earlier that afternoon, I had timed the moment from when a car was out of my line of sight, to when the garage gate completely closed. It was a window of about seven seconds. I knew that if I planned it just right, I could sprint across the street, down the ramp, and roll under the gate with perhaps a second to spare. It wasn't much, but just enough time to get inside and catch Julian coming out of his car.

So as soon as his bumper cleared the gate, I stood up and hustled across the street. By the time I got to the edge of the ramp, Julian's bumper was going around the inside corner of the garage, and the gate was about halfway down. I dropped, rolled, and slipped under the edge of the gate with two feet to spare.

There was no surveillance camera at the ramp, something I'd noticed after a couple of walk-bys earlier that afternoon. No camera meant that even though there was a concierge at the building's front entrance, he wasn't watching the parking garage entrance, and if he wasn't watching that entrance, I doubted there would be camera security within the garage itself. It worked in my favor, and was probably one of the reasons Julian would pick this building. He could drive in and out at all hours without anyone observing him, something that's almost impossible when you've got a prolonged stay at a hotel.

Once inside the garage - locked in really, since I had no easy way of opening the gate - it was time to put on my game face, pull on my latex gloves, and get to work. I glanced around the corner of the inner ramp. The garage appeared to be two levels, the one I was on, essentially the first basement level, and a second, sub-basement level below me that was accessed by going around on a ramp. If I were Julian, I'd want to be on the first level. It'd be faster to get to my car, faster to get out of the garage, and less time between vehicle and the interior of the building.

Which meant I had to move and move fast. I walked quietly down the ramp, scanning right and left looking for the black Audi. The exit leading into the apartment building proper was in the left corner, but no one was moving towards it. Either I had missed my chance and he was already inside, or he hadn't gotten out of his car yet.

Or maybe I was already being played.

The sensation struck me before I knew what it was. A tightening of the scalp underneath my wig, the prickling of my skin along my arms and across my neck, an eerie tightness between my shoulder blades. I felt my body flooding with adrenaline and my heart jumped into my throat, and I dropped to the oil-stained concrete ramp a split second before I heard two quick coughing sounds from my left, the sound of a suppressed pistol. I registered the whining sounds the flattened, spinning slugs made as they ricocheted off the concrete post to my right, and I heard one of them crack a windshield nearby.

I had followed the lion into the cave, hoping to catch him napping. Instead, he was springing at me from the dark, fangs bared and claws outstretched.

I knew I was fucked.

Chapter 19

Options, options. I can't believe in the no-win scenario. Hours of war games, if this then that. I needed to take back what little initiative I could. Julian would be coming for me in moments. Only the edge of the ramp, a few inches higher than my body, kept him from making the kill shot. I could tell he was off to my left, as the bullets had passed me and impacted to my right, so I drew the Beretta and poked it over the edge of the ramp. Working the trigger as fast as I could, I fired off six shots, half the magazine, in a couple of seconds as I dug in with my toes and got my weight onto my free hand.

Then it was time to make a break for it. I sprung up as fast as I could, bent double, almost falling over trying to take off at a dead sprint and crouch at the same time. I was trying to get myself behind a Ford Escape parked at my one o'clock about twenty feet away, something big enough to soak up some lead. I laid down covering fire as I ran, not bothering to look where I was shooting. I just pointed the pistol to my left and emptied it as I bolted, keeping my eyes where I wanted to go.

Three more shots snapped air past me as I ran, but I made it behind the SUV without catching a bullet. Dropping the magazine and catching it before it hit the ground (and letting Julian know I was dry), I stuffed it in my pocket and slapped home a fresh one. I was panting, sweating, shaking. I'd been shot at out in the desert, but that was nothing compared to this. There I was the hunter, here I was the prey.

What was Julian going to do? What would I do if I were him? I would circle around, work the flanks with my back to the garage wall, try to spot my target and get him in my sights before he could do the same to me. Fair enough. I knew I needed to perform the same maneuver; it would just be a matter of who managed to circle in on the other first, like two jets in a dogfight, each trying to out-turn and out-climb the other to line up a shot.

I considered my options; left or right. Moving to my right, I would reach the doorway that led into the apartment building after two cars. I didn't want to do that, because it meant I'd have to cover at least a dozen feet out in the open. Moving left, I'd be shifting slightly backwards and away from where I thought Julian was, but there were half a dozen cars in that direction before I reached the corner of the garage.

Time to commit and take action. Bracing against the side of the Escape, I kicked off and jumped, sliding across the hood of the BMW behind me before I flipped and rolled over onto the other side of the sedan. Almost before my heels cleared the hood, I felt and heard the ringing of slugs punching into the luxury auto's body. Julian had me zeroed in and would be shooting at me the moment I moved. But the BMW's windows were tinted, and taking a risk, I peered through the passenger-side window, looking diagonally through the car to scope out the other side of the garage.

I spotted Julian just as he slipped around the body of a Jeep Cherokee and moved to his left by one car, hunkering down behind the trunk of a Lexus. He moved fast and smooth, like I'd seen Richard move when we fought out in the desert. Julian had kept his gun pointed in my direction but didn't waste ammo laying down covering fire. Instead, he moved fast and low, getting into his firing position while I was getting settled behind my car. I saw his weapon for the first time; a compact black automatic, probably a nine millimeter, with a suppressor fitted to the muzzle.

For the first time, I knew where Julian was, and now I had the chance to return fire effectively. While windshield glass is designed to stay intact, laminated with a layer of transparent plastic inside the glass, the side windows are made differently, designed to shatter into tiny pieces too small to do serious harm. With this in mind, I shifted myself so I was braced against the next car, a dark blue Nissan of some sort, and taking careful aim I fired a round into the side window of the BMW's front passenger door, angling it a little so it would shatter the rear passenger window on the other side.

Although my pistol was firing a rather puny bullet it was enough to do the job. Both windows shattered into tiny glass pebbles. I followed up as quickly as I could, firing half a dozen rounds towards where Julian was hiding. A taillight shattered and the rear window of the Lexus starred from the impact of a bullet, and I could see paint chips fly from metal where the slugs punched into the car body. Julian's hand poked out, and before I could realign, he fired off six shots in rapid succession. The body of the BMW shuddered as the bullets impacted, and one slug tore through both rear doors, punching a neat hole in the door of the Nissan behind me.

His gun was another advantage Julian had over me. The nine millimeter was able to perforate the light cover of a car door, something I wasn't confident my .32 could accomplish. Shifting the Beretta to my left hand, I drew the .38 snubnose with my right. Although not a powerhouse by any means, it was loaded with high-velocity hollowpoints designed to get the most out of the revolver's short barrel. With the heavier, faster bullets, I hoped the .38 could put a hole through a car trunk and have enough steam left over to perforate my rival.

"You're one lucky motherfucker, you know that?"

Julian was hollering at me from across the parking garage. I didn't answer.

"I had the drop on you, had you cold," he shouted. "Another half step and you'd have caught a bullet through the head. Coming down the ramp like that, were you just taking a fucking stroll? That was some rookie shit."

He was trying to distract me while he came up with a plan. I realized he knew he was as pinned down as I was, and while his gun might pack more of a wallop than mine, shooting through a car body wasn't easy. Both of us had pistols poorly suited for this kind of duel. Moreover, I was halfway through my second magazine, but Julian had fired at least a magazine's worth of bullets, and I doubted he was burdened with lots of ammunition. Finally, there was the inevitability that a bystander would come along, a needless complication both of us wanted to avoid.

What I needed was a better angle. Right now the cars Julian was using for cover were parked not across from me, but perpendicular to me, so we were at a forty-five degree angle to one another. If I could work my way down the line of cars and fire from the end of my row, I would have the better line of sight. I checked how close to the wall the Nissan was parked, and saw there was perhaps a six inch gap; just enough to squeeze my shins through.

Shuffling back with my head down and my gun trained in Julian's direction, I worked my way to the front of the Nissan and slowly, carefully ma-neuvered between the front bumper and the wall, careful not to jostle the car and give Julian any sign of what I was trying. Although the remaining tinted windows of the BMW kept my movements mostly hidden, I was in a vulnerable position, and didn't want to get caught there. A couple seconds of work and I slipped free, now between the Nissan and a Range Rover. The Rover was parked close to the wall, but I did notice that with some effort, I could crawl under the body.

I dropped to the ground, balancing on the tips of my toes and fingers, and I peered under the Nissan as I prepared to slide under the Range Rover. Just in the nick of time, I spotted a pair of dark leather shoes sprint from where Julian had been to the other end of my row of cars. I realized I had been out-gamed yet again. Julian was taking the fight to me, while I was backing off and trying to come at him from another direction. I had tucked my Beretta in its holster and the .38 back into my pocket in order to maneuver under the Rover without making any noise. Now, I scrambled for the butt of the automatic and drew it just as I heard a loud metallic thunk thunk thunk. I realized Julian was leaping from the hood of one car to the next, racing at me.

Caught halfway under the Rover and at an awkward angle, I fired two shots at the wall, hoping to ricochet a slug at him or make him slow down, but he didn't buy it. Several shots slapped into the side of the Rover above my head. In spite of myself, I flinched down rather than keep my head up and ready to take the shot. I saw the muzzle of the suppressor just before Julian's head appeared behind it, and he fired at me the moment he had a sight picture.

Sometimes, you just get lucky. I managed to get off a shot, and I saw the bullet rip up the side of his sleeve just before he fired three times. The first shot slammed into the Beretta, wrenching it from my hand, and the second and third shots punched through the body of the Rover just inches from my right ear, paint chips spraying me. Julian jumped into the air to land between the cars and finish me off, and I did the only thing I could think of: I crawled under the Range Rover as fast as I could. On the other side, I pulled the .38 snub nose from my pocket and fired three shots, spacing them out along the body of the Rover in the hopes of a lucky hit.

Unfortunately for me, Julian wasn't standing on the other side of the Rover. If it hadn't been for movement reflected in the rear bumper of the Volvo next to me, caught out of the corner of my eye, I would have been dead then and there. But I saw the distorted reflection of Julian coming around the rear of the Range Rover, low and fast, and I fired at him, just an instant too soon. The bullet punched through the rear corner of the Rover inches from his face. I hoped it was enough to disorient him so when he came around I had him dead to rights with my last bullet.

But again my lack of experience came into play. He saw me lining up out of the corner of his eye, and with the gun in his right hand, his left hand shot out and slapped the revolver aside just as I pulled the trigger, putting the last .38 slug through the side window of the Rover and emptying the pistol. His gun came around, lining up with my face. In desperation, I stepped in close and shot my left knee into his belly, my left forearm going for his throat. Julian took the knee hard, but shifted away so my forearm slammed into his right shoulder instead.

Playtime was definitely over. Julian's left fist rocketed in and I saw stars from a crosswise hookshot to the side of my head. I staggered, trying to chop at him with the empty revolver, but Julian caught my arm before I could connect, and taking a page from my book, slammed me in the right side with his own knee, pulling me into the blow by my arm and adding force to the impact. It was a far better move, with a lot more power than I'd served up to him. The wind exploded out of me, and I staggered back, reeling against the Volvo. As I bounced off the car and tried to steady myself, Julian snapped his foot out and drove his toes into my gut. What little breath remained in my lungs exploded out of me.

I dropped to my hands and knees, the empty revolver clattering away.

I was done.

Sorry Mom and Dad. Sorry Danielle. I got cocky. Save a seat for me.

I looked up. The muzzle of Julian's suppressor was a foot from my face. Able to get a good look at Julian up close for the first time, I saw he was handsome, but there was a cold, dead quality to his eyes that gave it all away. He wore black Oxfords, a trim black suit, starched white shirt, and a pearl-gray tie, with silver cufflinks and a tie clip. A stainless steel Omega watch hung from his wrist. His pistol was a matte black SIG P228, compact and deadly.

Without the gun, he could have walked into any office in the Financial District and no one would have batted an eyelash. He was the spitting image of a young, affluent, predatory executive.

Julian was smirking at me as he savored his victory.

"Next time, spend some money on a better wig. I saw that fake the moment I turned the street corner. You look like one of those Beastie Boys in their Sabotage video."

I coughed, but didn't say anything. I wasn't going to give him any chit-chat.

Julian took a harder look at me, his eyes slightly narrowed, and a grin split his face.

"Oh, hah! You're the kid! The Lynch boy. The one who got away, in Paris."

He started chuckling. I said nothing.

"This is fucking rich! When I heard about Di-Marco, I figured a crime hit. When I heard about Pauly, saw the news reports, I thought damn, that was a real piece of work! Shotgun in broad daylight, you turned the inside of that Caddy into a butcher shop. But shit, you're just a fucking child!"

I just glared at him, saying nothing. Julian shrugged.

"Hey, you had a good run. You bagged five of 'em. If it wasn't for your little girlfriend, I don't think I would have thought to keep an eye peeled. Might not have noticed you, even with that bad wig. You might have had a chance today."

Girlfriend. That got my attention.

"Sophia," I said.

Julian's mouth split into a leer.

"Yeah, the fine Latina you sent after me. She should have been a little more careful silhouetting herself along a rooftop. I spotted her two days ago. She and I had a nice long talk last night."

My blood went cold. The expression must have been obvious, because Julian's grin stretched wider.

"Oh yeah, a nice long talk. She was one tough little Chiquita banana. Didn't give me anything. Lucky you, because I would've woken you up this morning with a bullet in your ear."

She was.

"You killed her."

Julian laughed out loud. "Put two through her sweet little face, my friend. Her head came apart like a fucking melon hitting the sidewalk. Wasn't so pretty anymore."

I wanted to say he was lying, but of course it wasn't possible. How could he have known she even existed if he didn't catch her spying? And now she was dead, killed working for Richard, just like she imagined. I couldn't tell which man to hate more; the one who killed her, or the one who sent her to be killed.

Or me, the guy who set the whole process in motion.

I must have had a particular glint to my eye, because Julian lost his smile and leaned back a few inches.

"Don't get me wrong, pal. She might've been a sweet piece, but I didn't take a bite. That's not how I do business. I worked her over and put her in the river, but I keep that shit professional."

I couldn't believe this. The guy was about to shoot me in the face, and he was concerned I thought he was a rapist?

"Yeah," I said through gritted teeth, "you're a real humanitarian."

Julian got angry at this, and jabbed the muzzle of his pistol into my forehead. "Hey pal, you step into the ring, you might get yourself knocked out, got it? The bitch might not have been a shooter, but she was in the game and she got dead. And now you're going to get dead too. A few more years and you might have been real talent, but you're just a lucky kid who skipped his dirt nap for a couple of months."

Looking at Julian now, in his Savile Row suit and hundred dollar haircut, was this what I would have become after a few years of stalking and killing? Was the only difference between the two of us a combination of experience and callousness?

I figured I'd never know, because Julian took another step back and leveled his pistol at me.

"Eyes open or shut, better pick now."

I sat back on my heels, hands on my knees. I kept my eyes open. I thought for a moment about the knife clipped in my pocket, but the idea was laughable. If I was going to die, better he made it quick and clean right now, rather than while I was flailing around with a pocket knife like an idiot.

At that moment, there was a sound off to the right, a click and a creak. It took a moment before I realized it was the interior garage entrance opening. My last thought was the regret that some innocent bystander was about to die because they stumbled across my execution.

"Hey, shitbird!" I heard a man shout.

Julian turned to his left, eyes wide, his pistol coming off me and swinging around for the shot. There were twin thunderclaps, two puffs of pearl-gray silk as Julian's tie came apart, two crimson bursts of flesh and tatters of black cloth from his back as a pair of slugs blew through his body. A heartbeat later, another thunderclap punctuated the arrival of a neat round hole in Julian's forehead, and an eruption of pink-white bone and bloody gray brain matter from the back of his skull. Julian's body bounced off the bumper of the Volvo and sprawled onto the concrete, his pistol skidding across the garage floor.

I sat there stunned, still on my knees. The smoking muzzle of a Colt .45 automatic appeared around the back of the Range Rover. Then there was a hand, an arm, a head.

I looked up.

"That was very kind of you," I said.

Jamie nudged Julian's corpse with his toe, then holstered his pistol.

"William, I think you owe me a beer."

Chapter 20

"Richard called me about six o'clock this morning."

We were sitting in a downtown Irish pub. Since this was Boston, you sometimes have to say "Irish", finger-quotes included, because the fastest way to improve your bar business in this city was to put "O'" in front of your name and slap it over the front door. "Authentic" was having a waitress with a Galway lilt and an Irish beer other than Guinness on tap. But, this place was pretty legit. It was an old, comfortable corner pub along Broad Street. The staff were entirely Irish-born and bred, the menu included black and white pudding and Irish rashers for breakfast, and a tall, cold Smithwick's ale sat in front of each of us. Live music provided by a singer and a fiddler over in the corner drowned out our conversation, and we were seated in a dark booth near the back.

Jamie told me he had made his way into the apartment building by pretending to be a courier, holding the concierge at gunpoint and locking him in a utility closet, then barging into the garage in time to execute Julian.

"It's amazing how close someone will let you get with just a messenger bag, a clipboard, and one pant-leg rolled half way up your calf," Jamie had said.

He'd been smart enough to wear a cap and sunglasses, and Jamie's bag had contained a change of clothes, but we wanted to avoid detection and keep off the streets, so we hunkered down here and hoped the one television in the corner stayed on the baseball game and not the evening news.

Now, though, we were talking about what had happened to put him square in the middle of something he'd worked so hard to avoid.

"Richard had put feelers into the Boston area police departments, into the local FBI bureau office, State Troopers, MBTA police, any law enforcement agency in the area, hoping to catch wind of any leads they might have on hunting you down once you went operational, or any moves the Paggianos might make once things heated up."

"Makes sense," I said. "Offer some cash for information, possibly call in a few government chits to add a little weight to his request."

"Exactly. Well, Sophia missed her scheduled daily phone brief, and after a few hours passed, Richard put the word out that he'd pay for information on a female matching her description. Around five in the morning, her body was pulled from the harbor out by the city's water treatment plant."

"Was it bad? Did Julian...torture her?" I dreaded

asking, but felt I had to say the words.

Jamie nodded. "She was beat up pretty bad. Her fingernails were torn away, and several of her fingers was severed. I guess from what Julian told you, she didn't give him anything. I suppose he figured once you start cutting off parts and they don't break, you've taken it as far as it can go. So he shot her twice and dumped her."

I sat silent for a long moment. Sophia and I had only seen each other in person that one night. Any requests I made, I sent through Richard using the disposable email accounts. That she had withstood a beating, torture, and was defiant to the bitter end in keeping me safe was, at the very least, extremely humbling. I couldn't rightly say whether I had what it took to do the same if our roles had been reversed.

Jamie could read the expression on my face. He picked up his pint and raised it between us. I followed his example.

"To the fallen," he said.

We clinked glasses and each of us took a deep swig. The dark Irish ale was just what I needed. I didn't want to admit it, but my nerves were shot. I had been, at most, a few seconds away from certain death at the hands of a man who had clearly been my better at every aspect of the game.

"He was good," I finally said.

"He was an idiot," Jamie replied.

"Every time I had a plan, he was ahead of me. He had seen me the moment he drove up to the garage. He had the drop on me as soon as I came inside.

While I tried to maneuver and find the perfect angle, he just came at me and threw my plan in the toilet. When we struggled, he knocked me around like a punching bag. I didn't have a chance."

"If he had just shot you and walked away, instead of engaging in an ego-stroking session, he wouldn't have been caught off-guard. He might have even been able to shoot it out with me. I doubt he would have won - I've put far better men in the ground than that shithead - but there was always a chance. Instead he got cocky and now he's dog food, and you're still standing."

"He couldn't believe I was the person who'd done all the damage to the Paggianos," I said.

"Julian was a bottom-feeder who hunted scumbags for a living. Drug dealers, crooked businessmen, greedy cons who swindled the wrong person. He hunted amateurs. You probably put up more of a fight than he'd ever faced. Rather than popping you and moving on, he fucked up and savored his victory before he'd actually won. Bad, bad move."

I nodded, taking what Jamie was saying to heart. Bad guys don't deserve long speeches before you pull the trigger.

We both paused a moment to take a sip from our pint glasses.

"So," I finally asked, "why did you come to Boston?"

Jamie was silent for a long moment, staring into the dark depths of his beer.

"When Richard called, he told me Sophia had been compromised. He said he didn't know if she

287

had talked, but if she had, the Paggianos might know where you were. He wanted to know what I thought he should do, since I was your family."

"Why didn't he call me?" I asked.

Jamie smiled at me. "He figured you'd do something stupid and reckless. Of course, you went and did that on your own."

I wanted to throw a retort at him, but I realized he was probably right, so I just nodded.

"Richard offered to find and hire some local talent," Jamie said, "someone who could watch over your apartment and make sure you didn't get hit. I told him that if they found the girl's body around five in the morning, more than likely they had dumped her hours before that, and if they had gotten anything out of her, you'd probably already be dead."

I nodded again, recalling Julian's comment about waking me up with a bullet.

"So Richard asked me again if I wanted him to do anything, or if I should leave you to handle it on your own, for better or for worse."

Jamie emptied his pint glass with a long swig, and motioned to the waitress for another. I caught up to him with my own beer and did the same.

"I sat on the phone for a long moment, and Richard waited, that bastard. He didn't say anything, but I could feel the implication over the phone just the same."

"What implication?" I asked.

"Richard always thought I was being a pussy by not going after the Paggianos on my own and leaving you out of the picture."

"He never said that to me."

"He didn't have to. I saw the way he looked at me when we sat and talked about it for the first time, the things he said. I knew he never liked how I left the life, how I retired. He always thought I was weak because I wanted out."

"Again, I never got that impression from him."

"That's because he was being polite. We go back a long way, almost thirty years. We met soon after I got back from Vietnam, when my blood was still running hot and I felt the need to keep kicking ass and taking names. I was young, I was hot shit, and I liked getting into trouble and fucking things up in a big way. But Richard was already a pro by then, and he knew his way around the shadow world. The two of us worked together putting boot to ass for a long while, but in the end, I found that I had boiled off all that anger, all that need to get into a fight for the fuck of it. I hung up my spurs and walked away before it ate me up. I saw it had swallowed him whole, and I wanted to get out before I was lost as well."

"That doesn't sound like anything he should give you trouble over. He said much the same to me, and he didn't seem to think less of you."

Jamie just shook his head. Our second round of pints arrived, and we took a moment to each take a long pull from our glasses.

"How much did Michael ever tell you about your family tree?"

I took another long sip and thought for a moment.

"Dad said his father was in World War Two, and

he and Grandma met in England. I know she was an American nurse, and after the war they moved to Providence to be with her family. A few months after my Dad was born, Granddad died in a car accident."

Jamie gave me an amused smile, taking a long drink from his glass.

"Did my brother tell you anything else?"

"Not that I can recall."

"Fucking typical," Jamie snorted. "Revisionist bullshit from my little brother. Just like Mom."

"I'm not following you," I said, frustrated.

"Your grandfather, Thomas Lynch, was a member of the British Commandos during the war. Did you ever hear that from Michael?"

I shook my head.

"I figured. Your grandfather tore shit up all across Europe for the whole duration of the war. At one point he even joined the SOE, the Special Operations Executive. That's the British version of the American OSS, what became our CIA after the war. He performed covert raids, assassinated German officers, planted bombs, hunted spies - he was a fucking war hero. And after the war, when he came to the States and started playing house, I think he couldn't take it anymore."

"Do you think he killed himself?" I asked.

"His body was never found. His car went over an embankment and into a river, but they never found him. Everyone assumed he was washed downriver, went out into the ocean."

"But you think something else."

Jamie nodded. "I think he staged it. I think he was asked to go back, to fight the Cold War, and he couldn't resist. After his supposed death, we learned that a massive insurance policy had been established, enough to make sure the rest of us would be able to survive. Mom got remarried a few years later, and that was that."

"Sounds like a real asshole move on Granddad's part," I said.

"It's what we do," Jamie replied.

"What do you mean?" I asked.

"After Vietnam, I did some digging about our family history. We go back a long way, the Lynch name, back to Ireland of course, and we have always fought. My grandfather, your great-grandfather, Liam, was in the Great War, going over the top in the mud and blood of the Somme. Later, he fought against the English during the Irish Rebellion, when he was killed. His father fought in the Boer War, and his grandfather in India and Afghanistan, and it goes back generation after generation. At least one Lynch, Killian, fought against the regiments of Napoleon. Before that I don't know, but I firmly believe we are a family of soldiers, of warriors, part of a legacy going back centuries. I imagine we fought the Normans, and the Vikings, and the Britons, and who knows who else, the Picts maybe. Fighting is in our blood, William, it is our family's destiny."

"That's why you weren't the least bit surprised when I told you I wanted revenge."

"After seeing what Vietnam did to me, or what

he thought it did to me, Michael didn't want you to join the army or do anything to follow in my footsteps, or his father's footsteps. I think you've got the old blood in you, the strong blood, the fighting blood. But your generation, your age, doesn't have a war to fight. You all fell into a pocket of peace, and now the closest thing to a war for men your age is on a PlayStation."

I finished off my second pint, throwing the last of it back down my throat and holding the glass up, signaling for more. This time it was Jamie who played catch-up.

"But now," I said, "now I've got my own war."

Jamie nodded, a cold smile coming to his lips.

"That's right. And Lynches don't lose wars. We finish them."

Chapter 21

We closed the bar that night, and I'm still fuzzy on how we made it back to the Fens and my apartment. I determined that somehow, some way, Jamie not only managed to get us back to where he left his Jeep, but he was able to drive us back to my apartment building. I remember scrawling some kind of note and leaving it on the dashboard, hoping the Jeep wouldn't get towed. Jamie offered to sleep in the cab of his Jeep with a gun drawn to make sure "no one fucked with his ride", but what little sense remained, prevailed, and he crashed on my couch around 3:30 or 4 in the morning.

I marveled at Jamie's ability to function stumble-slurring drunk like that. Jamie reminded me that "Back in 'Nam" being able to keep your shit together while on R&R, just you and a handful of other white guys carrying money - and ripe for the picking if you made a wrong turn - was literally a life-saving skill.

"Compared to Shanghai, Bangkok, or Saigon,

Boston is a city of pussies!" Jamie declared at the top of his lungs, as we made our way down Broad Street around 2 AM.

I was convinced someone was going to pick a fight, and Jamie would wind up unloading his pistol in the middle of downtown. Actually, looking back on it, I was drunkenly convinced that someone would notice my weapons, or Jamie's, and that we'd wind up getting arrested, the whole game lost at the eleventh hour.

Despite all the drinking, we were both up and awake by nine the next morning. I put breakfast together, coffee and OJ, toast and eggs and ham and some fruit. We were both ravenous, and everything disappeared in a shockingly short amount of time. I followed my breakfast with eight hundred milligrams of ibuprofen; my face and ribs ached where Julian had worked me over, my hip throbbed where it had slammed into the Volvo's bumper, and my head pounded like a kettle drum from all our drinking.

"I've never gotten my ass kicked before," I told Jamie while I examined the blooming bruises across my ribs, "and this hangover isn't helping my recovery."

"Every grown man should get his ass kicked at least once. Puts a little humility into him. The hangover is just for seasoning."

"I can say with some authority, it was indeed a humiliating experience," I replied.

"Stop it please, now you're beginning to sound like a complete fairy."

After making sure the Jeep was still untowed and in its parking spot, we packed a lunch and decided to drive up to Swampscott for the morning. Winding our way up along Route 1 and 1A, we eventually found ourselves cruising along the Atlantic coastline, driving past tourists and beachcombers down below the road along the rocks and sand.

Swampscott seemed like a comfortable little coastal town, cozy even, with inviting seafood shacks and ice cream stands, sub shops and pizza joints. We passed through the middle of town and continued on, further up the coast and into the nicer residential areas, where the lawns began to spread out and push the houses further and further apart, and the houses grew proportionately.

Eventually we found the Paggiano estate. The street-side property was enclosed with a heavy wrought-iron fence topped with sharp decorative spikes. The driveway itself was gated, operated with an electric motor and complete with a surveillance camera and intercom. Right inside the fence, next to the gate, stood the groundskeeper's cottage, home to the two bodyguards who manned the gate at all times. The windows were curtained, the lawn immaculate. No one was visible as we drove past, but we both got a brief glimpse of a chain-link fence further inside the property, presumably where the guard dogs lived during the day.

"Looks pretty, if you didn't know better," I said.

"Even if you did, it still looks pretty. Pretty can be a cruel fucking bitch when she sets her mind to it."

The area was deceptively quiet; not a lot of traffic, no kids playing in the yards, only the occasional dog-walking pedestrian. We made two passes through the neighborhood, cutting up streets one way and then coming back the other. Jamie drove while I took note of homes near the Paggiano estate that appeared unoccupied at the moment, without cars in the driveway or other signs of habitation. We found three possible candidates within a five minute walk of the estate, and a couple others further away. Not ideal, but acceptable if given no other choice in the matter.

We found a place along the shore to park and eat lunch. We didn't say anything while we ate. Rather, we just looked out over the ocean, watching the gulls swoop along the rocks and the sand, the occasional beachcomber wandering past. I thought back to our meal along the beach in Calais a lifetime ago, remembered how I imagined looking across the Atlantic Ocean somehow to gaze on the Paggiano estate, and now I turned that telescope in the other direction, looking back in time and across the water to see my uncle and I sitting there looking at us.

"At no point in my life," I said, "did my father ever sit on a shoreline with me and share a packed lunch."

"Does that bother you?" Jamie asked.

"I don't know. I guess my dad just wasn't that kind of person. He was always so formal, so meticulous in everything he did. This would be too outside the lines for him to be comfortable."

Jamie nodded and took a bite of his sandwich.

"Michael was a serious child. He was very little when our father supposedly died, and your grandfather, Thomas, well from what I gather I'm much more like him, while Michael was raised by our stepfather. He was a banker and was all about etiquette and decorum. I couldn't stand it, and maybe that's half the reason I signed up for the Army when I turned eighteen. He never really treated us like his own children, and we never would have gone on a seaside picnic, either."

"So I guess his brand of parenting rubbed off on my dad?" I asked.

"Yeah, and you have my sympathies, "Jamie smiled. "My brother was never a really fun guy to hang out with, anyway."

On the way back into Boston, we pulled into a gas station in Chelsea and used the payphone to contact Richard. After a couple of minutes being routed to wherever he was, I finally got him on the line, filled him in on the details of the last twenty-four hours.

"Glad to hear everything worked out in the end," Richard said.

"Everything didn't work out, at least not for everybody," I replied.

"I would have thought by now you understand that winning and losing in this game have very real and permanent consequences. She got dealt a bad hand and she lost out. She was in the game, and-"

"She was in the game because of you. She knew you'd be the death of her, and she was right. I suppose you can sleep with that knowledge, but it's wearing me a little thin."

There was a long pause on the other end of the line. Finally Richard spoke.

"Son, you need to get one fact real straight in your mind. That little girl, she was a professional. She worked for me because I paid her well, and she took risks because I paid her very well. If she had called me up five minutes before Julian found her and told me she was done working for me, forever, I would have wished her the best, told her to keep the advance fee I'd given her, and then shredded her file the moment I hung up the phone. You can go on and believe whatever you want, but that's the truth."

I stood there silently contemplating his words for a long moment.

"We're going to finish this business tonight. I just wanted you to know," I said.

"Do you need anything from me?" Richard asked.

"Just wish me luck, and have the apartment dealt with by tomorrow morning. We're not going to be going back there."

"Asking for luck is just an excuse for poor planning, but I'll wish you luck regardless. Someone will take care of the apartment by 5 AM."

"If we don't speak again..."

"Just aim low and keep moving, and you'll do fine."

"Goodbye, Richard."

"Be seeing you, William."

We got back to the apartment around three in the afternoon. Jamie recommended we settle in and take a nap. Throughout the day I had marveled at how well I was holding up considering the drinking and lack of sleep the night before, but as I considered tonight's agenda, sleep made sense. We set the alarm for eleven that night, and although I feared I'd not get to sleep, I must have nodded off moments after hitting the pillow.

When we awoke, we both took a quick shower and ate a small dinner, packing sandwiches and sports drinks into our travel cooler as provisions for the next day. After eating, we broke out my weapons trunk and the hardware Jamie had brought with him, and spread it all out on the bed.

Each of us would carry a suppressed Uzi submachine gun, and we would wear Kevlar tactical vests holding six spare magazines apiece, just like I wore when Richard and I attacked the meth lab. We'd each have a gunbelt with a suppressed Glock 19 automatic and two spare magazines, a small LED tactical flashlight, and a tanto-bladed fighting knife, just in case.

Rather than anything overly dramatic, we both wore dark blue jeans, dark long-sleeved shirts (mine was green, Jamie's was gray), and we each had a windbreaker we could wear over our tactical gear just in case we were seen moving to or from the estate. Rather than any kind of combat boot, we wore dark-colored trail shoes, sturdy enough for the job but with soles that allowed for a quiet step. With our windbreakers zipped up, at a casual glance no one would think twice about us.

In the last few minutes before we left, Jamie and

I gave the apartment a final sweep, making sure that nothing of a criminal nature remained. I used the de-gausser to wipe the laptop's hard drive, and I packed up any of the documents Sophia had provided me. By the time we went out the door, the apartment looked no different than when I had first walked in weeks ago.

We pulled out of the parking lot at 1:15 AM.

Chapter 22

By two in the morning, we were driving past the Paggiano estate, lights on, normal speed, just another neighbor coming home late. I used a pair of night-vision binoculars Jamie kept in the Jeep to scan the residences nearby, and we settled on one of the three homes we'd earmarked earlier as being uninhabited. A single light was left on visible through a downstairs window, but there was no garage and no car in the driveway. The light was simply a poor deterrent against burglars, and of course we weren't looking to break in, just use the driveway as a place to park the Jeep so it was out of sight.

We pulled into the driveway slow and with the lights turned off. Once we parked, I let myself out of the car, very carefully closed the door, and gave the house a quick once-over around the perimeter with the night vision binoculars. Satisfied that no one was home, I came back to the Jeep and gave Jamie the thumbs up. Time to get dressed.

We hadn't worn our tactical gear while we drove, so now we each pulled on a pair of thin neoprene gloves, then strapped on our vests and our gunbelts in the dark, giving the pistols a final brass-check before slipping them into their holsters. Magazines were loaded into our Uzis, but we left the bolts closed for now. Jamie slung a canvas satchel over his shoulder, similar to what Richard had carried out in the desert, and Jamie told me to leave the night-vision binoculars behind.

"Why? They might come in handy," I asked.

"William, I spent years in the jungles of Vietnam. I didn't need that toy then, nor do I need it now. In combat if you rely on those gadgets too much, you stop paying attention to everything else, and that's when you die."

I tossed the binoculars onto the front seat.

"What's in the satchel?" I asked.

"Some special-purpose munitions," Jamie replied.

"Like what, exactly?"

Jamie reached into the satchel and produced a small, round, dark object.

"Is that a fucking hand grenade?" I asked.

"Got a couple of frags, a flash-bang, and an incendiary. I keep a few around for special occasions."

"What, like a bottle of champagne in the fridge, just in case?"

"Yeah, but when you pop the cork on one of these bastards, you can lose more than an eye if you're not careful. That's why I'm holding on to them."

"Good to know."

Jamie reached into the back of the Jeep and pulled out a heavy-looking box with a collapsible antenna sticking out of the top.

"Here, you get to carry this instead."

"What is it?"

"A portable RF signal scrambler. It'll fuck up any cell phone, cordless phone, radio, anything like that in a three hundred meter radius. Might help give us a bigger window of operation time."

"You'll get no argument from me."

"Good, because you're also carrying this."

Jamie pulled another item from the back of the Jeep, a black fabric bag with something coiled and lumpy inside.

"What's this?"

"That's how we're getting over the fence. Now, enough questions, let's get moving."

I slung the scrambler over one shoulder, the black bag over the other, hefted my Uzi, and we set out across the lawn, looking to cut through the neighboring properties and strike at the Paggiano estate from the flank. We moved low, slow, and smooth, hoping to avoid attracting any unwanted attention from curious insomniacs. There was enough cover along the street that with a little planning, we could move and keep exposure to a minimum.

Ten minutes later, we had the wrought-iron fence in our sights. Jamie turned to me as we crouched next to a tree.

"The dogs are probably going to notice us any moment now. Attack dogs like those, they don't bark when they come at you, so you don't know

303

they're on your ass until their jaws clamp shut. We pull 'em in while we're on this side, and I'll pop them with singles from the Uzi."

"I still don't like the idea of shooting dogs. I wish we could use tranquilizer darts or something," I said.

Jamie shook his head and eased back the bolt of his weapon.

"Save that shit for the movies, William. Besides, we pull this off, the cops show up, those dogs are going to be put down anyhow. At least this way, they get a soldier's death."

Jamie stalked across the lawn, keeping low and behind a hedge, until he was within a few feet of the fence. Getting down on his belly, he crawled right up to the edge, then softly dragged the suppressor of his Uzi across the wrought iron several times.

It took a few seconds for me to notice them, as they made no sound even at a dead run. Two lean, dark shapes flashed across the lawn heading in our direction. I eased back the bolt on my own Uzi until I heard it click home, despite the fact that I didn't think there was any way the dogs could get over or through the fence.

At a distance of about thirty feet, Jamie fired three fast shots at one dog. The animal tumbled into the ground and rolled tail overhead, coming to rest in a boneless heap. The second dog didn't even break stride, arrowing in on Jamie like a Tomahawk cruise missile. Just as the dog pulled up to keep from slamming into the fence, Jamie fired a single shot that tore through under the animal's jaw, blowing out the back of its head and dropping the corpse to the ground, twitching.

"Hold position," Jamie whispered back to me.

We waited. I could see thin wisps of steam rising in the cool night air from the crater in the dog's skull. Nothing moved, no sound reached us. A minute passed, then another.

Jamie motioned me forward. I moved up next to him, scanning the grounds for a target.

"Let's get over the fence," Jamie said.

I unslung the black bag, and Jamie pulled out its contents. A black nylon rope ladder uncoiled onto the ground. Taking one end, Jamie threw it over the fence. Giving the ladder a tug, one of the rope rungs caught the spikes at the top, anchoring the ladder.

"Cover me," Jamie said.

Slinging his Uzi, Jamie climbed up the fence and gingerly swung a leg over to the other side. As he put weight on the other end of the ladder it slid down a foot until another rung caught and stopped his fall. Jamie maneuvered his other leg over the spikes and climbed down onto the ground.

"Your turn."

I followed Jamie's example. Except for the moment when my weight shifted the ladder's position, I made it to the ground without a hitch.

"We're going to leave the ladder in place," Jamie said. "Remember this location, because we're going to exfil from here if at all possible."

I nodded.

The groundskeeper's cottage was thirty meters

away. Because of the information Sophia provided us, we knew there were two cameras at the cottage. One faced the grounds back up the driveway towards the main house, and another faced the gate. Given their angles, we hoped that coming straight at the cottage from the side would minimize our chances of showing up on either camera.

Jamie went first. Crouched with the Uzi up to his shoulder, he raced silently across the lawn and the driveway, coming to a stop at the corner of the cottage. We waited, neither of us moving, for a full minute before I saw Jamie motioning for me to cross the grounds.

I followed his example again, moving across the manicured lawn in a combat crouch, my Uzi sweeping from side to side, eyes always looking where the muzzle was pointing. I was waiting for the shout, the floodlights coming on, like something from a prison movie, but nothing happened. I tucked myself next to the building with Jamie and listened for any movement from inside the cottage, but all I could hear was the quiet murmur of a television set. Something seemed unusual about the sound, and it took me a moment to recognize it for what it was - sex.

"They're watching porn," I said.

Jamie chuckled and checked the bolt on his Uzi.

"At least they'll be distracted."

"So how are we going to get in?" I asked.

We came around the side of the building, staying directly under the camera that looked back up the property towards the house. There were three low steps and a small porch in front of the door, a sturdy wooden affair with a curtained glass window. Jamie pointed at the doorknob.

"No deadbolt. Let's see if we can be subtle about this."

We both crept up onto the porch. Reaching into a back pocket, Jamie produced a small pouch. Inside were a number of small metal picks and wires. It was a lock-picking kit.

"Jesus, you know how to pick locks?" I asked.

"My career became rather colorful after the war. Now cover me, this takes concentration."

For the next two minutes, Jamie quietly worked at the lock. I remember talking to a kid in college once who had a friend from MIT. Apparently over there, lock-picking and sneaking into places you shouldn't go was common practice, and so he told me a few things about how the process works. You need to insert one wire to put tension on the tumbler from inside, meaning the pins in the lock will stick inside the tumbler when you poke them, and another pick fitted inside the tumbler to do the poking. The key is that once you maneuver all the pins into their proper alignment, you then have to use the picks to turn the lock without letting the tension slip, popping all the pins back where you don't want them.

I had no idea how long it had been since Jamie worked a lock, but he apparently never lost his touch. With a deft twist and a roll of his wrists, the wires turned the doorknob just as easily as a key. Jamie looked at me, and I reached up with my free hand and held the doorknob in its open position so Jamie could remove his picks and put them away. Jamie then raised his Uzi and nodded to me. With infinite care, I eased the door open, cringing, waiting for a telltale squeak or creak to give us away.

But there was nothing. As soon as there was enough room, Jamie slipped through the entrance, and I followed him in, easing the door shut as quietly as possible before bringing the Uzi up again in a two-handed grip. We were in a dark entrance way just off the kitchen, where a single dim bulb over the stove illuminated the room. Straight ahead there was a hallway that led, as best as we could see, towards a dining room and the front door. There was another doorway to the left, and through that we could see the flicker of the television coming from further inside the cottage. As best as we could tell, our quarry was in the corner of the first floor, opposite from where we were standing.

We glanced through one doorway, then the other. It seemed like off to the left of the front door, the glow of the TV was more pronounced and the sounds of a ridiculously faked orgasm a little more audible. With nods and hand gestures, we both agreed that the television was facing in our direction, meaning our prey was looking towards the front of the cottage, away from our avenue of approach.

Jamie stepped in close and whispered in my ear.

"One of them is probably asleep, the other one watching his fuck show. The guns are going to be too loud even with the cans attached. I'm going to do the jerkoff artist with my knife. You cover the stairs in case it gets loud."

"Works for me," I said.

"I'm going to come up on him low and from behind. I want you to work your way down the other hall so you can see him from the side. I'm guessing the stairway comes down towards the front door, so you'll be right at the base of the steps and to the side in case this goes badly."

I nodded and gave Jamie the thumbs up. He smiled and gestured that I should get going. We were separating from each other for the first time today, and despite the fact that we'd be less than twenty feet apart, this made me incredibly nervous. I had originally thought to do all of this on my own, but now that I was working with my uncle, I couldn't imagine how I'd have gotten this far tonight without him.

Jamie went to the left and began creeping down the hallway towards the living room. I moved ahead and slowly padded my way along the hall, past the bathroom and next to the staircase, into what appeared to be the dining area. A long dining table was pushed against the wall, and a number of television monitors, VHS tape recorders, and other electronic gear was set up as a surveillance center. Everything was turned on and the video was recording footage from the two cameras mounted on this house. In addition, another set of monitors provided the feed from the cameras mounted around the mansion. There was also a monitor and intercom that covered the front gate and another

VHS deck that recorded the feed.

Presumably, the guy now in the living room should be sitting and paying attention to the security camera feeds, but it seemed like he had another kind of video viewing in mind tonight.

Eventually I came to the edge of the stairway and peeked around to the left, slowly easing one eye around the wall just enough to see. There was a big screen television set up facing away from the front windows of the cottage, a coffee table immediately in front with a pair of remote controls, some magazines, and a short-barreled pump shotgun at the ready. I could make out some kind of sex scene on the television screen, although at this angle the details were unclear.

Easing out another half inch, I saw the guard. He was a beefy, middle aged guy with a bit of a paunch in a wife beater and boxer shorts, laying back on the couch with a hand down his shorts, mouth slightly agape. This was the guy making sure the Paggianos slept safe and sound at night? I was shocked someone hadn't wiped out the family already.

Seconds ticked by, and I waited, ready to bring my Uzi around and spray the guy if he spotted me. Thankfully, he was oblivious to anything but what he saw on the screen in front of him. I wondered how long it would take Jamie to cover the distance. I assumed he was doing some kind of crab-walk across the floor, staying low and behind the couch, but I couldn't risk leaning out any further to see behind the man.

And then I spotted Jamie, or rather his hand,

coming around behind the couch. He was reaching to cup his hand over the man's mouth and keep him silent, when circumstances suddenly changed for the worse. The television screen, which a moment before had been bright and filled with moving flesh, went to black as the scenes changed. In that moment, Jamie's image was reflected in the darkened glass of the television screen. The man suddenly jerked upright, his eyes snapping wide and his mouth opening in a scream. He threw himself forward, reaching for the shotgun lying on the coffee table.

I started to raise my gun up and step out from the stairs, but before I could bring the Uzi into play, Jamie leaned over the back of the couch, his gloved hand clamping across the guard's face from above, fingers splayed across eyes, nose, and mouth. With a heave, Jamie jerked the man's head back against the sofa, and with his other hand, Jamie drove the seven-inch blade of his fighting knife into one side of the man's neck and out the other.

The guard's eyes bulged even further from behind Jamie's fingers, and he tried to scream, but the sound was just a gurgled hiss. With a grunt and a heave, Jamie ripped the blade forward and out, the razor-sharp edge slicing through muscle, blood vessels, and trachea before tearing free in a gleaming spray that slapped across the coffee table, television, and window curtains. Thick pulses of blood fountained from the sides of the man's neck and out his mouth. His arms and legs flailed as he struggled, while Jamie's hand stayed clamped across his face, pinning him to the sofa.

This was probably the most awful thing I'd ever seen, more horrible and grotesque than the damage my shotgun had done to the men inside the Cadillac. That, at least, had been over in a couple of seconds. This struggle seemed to last forever, but I thought at least we'd managed to kill the guard quietly, until his flailing foot made contact with the coffee table. With a loud thunk, the table flipped over, the remote controls clattering onto the hardwood floor, the pump shotgun making a racket as it landed and slid several inches.

Almost immediately, I heard a creak from the second floor, and a bedroom door opened. A voice boomed down the stairs.

"Hey Marco, you fucking asshole! I don't care if you're jerking off to your titty teevee, but I'm trying to fucking sleep up here! Stop knocking shit around!"

I poked my head around and looked at Jamie, who was wiping his knife on the sofa and keeping the guard still while the man made his last feeble movements, the pulsing blood now slowed to a trickle. Marco's shirt, shorts, and most of the sofa were soaked with dark crimson. The odor of hot, freshly-spilled blood finally hit me, and I clamped my jaw against the reflexive desire to gag from the smell.

Jamie's eyes darted to the stairs, and he pointed up with his knife and jerked it in the air several times, mimicking gunfire.

"Hey, Marco? What the fuck, asshole. You finished whacking off? I need to take a piss, and I don't want to see your teenie weenie waving around when I come down there."

I heard a couple of footsteps. A stair creaked, then another.

"Marco? You in the shitter now?"

I felt the fire selector with my thumb, making sure it was set to full-auto. Then I stepped back from the stairs, brought the Uzi up and pointed in the right direction, and shifted my position half a foot to my right. The moment I laid eyes on the man up the stairs my gun was already on target. He was another big guy, shorter and paunchier than the man on the couch, but strong-looking, with powerful muscles under a layer of middle-aged fat. During his prime, he was probably a terror in a back-alley scrap, but now he was about to become dog meat.

I squeezed the Uzi's trigger and stitched him with a half-dozen slugs from crotch to throat. Even suppressed, the Uzi's roar was still surprisingly loud in the confined staircase. The man jerked from the impacts and collapsed, tumbling down the stairs like a bag of bowling balls until he sprawled across the floor at my feet, twitching and bleeding out. I brought the Uzi around and fired a burst of three slugs through the back of his head, fragments of skull and flesh scattering across the hardwood floor.

Jamie looked at me from across the two dead bodies.

"I think you got him, killer."

"You can never be sure," I replied.

We stood there, stock-still and silent, for two solid minutes, listening and waiting. Just because our intelligence had told us there were only two men in the cottage at any one time, that didn't necessarily mean it was true tonight.

Finally Jamie looked at me and nodded.

"I think we're clear here. Someone would have made a move by now."

"So what do we do?" I asked.

Jamie took his hand off the face of the dead man on the couch, wiping his hand across a clean patch of sofa fabric to clean some of the blood from his glove, then sheathing his fighting knife with the other hand.

"Now, we set up the RF scrambler, and make our move."

I unslung the heavy case from my shoulder and set it on the kitchen table next to all the security monitors and VHS decks. Jamie opened the case. The controls seemed simple; a timer, a duration counter, and an activation switch.

"I'm not going to bother setting a delay. We'll just fire it up and let it run until it drains the battery."

"I'm sure it'll help some, but isn't this going to be a valuable piece of evidence when the police finally come along?" I asked.

Jamie smiled and flipped the case over. There was a panel on the bottom, which he popped open. A rectangular metal object was fitted into the base of the scrambler, a pin fitted through a gap had a pull-ring at the end.

"That looks like a grenade pin," I said.

"Because that's sort of what it is," Jamie said. He pulled the pin and I heard a ping from inside the metal object.

"What did you just do?" I asked, suddenly nervous.

"Armed a thermite charge. When the battery winds itself down in roughly an hour, it won't be able to keep a pair of contacts apart, and when the circuit closes, that charge will ignite. This thing will be a puddle of molten metal twenty seconds later."

"I'm guessing anything around it..."

"Yeah, it'll burn this fucker to the ground. So long incriminating evidence. This bastard burns at a couple thousand degrees. They aren't getting shit outta this place."

Jamie extended the antenna from the scrambler and flipped it on. Immediately, the monitors all went slightly fuzzy, the electromagnetic interference so strong this close that even wired electronics were being affected. Jamie took the scrambler and set it behind the table, tucked inconspicuously away where no one would pay it any attention.

"Will it knock out their cameras?" I asked.

"No, they might get a little snowy. Probably not enough to help us."

"So what do we do?"

Jamie smiled, unslinging his Uzi and bringing it up in both hands.

"As they used to say, 'hey diddle diddle, straight up the middle'."

"Seriously?" I asked.

"William, with the two of us on point, they don't have a fucking chance."

Chapter 23

We walked out of the house and began to move up the drive, a distance of five feet between us to keep from advancing too close together. Jamie swapped out his partially-emptied magazine for a fresh one, and I did the same.

As we moved through the darkness, Jamie spoke to me in a hushed tone, his eyes gleaming in the starlight.

"In 1970, I was twenty-one when I went into Laos as the second in command of a SOG recon team. We hunted the NVA, the North Vietnamese Army, in a country that denied they existed there. When we found them, we would call in airstrikes, or Hatchet Force assault teams, whole platoons or companies of Green Berets and Montagnard tribesmen; those little guys were some of the most fearless motherfuckers you'd ever see.

"This time, a team of us, three Green Berets and five 'Yards, we choppered into Laos, hunting for the enemy. Twelve minutes after we hit the ground we found 'em, a whole battalion of NVA, probably expecting us. Army intelligence was so riddled with South Vietnamese who were paid off or North Vietnamese agents who'd slipped in, the NVA often knew where the recon teams were going before we did.

"Within the first thirty seconds, two of us were dead and two more hit so badly I knew they weren't making it out alive. I was the only Beret still standing, so we tried to drag our wounded with one hand while laying down fire with the other, our rifles smoking and steaming as we burned ammo. Both wounded caught lead as we tried to make it out, almost a relief since if we had kept trying to get them out, we'd all have been killed.

"So we ran, and fought, and ran some more. Twelve hours, and by the end I was left with half a mag and my pistol was dry, and we scrambled onto a Huey that took so many hits getting us out, it crash landed in South Vietnam, so we had to be picked up by another slick. All that was left of the recon team was me and one wounded 'Yard, and I had taken a bullet fragment through my calf that bled like a bitch."

Jamie stopped walking, then he turned and looked at me. His features were alive, more alive than I've ever seen him before in my life.

"But we fucking made it out, the two of us against five hundred men. That shit was the stuff of legends: fucking Thermopylae, Agincourt, Antietam, Bastogne, all rolled into one. I know for a fact I killed thirty-two men that day, wounds they couldn't walk away from. Who knows how many more that I didn't know for sure."

I didn't know what to say.

"That was my zenith, my greatest battle. I fought men before and after that day, but nothing will compare to what we did during those hours in the jungle. I have always looked back and relived that moment in my mind, countless times, and secretly I wished I could go back in time and fight that day again, over and over like my own Valhalla, fighting all day and drinking all night until the end of time."

A chill of fear ran up my spine. Had Jamie finally cracked after all these years? He stepped over to me, put his hand on my shoulder, and looked me in the eye.

"Well, that was then. But what we do tonight, it makes all that pale. We are avenging our family, just like you wanted, like I wanted to do, but I couldn't face that truth. I had been through so much war and death, I was a goddamned coward. But you, so young and innocent, you were more than ready to leap right into the mouth of Hell, and in the end I knew I couldn't live with myself even if you came through it alive. So we do this together, the last of our family. I'm proud to be here with you at the end."

I could feel the tears in my eyes, and I saw them run down Jamie's own face.

I moved to embrace my uncle when I heard a door slam open. We turned in the direction of the mansion, perhaps sixty feet away, and saw the front door wide open, a man standing on the porch, a shotgun in his hands. Tall, broad-shouldered, wearing slacks and shoes but only a t-shirt, he was obviously one of the Paggiano's security guards.

"Hey, who the fuck are you?" he shouted, racking the shotgun's slide but failing to bring his weapon to bear.

Big fucking mistake.

Jamie winked at me and turned to face the man.

"Hey, don't worry, we're the travel agency!" Jamie shouted back.

"The fuck you talking about, travel agency?" the man hollered, taking two steps down from the porch.

I brought the Uzi up. The man gawked. His shotgun moved, far too slow. A three-round burst knocked him back, sent him sliding down the steps to the granite walkway below.

We sprinted the distance, guns up, scanning the windows and the doorway for any threat. By the time we reached the foot of the porch, the man had managed to prop himself up on an elbow, his white shirt soaked in blood, dark foam bubbling from his lips. I could see the question in his eyes. I leveled the submachine gun in his face.

"We're sending you all to Hell."

The Uzi snarled.

There were footsteps coming from inside the front door, shoes slapping against a hardwood floor. Muzzle blasts disintegrated the cut and frosted glass windows that decorated either side of the doorway. Pistol fire sent slugs whining past us, fanning the air so close I thought I could feel it.

Jamie and I threw ourselves out of the way, each of us jumping in a different direction. I rolled across the dew-wet grass, brought the Uzi up, and riddled the front of the porch with two dozen slugs. Paint chips, splintered wood, and shattered glass went spinning through the air. I made out a man's holler of pain and somewhere more distant, I heard a woman's scream from deep within the house.

I got to one knee and fumbled for a full magazine, drawing it from my vest, slapping it home, and racking back the bolt. Jamie was on his feet, putting burst after burst of auto-fire through the doorway.

"Into the breach!" he shouted at me.

I scrambled to my feet. There was movement at the doorway, but I couldn't make out what was going on. We moved up the porch, one of us on either side, weapons at the ready. Jamie glanced through and fired a long burst diagonally across the doorway. I heard a thump, a cough, and a gurgle.

"Left side clear," he announced.

I looked through the doorway from behind the cover of the exterior wall. There was a hallway leading into the house, with a sitting room a short distance inside. Narrow hallways led away from the left and right side of the front entrance. The right hand hallway was empty. I nodded to Jamie.

"Clear on the right," I said.

"In we go," Jamie said, and stepped through the doorway, Uzi up and moving everywhere he looked.

I followed him in, a step behind and to the left, my

own weapon up and following my eye-line. I saw a younger man, probably in his early 30s, sprawled in the left-hand corridor, a stainless steel automatic next to his hand. He had two bullet wounds in his left thigh, and most of his face and upper chest were shot away. From up above, we could hear shouting and running footsteps, doors slamming and heavy objects dragging across hardwood floors.

"They're barricading themselves into a room," I said.

Jamie shook his head. "Only the women and children. The rest are going to come for us. They can't button up. Even these chatterboxes will shoot right through interior walls. We'd just dump a few mags in and rip them apart."

We advanced through the short hallway and into the beautifully furnished parlor at the end. To our left, I could see the grand staircase leading up to the second floor. Light was coming from silver wall sconces and a crystal chandelier illuminating the whole room. I felt awkward and exposed. Reaching ahead of me, I turned off the parlor lights with a nearby wall switch.

The deafening boom of a shotgun came from the top of the stairs, ripping through the wall right above the light switch. If I hadn't reached out, and instead stood in front of the switch, the buckshot would have ripped out my throat.

"They know where all the light switches are," Jamie said. "This is their house, remember that. Indian territory."

I crouched down low, edged an eye around the

wall. I saw a man in a bathrobe kneeling at the top of the stairs, a riot-style pump shotgun in his hands. The muzzle flashed and buckshot shot tore up the hardwood floor an inch from my knee, the muzzle blast so loud I could feel the air buffet my face like a hurled pillow. I rolled back out of the way a second before another load of buckshot punched a fist-sized hole in the wall.

Jamie waited until the next shot came, then he stepped out and calmly ripped two quick bursts into the man in the bathrobe before he could rack the shotgun's slide. The pump-gun clattered down the stairs, the action left open. The man had flopped backwards, slipper-shod feet hanging over the top steps. Jamie reloaded his Uzi and motioned me forward.

"I'll go up first, you follow. Break left, I'll take right. They'll try to pin us at the top, so get ready to open up as soon as you get there and keep their heads down."

"Got it," I said.

We went up the stairs swift and silent. Jamie picked up the shotgun, holding it by the barrel, and just before we got to the top of the stairs, he flung it up and against the wall across from the stairway. Immediately, there was a fusillade of shots coming from the right, some kind of high-capacity pistol or carbine. Wood and plaster rained down the stairs as the walls were riddled.

Jamie looked at me and gestured with his hand. Aim right there, he was telling me. We both raised our Uzis and cut loose through the wall at the same time, each of us firing a dozen shots on full-auto. There was a man's shriek, and a body hit the floor. At the same moment, Jamie and I stepped out and fired another long burst at each end of the hallway, sweeping from one side of the hall to the other. Century-old paintings, in gleaming wood frames decorated with gold leaf, exploded into tatters of canvas and tinder as they were with bullets. A small decorative table at my end of the hallway collapsed, one of its legs shot away. A flower-filled crystal vase fell to the floor and shattered, water soaking into a runner that stretched from one end of the hall to the other. Nothing moved on my end.

Glancing over my shoulder, I saw another middle aged, beefy man in a sports coat and slacks leaning against a hall doorway, perforated in half a dozen places. He raised his head with great effort and looked at us, a hand feebly reaching for the nine-millimeter carbine on the floor next to him.

"Nuh-uh," Jamie said, and popped two slugs through the man's head.

The mobster's skull blew apart, and the body slumped back into the room.

"Hose the walls. Try to draw anyone out," Jamie said.

We both emptied our Uzis, raking the walls to our left and right. I could hear the slugs punching through the interior walls, hear things shattering and breaking inside the rooms. At the end of my stretch of hallway, I heard a grunt.

"Think I heard someone," I said.

Jamie nodded, then jerked his thumb. On his side

of the hallway, there was another flight of stairs, leading up to the third floor.

"You check your room, I'll cover the stairs."

I gave him a thumbs up. Swapping magazines, I reloaded as I moved down the hall. The door was closed, at the end of the hall to my left. I had no idea where my quarry might be within the room, but I was fairly sure he was wounded.

It was time to do this the hard way. I reared back and kicked in the door, then flung myself to the side. No shots answered my actions, and after a moment I came around the door jamb, Uzi up and sweeping the room. In the corner, slumped against a opened nightstand, was an elderly man, perhaps in his seventies. His hands were by his sides, and blood pooled around his thigh where a bullet had caught him and brought him down.

It was the Paggiano's butler, I realized. I wasn't quite sure what to do with him. I didn't really consider servants as part of my crusade, despite the fact that this man had worked for decades in a house where he knew exactly what sort of people employed him. My hand still hesitated, though.

"Please, my leg...you've shot me!" he groaned.

I took a step into the room, my Uzi lowered a fraction. Maybe if I thumped him over the head -

A shot rang out, and the wall next to me sprayed paint and plaster. The old man had a revolver in his hand, fired from the waist. A simple .38 snub, taken from the nightstand drawer. He had concealed it behind his thigh until he could lure me into the room.

I ripped a burst into him, shredding his heart and lungs. The old man flopped once and died. I put a single slug through his skull, just to be sure.

There was a long, deafening roar of automatic gunfire from the direction of the stairway. Rushing from the room in a crouch, I saw Jamie scramble back down the hallway and pull his body into a tight crouch. Auto fire was tearing up the lip of the stairs and blasting through the walls, coming not from above, but from down below.

"We've been flanked!" Jamie shouted.

Someone must have taken a back stairwell, or somehow roped down out of a third-story window, or maybe we just missed someone hiding on the first floor or in the basement. Whatever the reason, we were separated at both ends of the hall, and whoever it was had an automatic weapon, a full-blown assault rifle of some kind.

I put my fist to my mouth, mimicked pulling a grenade pin with my teeth and lobbing it down the stairs. Jamie nodded, dug into his satchel, and produced one of the lethal green eggs. He moved forward, glanced up the third floor staircase, and spun out of the way just before a fusillade of pistol fire tore up the floor and opposite wall.

They were getting smart. Someone was down below, firing up the stairs, while someone else was up above, firing down. We were pinned on the second floor, separated from each other. Something had to be done, and fast. I let my Uzi hang from its sling and held my hands out, knees bent, obviously wanting Jamie to toss me the grenade.

He shook his head no, obviously not trusting me with that delicate task, but bursts of gunfire from below, and then shots from above, shredded through the walls and floors in an attempt to keep us away from either stairway. Finally, Jamie nodded. Standing, he gave me a one, two, three, and tossed the grenade to me. Bullets tore across the space, but none hit the deadly missile, and I caught the heavy metal egg in my gloved hands.

Remembering every grenade-related war movie moment I could think of, I gripped the grenade firmly and kept the lever under my fingers. I pulled the pin with a hard yank and I looked to Jamie, who mimicked holding the grenade, lifting his fingers to let the lever fly while holding the grenade in his palm with a thumb. He raised one, two, three fingers in the other hand, then mimicked throwing it down the stairs.

I nodded, then did exactly what he showed me. I let the arming lever flip away, heard the striker impact, saw a thin wisp of smoke curl away as I counted. On three, I leaned over and tossed the grenade down the stairway with an underhand throw, aiming to bounce it off the stairway wall opposite me so I didn't have to expose myself. I heard the grenade thump down the stairs and I saw Jamie frantically gesture for me to back up. I threw myself down and away from the stairs, and just as I slapped my hands over my ears, I felt the whole house shudder from the explosion.

A hideous, keening wail came up through the floor, the sound of someone suffering an unimaginable amount of pain. I sat up from the floor and looked at Jamie. He was changing magazines, and he gestured towards me, towards his eyes, and towards the first floor stairs, then placed his hand low to the ground. Getting the hint, I got down low, then slowly eased my eyes around the corner of the stairwell.

Down at the base of the stairs, I saw who, or rather what, was making all the noise. What was once a man lay in ruins at the foot of the half-destroyed staircase. His legs were shredded by the grenade, his intestines splashed across his lap and a good portion of the floor, his chest a horrific red ruin. But somehow, the wounds hadn't killed him outright. A short-barreled AK assault rifle with a folding stock lay next to him, the receiver and magazine torn and perforated by the grenade, rendering the weapon useless. The man rolled his head back in my direction, and through the sheet of blood across his lacerated face, I recognized John Paggiano, Pauly's older brother and next in line whenever old man Dominic gave up his position as head of the family.

So much for that plan, I thought. Drawing my suppressed Glock, I pointed it down at John. The man looked up at me, but I could tell the shock of the blast had rendered him senseless. I fired a single round that caught him above his nose and blew the back of his head away. Then I rolled away from the stairs, holstered my pistol, and picked up my Uzi again.

Jamie and I both heard movement at the top of

the third floor staircase at the same time. We tensed and looked at each other, preparing for an assault or a storm of gunfire. Instead, a white t-shirt, knotted into a ball at one end to help it fly through the air, fell to the bottom of the stairs.

"We want a second to talk!" a woman shouted. I guessed it was Mary, John's wife. Actually, make that widow.

Jamie shook his head and put a finger to his lips. Don't say anything. We waited.

"We just want to know why you're doing this! We can work something out before anyone else has to die!"

I had to admire her courage. After the grenade went off, she had to know her husband was dead, but instead of crying or begging, she had the state of mind to seek some kind of parley, to perhaps buy time for someone else to maneuver into an attack position. Seconds passed, and we still said nothing. I looked at Jamie and shrugged. He patted his Uzi and brought it to his shoulder, and I followed suit. Jamie raised three fingers, and closed them one by one. Together, we fired through the walls of the stairway, riddling the top of the third floor landing with a blizzard of slugs.

As soon as we were dry, we both reloaded, and as one, popped around the corners, rushing up the stairs as quickly as possible. Mary Paggiano had joined her husband in Hell, riddled from head to foot. At least twenty slugs had struck her, soaking her white nightgown and pink bathrobe with bright crimson. A nickel-plated automatic was clutched in her hand.

We made it to the top of the staircase and I rushed past Jamie, into a bathroom at the head of the stairs. I hunkered down at the doorjamb and covered us from the right side of the hall while Jamie held position at the top of the stairs. The hallway extended off to the left of the stairs, with multiple doors along both sides of the hall, and a door at the far end.

Without warning, the bathroom wall next to me disintegrated, a hail of gunfire cutting through the wood and plaster from the room next door. Someone was firing at me with a heavy-caliber automatic, probably a .45, and the toilet's water tank exploded in a spray of porcelain fragments and a rush of cold water, soaking my pants as I lay on the floor, taking cover behind a cast iron bathtub. I looked at Jamie, and he leveled his Uzi, ripping off half a magazine into that room at waist height. I rolled over onto my back, brought up my own Uzi, and fired half of my magazine over the lip of the tub and through the wall.

There was a shout and some cursing, and suddenly the hallway door burst open. I heard a man scream "Motherfucker!" before a short burst from Jamie's Uzi silenced him, and I heard a body hit the ground.

I rolled back onto my stomach and looked at Jamie, crouching at the head of the stairs. He drew a line across his throat. I pointed at his satchel, mimed pulling a grenade pin and rolling it down the hall towards the door at the end of the hallway. At first Jamie shook his head.

"This place has to sound like a war zone!" I hissed. "We need to end this and get the fuck out of here. Someone's bound to have called the cops by now. Toss it and the door will go away, then we hose the fucking room and charge."

Jamie let out a muttered curse.

"Get behind that bathtub, and cover your ears!" he said.

I squirmed back on my hands and knees and covered my ears with my hands. I saw Jamie pull his last frag grenade from the satchel, yank the pin, let the lever fly, then soft-pitch it down the hall. He then threw himself back down several steps and out of sight. A moment later, the house shook again from the blast, tiny grenade fragments tearing through the walls above me.

I got to my feet, leaned out into the dust-choked hallway, and burned the rest of the Uzi's magazine through the doorway at the end of the hallway. Leaning back into the bathroom, I changed magazines while Jamie came back up the stairs and emptied his magazine down the hall. I waited for him to change mags.

"The stun grenade!" I shouted.

My ears rang from the grenade blast despite being covered, not to mention all the gunfire in such an enclosed area.

"I've only got the one!" Jamie shouted back.

"Now's the time to use it! Toss it in and we'll charge through."

Jamie took the flash-bang out, pulled the pin, and threw it overhand into the room at the end of

330

the hall. We covered our ears, and as soon as the grenade went off, we snatched up our hanging Uzis and rushed the room, Jamie leading the way.

The room was a spacious reading room or study, bookshelves lining three of the four walls, with the fourth given up to a desk, a small end table, and a standing lamp. A shattered office chair lay on the floor in front of the desk, and a flayed leather recliner stood by the lamp. A low wooden chest had been dragged in front of the door as a makeshift barricade, but the grenade had blown it into kindling. The shelves of books were all shredded, either by gunfire or by grenade fragments, and there was a thick cloud of dust and smoke hanging in the air. A body lay sprawled across the reading chair, no doubt one of the last bodyguards, a short-barreled shotgun in his hands. He must have been waiting for us to charge through, but grenade fragments and Uzi fire had torn his body into pieces of bleeding meat.

I heard the boom of the heavy magnum revolver as I cleared the doorway. I saw Jamie's body jerk, but it wasn't until the second and third shots that I realized he was hit. Jamie went down hard, sprawling face first into the room, sliding into a bookshelf. I saw the revolver poking around the corner fire once more, and the Uzi in my hands was torn away by the slug. I threw my body to the left, out of the line of fire, and scrambled for the Glock at my hip. The shooter, thinking he'd hit me and knocked me down, emerged from behind the wall. It was Adam Paggiano, son of John and Mary, youngest member of the family. Fourteen years old, he wore boxers and a t-shirt, and his feet were in slippers.

Adam stepped over Jamie and froze as he looked out of the room and down the hallway. I knew the body of his mother lay there, shredded by gunfire and the blast of the grenade. I began to draw my pistol, but the movement caught Adam's eye and he turned, bringing the heavy stainless steel revolver, a Ruger .357, in line with my face. His eyes were cold and dead-looking. I thought his expression must resemble how I'd looked when I learned my family was dead. Vengeance had come full circle.

The boy let out a cry and staggered. I looked down and saw that Jamie had rolled onto his back and had driven his knife through the boy's thigh. Staggering, Adam brought the pistol around and fired a shot point-blank into Jamie's chest, my uncle spasming from the gunshot.

I finally managed to get the Glock clear of its holster, the long suppressor making the draw awkward while on the floor. I brought the pistol up and fired twice into Adam's 10-ring. The boy jerked back, but remained on his feet, and the magnum swung back around towards me. What was the line from Dirty Harry? Six shots, or only five? I didn't want to find out. I fired twice more, both shots catching the boy in the face. He flipped backwards and sprawled across Jaime's legs, then lay still.

I rolled over and got to my feet. Jamie was trying to get himself out from under the boy, but he was too weak. I could tell he had been badly wounded. I grabbed Adam's ankles and dragged him off of

Jaime's legs, then tried to examine my uncle. There was blood sheeting his lower abdomen and groin, and I saw another wound in his thigh, but the shot to his chest looked to have punched into an Uzi magazine, finally stopped by the body armor underneath.

"Jamie, you've been shot, let me take a look," I pleaded.

Jamie was pale and clammy, his eyes glassy and unfocused. He tried to push me away.

"Finish it. Finish the mission. Clear the target area."

Jamie pushed his Uzi towards me. I picked it up, checked the breech to make sure it was clear, and then holstered my Glock.

"I'll be back for you."

"Finish it boy. Finish them all," he said.

I stepped over my uncle and walked into the next room, Uzi at the ready. It was a large bedroom, the master bedroom of the house, with a bureau the size of a Buick, an armoire over in the corner, an end table with a lamp and a couple of sitting chairs, and a massive king-sized bed dominating the room. A small bathroom was visible off to the side, the door open. A number of slugs had made it through both rooms and punched holes in the walls, shattering a mirror and destroying a few objects of finery; a porcelain vase here, a jade statuette there.

There were two people on the bed, an elderly man and woman. The woman was clutching her belly, a crimson stain soaking through her nightgown. She lay across the lap of the man, who was sitting on the edge of the bed, next to the night-stand. A small, vintage-looking automatic was in his hand, but his arms were wrapped around the dying woman, tears streaming down his face.

Dominic and Maria Paggiano.

Dominic looked up at me.

"The boy?" he asked.

"Dead."

"Johnny?"

"Dead. Mary too," I said.

He was wracked by a sob, then another. The old woman lifted her head.

"Who are you?" she whispered.

"William Lynch."

It took a moment to sink in, but finally, Dominic nodded in understanding. The old couple looked each other in the eye, each giving the other a soft, sad smile.

For a man of seventy-nine, Dominic Paggiano was surprisingly fast with a gun.

Unfortunately for him and his wife, I was considerably faster.

When it was done, I walked back into the study. Jamie lay on the floor, a pool of blood around his lower body. I dropped the smoking Uzi onto the floor next to him.

"It's finished," I said.

Jamie nodded, his eyes rolling around in his head.

"I can't move my legs," he said.

I knelt down and rolled him over. I saw immediately what was wrong. There was an exit wound the size of a silver dollar in the small of Jamie's back. The bullet had come in right at the bottom edge of the vest, below his belt, and shattered his spine.

I rolled Jamie back over and he saw my face. He gave me a weak smile.

"I've seen that face before. Often made it myself. I'm a dead man."

"The bullet severed your spine."

Jamie nodded.

I moved to stand up and grab his arms.

"I might be able to carry you out, but we've got to hurry," I said.

Jamie shook his head.

"I'm staying here," he replied.

"Let me at least get you down to the lawn. The police will find you and take you to a hospital. Otherwise you might bleed out before they clear the house."

Jamie shook his head again. Feebly, his hand reached into the satchel and he drew out the incendiary grenade. He handed it to me.

"Get out. Pop this on the first floor. It'll burn the house down quick. I'm not going anywhere. When they find me, I'll be just a lone, whacked-out vet who took the law into his own hands. Go back to my cabin, get your story straight, and you'll be fine."

I looked incredulously at my uncle. "You can't tell me you planned this from the beginning? Getting shot and dying here so you can take the blame?"

Jamie smiled and shook his head.

"I never planned on this, no. But it looks like Fate improvised."

I knelt there for a moment, holding my dying uncle's hand. To have lived through so much, only to meet his end at the hands of a teenage boy. Of course, it could have been a Viet Cong teenager with an AK thirty years ago, but the thought wasn't very comforting.

We both heard it, the sound of a siren off in the distance. Jamie gave my hand a feeble squeeze.

"Get going. Get to the fence. Remember the ladder. Stay low. Slip away before they can see you. Get to the cabin. Get your story straight. A letter under the turntable. Everything you need."

I nodded. Leaning over, I drew my uncle's Glock and put it in his hand. He said nothing, but nodded. A warrior shouldn't meet his end without holding a weapon. I picked up the functioning Uzi - someone might ask questions if they found two of the same weapon in the ruins - and looked at my uncle one last time. He waved the muzzle of the Glock towards the doorway.

"Go on...move...damn you..." His eyes wandered away from me and his head sagged and lolled, dazed from the shock and blood loss, his speech slurred.

"The chopper...won't wait forever. Get to the..."

Jamie trembled and went still. His eyes remained open, staring into a jungle half a world away and a lifetime ago.

I stood and left the room. I walked past the corpse of Mary, down two flights of stairs, past the corpse of John. I pulled the pin on the incendiary grenade and dropped it into his lap as I walked past. Instead of heading for the front door, I went out the kitchen entrance, shutting the door behind me just as I heard the whump of the grenade as it showered the inside of the mansion with burning fragments of white phosphorus.

I walked to the edge of the house and peeked around the corner. Down at the end of the drive, I could see police cars lined up along the street outside the gate, and about a dozen flashlights shining all around. Too close and too many. I'd be spotted for sure if I tried for the ladder. I might be able to find a board or some other means of getting to the top of the wrought-iron fence, but I'd have no way to put it back, and it would be completely obvious that someone left the scene of the crime.

"Y'know, this here ladder sure ain't going to climb itself."

I peered into the darkness. On the other side of the fence, the rope ladder hanging next to him, stood Richard. He'd dressed as he did when we raided the meth lab, a black-clad commando out for a stroll in the wee hours of the morning.

"Well fuck me," I said.

"You're a handsome kid, but not really my type. Come on, before they park a police helicopter with infrared over us and the whole gig is up."

So away we went, off into the night, as the Paggiano mansion burned to the ground behind us.

Chapter 24

It was a long, miserable summer.

Richard drove me back to Maine in an airport rental. He had decided to fly in right after getting off the phone with me, and set himself up in an observation point to watch and see what happened. When he saw the police were closing in and we hadn't made our escape, Richard grabbed the rope ladder and waited for us.

When I emerged alone from the house, Richard knew what must have happened, but he focused on the mission, and at that moment, the mission was to escape without being caught. I went over the fence, we cut across a couple of lawns, and we reached Richard's car, parked in the same driveway as Jamie's Jeep.

Before hitting the road, I changed into a fresh set of clothes and shoes, while everything - clothes, guns, gear - went into a trash bag in the trunk. Before we left, Richard broke into Jamie's jeep, grabbed something from underneath the driver's seat, and then planted a little "present" in the glove compartment: a timed thermite charge.

"It'll look like Jamie planned on torching his own car if he knew he wasn't making it back in time. This way, there'll be no evidence left that you were ever in the vehicle."

Richard had rescued Jamie's pistol from under the driver's seat. It was the gun he had used to kill Julian, a slightly customized Colt 1911 .45 automatic. Richard handed it to me while we drove away.

"That pistol has a long and distinguished pedigree. Hold onto it, for his sake at least."

I just nodded.

The drive north to Jamie's cabin took about five hours, and we pulled in around 8:30 in the morning. The battered pickup was there, parked next to the shed, and everything looked just as it did when I left over two months ago.

Except, of course, that nothing was the same. Jamie was dead, the Paggianos were dead, and I'd killed over a dozen people in the last month. I didn't know whether to laugh or cry, to thank my uncle for helping me or damn him for not stopping me cold the moment I suggested the idea back in Calais. I sat in Richard's rental sedan and simply stared at the front door.

"You're going to have to get out sometime. I've got to return the car," he said.

"I have absolutely no idea what to do with my life from this moment forward," I replied.

Richard pondered for a minute. "You're going to be approached by the police, probably the FBI.

They're going to ask you a lot of questions, but the most important thing to remember is that you've never had anything to do with this, officially anyways. No fingerprints, no paper trail, no money with your name associated with it. Jamie paid me for your training out of his own funds, assuming he'd be able to recoup the costs as the life and home insurance policies and family assets became available."

"But what about an alibi?" I asked.

"Your gardener has been coming up here once a week since you left, long enough to go out boating with Jamie, be seen at a distance by some of the locals, drive by some houses or through town in Jamie's truck. As far as anyone knows, you've been grieving in seclusion for the last two months. If you're asked about your uncle's whereabouts, just tell them that he would drive down to Providence now and then for a few days to take care of family-related business, or at least that was the case as far as you know."

"Do you really think they'll buy that?" I asked.

Richard shrugged.

"At the end of the day, they'd not only have to suspect you, they'd have to prove you were involved. What is the more likely scenario? A white-collar college kid goes on a shooting rampage and wipes out an organized crime family, or the reclusive Vietnam veteran, ex-Green Beret? No one is going to miss the Paggiano family, and your uncle has already given the FBI the suspect they'll want in order to pin this on someone. Play it cool through the rough patches, don't make any stupid mistakes, stay out of the media as much as you can, and you'll be fine."

I nodded and climbed out of the car. Leaning in at the door, I offered my hand to Richard.

"Thank you for coming here. I don't think it would have gone well for me if you hadn't."

Richard turned the engine over and put it into gear.

"That would have been a piss-poor way to protect my investment."

"Investment?" I asked.

Richard just smiled.

"Be seeing you," he said.

I watched the rental back down the driveway, and soon it was out of sight among the trees. I acquired Jamie's hidden key and let myself into an empty home.

My empty home.

The FBI, when they arrived a day later, were surprisingly polite. A team came into the house, carefully and thoroughly went through everything they could find with a fine-toothed comb, including the shed and the surrounding property. They boxed up a number of items, but I could tell they were somewhat disappointed. They kept asking me if I knew any other place where my uncle kept things, or if I ever saw him leave with documents and not return with them, but in all honesty I told them no. A number of my uncle's guns were taken away, but none of them, I knew, would be part of the criminal investigation, and they were all eventually returned to me.

Jamie's Colt automatic, along with a number of other weapons, documents, and souvenirs, was now buried in a sealed plastic container half a mile into the woods, on a piece of land that was owned only by the state. The morning I arrived, I read the letter Jamie had hidden under the turntable. The contents were fairly simple, just directions to his cache. I found not only the .38 revolver we used during my visit, but a Russian Tokarev pistol and a couple of other guns, about fifty thousand dollars in cash, some gold coins, survival gear, packaged food and bottled water, several alternate identities, and information on how I could access two different offshore bank accounts, each of which carried a balance well over half a million dollars. Between that and the insurance money, I found myself, at the age of twenty-one, a multi-millionaire.

After several stupefyingly long interviews and a detailed written statement, all I had to endure was several weeks of unpleasant media scrutiny. The news vans and the helicopters swarmed, as I knew they would, but I stayed inside, phoned the local grocery store to have my food delivered, and waited it all out. I gave no interviews, I made no statements, and I barely showed my face through the door when the grocer arrived. After a while, pressure from the locals towards the media to leave me alone did its work, and the reporters dwindled away, happy enough to feast in the carcass of my uncle's reputation, which they tore apart.

At the time, I read nothing written on the subject of the Paggiano killings. Several years later, when

I found myself in a quiet period of my life, I did some research online and dug up a number of the old articles. I read about the killing of my family, the speculation on where I was and a simple, brief statement from my uncle to the media about how I was "traveling abroad". Apparently a number of my college friends were interviewed, with the usual bullshit statements about how they were sorry for my loss. The speculation was, of course, that it was done by the Paggiano family, but without solid evidence, nothing ever came of it, and of course, the rape and murder investigation stalled out, witnesses suddenly becoming much more "confused" about the events that occurred.

I had seen the news media coverage about Donnie and Pauly, but the stories about the Paggiano mansion "massacre" were new to me. I discovered, with mixed feelings, that the cook and the maid were both killed in the assault. I hadn't seen them and assumed they were either not in the mansion that night, or they had somehow escaped during the shootout. I could only guess that when Jamie and I sprayed the rooms on the second floor with automatic fire, the two women were either killed outright or wounded to the point where they couldn't escape the fire, or they'd hid until the smoke and flames made escape impossible. I felt sorry they had died. Neither of them had so much as showed their faces, as opposed to the butler. On the other hand, no one works for a family like that for so many years without knowing full well what was going on.

Reading about my uncle though, that was the hard part. He was crucified from the moment his identity was revealed, painted as a gun-loving loner, lurking in the Maine wilderness, self-secluded from society to protect the world from his kill-crazy proclivities. Although my uncle had, at the time, never been suspected in the first two attacks against Donnie and Pauly, he was retrofitted into the investigations, his special forces training considered exactly what was needed to pull off both of the hits.

When it came to the attack on the mansion, the descriptions of the assault as "carried out like a military operation", my uncle "returning to his days as a Green Beret" were both further from the truth and yet closer to the truth than they realized. Yes, Jamie put his experience and training to good use, but the attack was never a re-visitation of Vietnam.

At least, not until he laid bleeding and dying in Dominic Paggiano's study.

In the end, it didn't matter. Article after article spun a web of paranoid violence and conspiracy around my uncle. There were theories that a second shooter was involved, but rather than implicating me, the speculation was that Jamie had contacted an old Vietnam War buddy to help him. The transfers of money to mysterious accounts that led the FBI nowhere seemed to support this theory, but it was never accepted as fact since there wasn't enough forensic evidence to support the theory, and all the ballistic evidence - ammunition casings and bullet fragments - were destroyed or rendered unusable in the fire. Some thought the money was simply spent on acquiring information and weapons, while others concocted even stranger theories. Even today, a decade later, a little investigation on the web into various true crime forums shows people still talking about the killings. Someone even tried to contact me a couple of months after the attack with a proposal to option the story and make it into a made-for-television movie, but I simply ignored the request.

After the media circus died down, my life became rather dull, and most of the month of August was spent sitting around Jamie's cabin, listening to vintage records, and leafing through his Vietnam documents and letters. I felt hollow and rudderless, all the money I could ever need, but no motive to spend it on anything or anywhere.

I didn't hear about the attacks on September 11th for two days. I had gone hiking that morning, and when I returned on the evening of the 12th, I had simply showered, unpacked, and went to sleep after a couple of beers. Jamie didn't have a television, and rather than listening to the radio I usually just put a record on the turntable if I wanted some music. It wasn't until the morning of the 13th, after I drove into town to buy some groceries, that I saw the headlines plastered across every newspaper. I picked up a copy of each paper and returned back to Jamie's cabin, turning on the radio for the first time in three months.

The news of what happened - the fall of the Towers, the crash at the Pentagon and Flight 93's rebellion - it all sank in with a curious dullness. I was shocked at what happened, almost amazed at the scope of the disaster, but my own personal tragedies were simply too fresh, my desensitization to violence a little too thorough. I read the stories in the papers, listened to the radio news and the various commentators. In a perverse way, hearing about so much tragedy and loss helped push my own suffering into the background, a sick form of schadenfreude.

I woke up the morning of the 14th and drove into town early to pick up the paper so I could bring it home and read it over breakfast. I had just finished my coffee when the phone rang. After the initial storm of calls from newspapers and other media trying to get a statement, the calls had died down for several weeks now, so I went ahead and answered the phone.

"I hope you've picked up a paper or turned on the radio this week."

It was Richard.

"Yeah, I've been following. Was out in the woods for the first couple of days."

"Gone caveman, have you? Running around in the wild wearing a deerskin loincloth and carrying a spear?"

"Just getting out of the house a little. There isn't really a booming social scene around Moosehead Lake if you're not into fishing."

There was a pause on the line. I could tell Richard was trying to find a way to say something.

"Just come out and say it, Richard."

There was a quiet chuckle on the other end.

"Well, if you're going a bit stir-crazy in the woods, maybe you'd be interested in some work?"

I thought for a moment.

"What kind of work?" I asked.

"You're reading the news, seeing what's happening. What do you think the fallout is going to be, after these attacks?"

"There's going to be a lot more work for Delta Force, I guess?"

"There's going to be a lot more work for anyone who knows how to kill people, period. This is going to make the Cold War look like the Great Depression for mercenaries and Special Forces types."

"I'm still not really following you."

"Governments everywhere are going to be throwing money at anyone who claims to be an anti-terrorism expert, or mercenary or private security groups willing to help fight terror. Money is going to be shoveled into those black book budgets in sums you aren't going to believe. Much easier to hire freelance someone of dubious moral standards to do the CIA's dirty work than use government agents who've got to fill out paperwork."

"So what does this have to do with me?" I asked.

"I'm going to be really blunt here, son. Come work with me, put in a few more weeks of training out here in Texas, and I can put you in touch with the right people. The kind of people who would pay very, very well for an operator who has, shall we say, cut some notches on his belt."

"You mean they want someone who's actually

killed people before."

"Aced it in one. There are a lot of posers out there in the private sector. And the buyers want to know they are getting the genuine article."

"And you can give them that assurance, I suppose?"

"Ever since I retired, that's been my specialty."

"A pimp for killer mercenaries?"

"That's one way to look at it. I do skim a finder's fee off the top, help make the arrangements. Travel, contract negotiation, arms dealing."

"A regular paramilitary entrepreneur, you are."

"That's right. That's exactly what I am, William. And what are you? A vigilante killer, with a score of rotting bodies to your name."

"That's pretty cold, Richard."

"You're right. Downright arctic. But I'm still waiting for an answer."

"I'm not sure this is the direction I want my life to go in right now."

There was another long pause on the other end of the line.

"Take a real long look at your life right now, William. Tell me, just what is it you do intend on doing for the rest of your days?"

It was my turn to give pause.

"I've no fucking idea," I finally said.

"Good," Richard replied. "Plane lands at nine tonight. Pack light."

AUTHOR'S NOTE

The genesis of Killer Instincts came from an idea I had to create my own Men's Adventure genre hero: a young, hard-bitten mercenary. Having never served in the military, I had decided to create a character who'd also never been a soldier, and I struggled to come up with an origin story to explain their career path and skill set. Eventually, I landed on the idea of a revenge backstory, where a college kid takes it upon himself to avenge the deaths of his family against a criminal organization. With that notion, William Lynch was born.

I knew the idea of a white-collar family college student suddenly becoming a vigilante killing machine wouldn't hold any water, so I decided he would find a mentor, a veteran mercenary who would train him to carry out his plans for revenge. Richard was inspired by a certain other Men's Adventure protagonist who also lacked a military service record. Certain readers have picked up on who Richard is supposed to be, but I will neither confirm nor deny any suspicions, at least not on the record. I created Richard with the idea that this person had finally retired from their mercenary lifestyle and, now an old man, instead ran his own mercenary contracting service.

As the story developed, it became apparent the primary conflict of the story was not, in fact, William against the Paggianos. Rather, it was William struggling to maintain his humanity while Richard attempted to tear it down in order to fashion William into the lethal instrument he needed to become. The idea had percolated in the back of my mind for some time, but one day, while reading an article on character conflict, when asked who the lead antagonist was in my story, I found myself answering, "Richard".

With that in mind, Killer Instincts became less a story of simple vigilante justice, and more a Faustian tale, with William in the titular role and Richard serving as his Mephistopheles. Getting inside William's head, seeing his rationalizations and excuses and the transformation (or, perhaps, the corruption) of his morality was a sobering experience. There is a quote that sticks with me, a line in Edward Abbey's novel The Monkey Wrench Gang, as the character George Hayduke contemplates "...a not-so-secret longing to cut at least one notch on his gun butt. He too wanted a tragic past. At another man's expense". That, to me, became the visceral appeal of William's story: to experience vicariously his quest for revenge and the loss of his innocence and humanity.

Vigilantism is a curious thing. Our popular culture is rife with tales of vigilante justice, a theme that seems particularly well suited to pulp Western tales and carries right on through to the more recent Men's Adventure stories, which became popular in the '60s and '70s. Don Pendleton's Mack Bolan, the Executioner, served as the template for countless fictional vigilantes in the Men's Adventure fiction genre, while Brian Garfield's short paperback thriller DEATH WISH served as a more intellectual and emotional investigation of vigilantism in society. Even the first film bearing that title was a more staid exploration of the concept, more a violent drama than action movie. Of course, there have been countless other books, films, television programs, and other media that involve vigilantism and its consequences.

But as an actual crime, vigilantism is rare in our society. There are revenge killings and crimes of retribution, of course, but planned, methodical, violent vigilante crimes or crime sprees carried out by otherwise normal, law-abiding citizens are exceedingly rare. There are no doubt many psychological and societal factors at play to explain this, but it is interesting to see that such an act, so popular in our pop culture media, is yet so rare in real life.

Killer Instincts took me a year to write and another year to edit, during which time I actually wrote and edited another novel – the first of the COMMANDO series, Operation Arrowhead. The genesis for that book came from mapping out William and Jamie Lynch's lineage back generation by generation. The "Thomas Lynch" Jamie talks about with William is, of course, the main character of my British Commando series. Since the summer of 2012, when both books were published, Operation Arrowhead quickly became the more popular of the two, which is why it is now a multi-book series. Inquiries have been made about a sequel to Killer Instincts, but such a project may have to wait on the back burner for some time to come.

In conclusion, I wish to thank everyone who supported me in writing and publishing this book – all my friends and family members, all the folks I met through various social media outlets, and everyone who has taken the time to write me about the book, or who has left a review. A writer without readers is simply someone who puts their imagination down on the page – a noble act, but a lonely one. Being able to share this story with you all has made the world a less lonely place.

- Jack Badelaire

A LOOK AT: COMMANDO: THE COMPLETE WORLD WAR II ACTION COLLECTION SERIES, VOLUME I

Hitler's Blitzkrieg has ground Europe into submission under hobnailed jackboots and steel tank treads. With the evacuation at Dunkirk, Britain stands alone, a small island nation defiant in the path of a ruthless juggernaut.

Unable to mount a counteroffensive against the Germans, but unwilling to let them rest easy and reinforce their positions unmolested, the British military began the formation of small, independent companies of light infantry raiders.

The men who formed these raiding companies were volunteers, men who were not willing to wait at home on English soil for the eventual invasion of Europe, but instead felt the call for action in their blood, the need for danger and adventure, the chance to strike back against the Third Reich.

These men were known as Commandos.

AVAILABLE ON AMAZON FROM
JACK BADELAIRE AND WOLFPACK PUBLISHING.

ABOUT THE AUTHOR

Jack Badelaire first began writing online in 2005, moderating a message board dedicated to Men's Adventure paperbacks of the '60s through the '80s. He created The Post Modern Pulp blog in 2007 and the fantasy, science-fiction, and wargaming blog Tankards & Broadswords in 2008. In 2011, Badelaire published his first fictional work, the horror short story "Rivalry", through Amazon's Kindle Direct Publishing. In 2012, he published his first novel, KILLER INSTINCTS, followed shortly thereafter by OPERATION ARROWHEAD, the first in his successful WW2 British Commando series. Badelaire has since written seven other novels, three novellas, and multiple short stories, mostly in the field of historical adventure fiction.

READ MORE ABOUT JACK BADELAIRE AT
WOLFPACKPUBLISBHING.COM